PRAISE FOR **THIS IS WHAT WE DO**

"A tight retro noir that's as equally comfortable channeling *The Stranger* as it is George V. Higgins. But there's also a sly anarchic subtext rumbling below the drugs-and-molls narrative, a welling need to bring plutocrat America to its knees. Where, of course, it belongs. *This Is What We Do* is a love story. Or, to be more accurate, it's a story that's in love with its own existential indifference. But it's also *Atlas Shrugged* jammed in reverse and with the tires smoked. It's Ayn Rand for people with a brain. And a gun. It's a kick. Read it."

—**SEAN BEAUDOIN**, author of *Welcome Thieves*

"Hansen's debut novel covers even wilder, trickier ground than his memoir, *American Junkie*. Anti-hero James Nethery seems an ordinary, lonely man drinking Coke at the bar, until he meets 'Lily,' a Ukrainian prostitute, and what began as a quiet, atmospheric meditation on down-and-out expats in Paris explodes into a nonstop, genre-blending noir-crime-vigilante-political-sexy-nihilistic-almost surreal thrill ride, infused in equal measures with brutality and beauty."

—**GINA FRANGELLO**, author of *Every Kind of Wanting*

"'There's what people say, and then there's *what they do*. The phrase will infect your consciousness, contorting and twisting itself around to take on more and more dimensions. What does it mean to act on our desires when one person's wish fulfillment means another's nightmare? What does it mean to be free, or to escape? At its core, *This Is What We Do* gives us two people left with nothing, cutting close to the uncoolness of loving without fear."

—**GRACE KRILANOVICH**, author of *The Orange Eats Creeps*

THIS IS WHAT WE DO

THIS IS WHAT WE DO

A NOVEL

TOM HANSEN

COUNTERPOINT
BERKELEY, CALIFORNIA

THIS IS WHAT WE DO

Library of Congress Cataloging-in-Publication Data
Names: Hansen, Tom, 1942– author.
Title: This is what we do : a novel / Tom Hansen.
Description: Berkeley, CA : Counterpoint Press, [2017]
Identifiers: LCCN 2017024771 | ISBN 9781619029415
Subjects: | GSAFD: Romantic suspense fiction.
Classification: LCC PS3608.A7223 T48 2017 | DDC 813/.6—dc23
LC record available at https://lccn.loc.gov/2017024771

Cover designed by Jim Tillman
Book designed by Tabitha Lahr

COUNTERPOINT
2560 Ninth Street, Suite 318
Berkeley, CA 94710
www.counterpointpress.com

TO BE IS TO DO.

—Immanuel Kant

FOREWORD

by Lenore Zion

There's this inane thing in the literary zeitgeist now; a sense that writers appear to have been brainwashed into believing that it is their moral responsibility to provide a comfortable, inclusive reading experience to any and all who open their books. This expectation that a novel should generate the sensation of being rocked to sleep by some sort of anesthetizing mother figure, singing you a soft lullaby, the lyrics of which are designed to personally flatter and validate as your protective mother figure shields you from facing the abrasive ghosts of reality that howl at the door.

Usually I am able to ignore this silliness, as it doesn't affect me personally in any significant way, and really, when something over which you have no control is irritating to you, you're an irresponsible asshole to keep staring at it until you become upset. But Tom Hansen's *This Is What We Do* contrasts so gloriously with this embarrassing trend in literature that it's impossible for me not to make a point of it.

It is fitting that Tom Hansen's female protagonist, Lily, is harshly Ukrainian. She was a model, and now she's a sex-worker—and you won't catch her crying about it, because Lily was never under the impression that this outcome wasn't the most likely scenario. The way Lily sees it, her physical beauty has always been her most easily exploited asset. She's not thrilled by this, but she's not so stupid that she won't use to her advantage a lucky characteristic that can effectively be employed as a cash machine.

Lily is my favorite example of what I find so exciting about Hansen's writing. She is, at once, a walking manifestation of the type of supernatural beauty standards by which less genetically blessed women feel crushed, and the aggressive reality of existing inside such a coveted female form. It's this eye for the contradictory nature of reality in Hansen's writing that engenders that low rumble of psychological discordance that I find appealing in a book. With this, Hansen offers a bona fide, complex emotional reaction, delivered subtly through the reflection of an honest and unflattering piece of the human experience.

Hansen was very thoughtful and purposeful when he designed his characters, but he successfully avoided the narcissistic temptation of falling in love with his own creations. As is true of any meaningful relationship in real life, Hansen hates his characters as much as he loves them. The consequence of this decision is that his readers now also must struggle with their own complicated feelings toward Hansen's characters—but, from a writer to a reader, this is a gift. Rather than cushion us in a warm, fatty womb with easily-understood characters in an easily-understood world, Hansen has given us the permission and the freedom to love, hate, and hate-love his characters, for whatever reasons are real to us. In assuming his readers can handle the brutal image of the world he writes for us, he offers us what so many writers now rob us of: respect.

PART I
A RESURRICTION

He opened his eyes, looked at the table. The vague black shape meant nothing to him. He tried to focus on it, but it was futile, as if along with everything else he'd lost and given up, he no longer had the desire to see things clearly. It was the sound that had brought him back. A Vespa had driven up onto the sidewalk and stopped right on the other side of the barrier that acted as a corral around the tables. The rider sat there, letting the engine idle and fiddling with the strap on his helmet. Finally, he turned off the machine, chained it to a lamppost, and disappeared into Le Petit Poucet.

He'd been daydreaming, of what he couldn't recall. It had been happening more and more often lately. He would float away to a pleasant and unnamed place, where his thoughts folded inward into the fog. Following the *question* that had been haunting him. It always seemed to lead him into a kind of trance, a state of non-being, something that resembled a brief fugue state. When he returned, he had no recollection, and it always took a few moments to get his bearings again. The waiter was standing next to the table. He stood there, hovering like an ominous golem. He said something. Nethery didn't know how long he'd been standing there, or how many times he'd tried to get his attention, but it finally pulled him into the present.

"What?" Nethery asked, looking up, slightly perturbed, the waiter's features slowly coming into focus.

"Your cigarettes," the waiter said, indicating the pack on the table. He smiled and made a motion with his hands, a back and forth, that indicated he wanted to exchange. He was holding a pack of Camels as well, and Nethery looked at him, confused.

"The Camels from America are better," the waiter said, and then he kept standing there. Without thinking Nethery gave the waiter his half-empty pack of American Camels, the waiter gave him his pack of Somewhere Camels, and the waiter said *"Merci"* and walked away. Nethery examined the pack of Camels, removed a cigarette, placed it between his lips. The Zippo made the familiar *plink* as he flipped open the top, he sparked the wheel with his thumb, waited for the flame to get going, and then he lit the cigarette and took a good long drag. It was horrible. Somewhere made a very poor cigarette.

Nethery was dog tired and he couldn't understand why. Earlier he'd taken the Metro out to Barbès and had lunch, but that was all, and somehow it had completely exhausted him. He slouched in his chair and found himself looking at the shoes of people as they passed on the sidewalk. Eventually he raised his head and gazed toward the monument in the center of Place de Clichy. The sun had passed overhead, and the tall bronze and stone memorial cast a shadow that stretched like a spear toward Brasserie Wepler. Nethery closed his eyes and was able to hear everything around him—cars honking, voices of people passing the café, shouting into their phones, a coin hitting the sidewalk, paper rustling, footsteps coming from every direction, the engines of buses, the engines of cars, the engines of scooters. The noise continued to build, seeming to squeeze in upon his head. He knew that if he didn't do something, it would only get worse.

He finished his coffee, stood, and was about to walk into the café when he spied an ant crawling across the table. He gazed down at the insect, and found the little creature irritating for reasons he could not fathom. He considered crushing the ant under his thumb, but decided against it, and set his empty coffee cup down on top of it, trapping it underneath. He walked into the café and sat on a stool at the center of the bar, near the taps. The bartender was at the far end chatting with a customer. He was young and handsome, with shiny black hair. When he saw Nethery he glided down the bar, smiled, and rattled off a stream of language that seemed like one long word.

"Um, sorry. I don't speak French," Nethery said.

"You are American?" the bartender said. Nethery nodded.

"I was a bartender in Los Angeles for many years," he continued. "Can I get you a drink?"

"No, that's okay," he said, nodding at his coffee, "I just had to come inside. It's . . . too fucking noisy out there."

"Ah, *oui.* Yes, it can be quite loud," he said and smiled again. He looked down and began washing glasses in a small sink. Nethery stared at the top of his head. After a few moments the bartender looked up, his hands full of wet wineglasses, three in each hand, his fingers wrapped around the stems. He set the wineglasses down on a drying mat on the counter behind the bar.

"What is there to do around here?" Nethery asked, and the bartender looked up at him, not failing to understand, but sizing him up.

"Something I won't find in the *Lonely Planet Guide*," Nethery continued, "if you know what I mean."

The bartender smiled, looked down, and began drying one of the wineglasses with a bar towel.

"Ah, yes. Girls?" he said.

"Yeah, sure. That'd be good, I guess," Nethery said, "but not like the Moulin Rouge, or that crap down in the Pigalle."

"Yes, you don't want to go down there," the bartender said, "bottle of champagne is costing thousand euro."

The bartender's hands gradually slowed. He carefully finished drying the glass in his hands, set it on the drying mat, looked up, and his eyes met Nethery's.

"La Lampe," he said, and he looked up and down the bar, to see if anyone had heard him. He leaned over the bar.

"You will like," he said quietly. "Is not far. Go up Rue Biot and then Rue Lemercier," he continued, "turn . . . left on Rue La Condamine. Number 13. There is a red lamp above the door. Next to door there is . . . painted . . . a figure of a man . . . with no face, on window. Go there and you will see. Very nice girls. Very nice," he said, nodding. He pulled a business card out of his wallet and scrawled something on the back.

"Give this to the man, he will help you."

The bartender was called away. Nethery examined the card. There was nothing on the face of it except a lamp, an old-fashioned gaslight, and an address. The bartender had signed his name to the back. Nethery sat for a few more minutes, debating whether he wanted to see what it was all about. It was probably just another rip-off joint, he suspected, like the Moulin Rouge, and all those sex shops in the Pigalle. The bartender could just be getting a cut for sending in customers. Then they get you inside, make you pay with your credit card, and when you get home you find a bunch of bogus charges.

But he was bored, or at least he thought he was. He finished his coffee, left some money on the bar, and walked out of the café and headed up Rue Biot. The street made a slight shift by the Hotel Eldorado and became Rue Lemercier. The street was fairly quiet. There was an occasional shop but they were all closed. He continued up the street and after five minutes he reached Rue La Condamine. It was quiet, darker, and more run-down than the others. He passed an old hotel that looked closed but for a faint light shining inside. The name was undecipherable, done in a mosaic of chipped and missing tiles on an arch above the doorway. He began down the street again and became aware of an intuitive feeling rising from somewhere inside him, a growing unease that he was returning to a familiar past instead of moving forward into a new future. His walk slowed and came to a stop. He looked down at the worn gray cobblestones of the street. He wondered how long they'd been there, and if blood had flowed between them in a previous century.

What was he doing here? It certainly wasn't to see the Eiffel Tower. He'd had his fill of monuments. But *the question* encompassed much more than simply place. It encompassed this world, this body, this skin. A vivid form of anger built up in his gut and flowed outward to his extremities. He wanted his life to move— somewhere, anywhere, forward, backward, sideways, he did not care. It was stale and stagnant, frozen by a warm and familiar kind of fear. His life had been exceedingly comfortable, and very nice to look at. All the bells and whistles, all the adornments. But it never moved, never advanced toward anything, and under the shiny surface it was doing nothing but rotting away. He knew this now, and he also knew it had been this way for a very long time.

He stood there and looked up and down the street. The realization hit that despite the boredom, despite everything, this was not the way. There was nothing on this street but more of the same, more of what had prompted him to come here in the first place. He thought for a few more moments, and he set off again, continuing the way he'd been, which he guessed would lead him back to Avenue de Clichy and from there he could find his way to the apartment. And then he saw it, a short way farther down the street, a red lamp glowing above a doorway.

It appeared to be an art gallery, although it looked slightly more run-down than one would expect, and on one of the cloudy windows was painted a large wooden mannequin about a meter tall. Under the red lamp were a few steps leading down to a battered and unmarked steel door. Nethery descended the steps and put his ear up to the door. There was music coming from somewhere in the bowels of the building. He raised his fist and hesitated. He lowered his arm and looked down at his shoes. He raised his fist again, knocked, and immediately took a step back. He was about to climb back up the steps and leave when the door screeched open. A very large man stood in the doorway. His broad face appeared wet, like pockmarked plastic, and he had lifeless and clouded bloodshot eyes.

"*Oui?*" he grunted.

"*Parlez-vous anglais?*" Nethery asked, trying to disguise his accent.

"*Nyet, nyet,*" the man spat, putting his hand on Nethery's shoulder, trying to turn him back and push him back up the steps.

"Wait, wait," Nethery said, whipping the card out of his pocket and holding it up. The man removed his hand from Nethery's shoulder, took the card, held it up into the red light, and looked at it.

"Okay, you come," he said with a Russian accent, and he put out a big meaty arm and used it to sweep Nethery toward the doorway. Nethery squeezed past him, and the big man wrenched the door closed behind them with a loud slam. Inside it was dark, and once his eyes adjusted Nethery found himself on a small landing of sorts. There was a passage to the right, which led to some stairs leading underground.

"One hundred euro," the doorman said, holding out his hand. Nethery dug some bills out of his pocket and counted them out. The man scrunched the bills into his fist, looked at Nethery, and smiled a frightening smile, the expression incongruous with the rest of his face.

"You are . . . American?" the man grumbled.

"Yes," Nethery replied.

"Hmph," the man grunted. He took his arm and steered Nethery toward the staircase.

"Have—good—time," he said slowly, one word at a time. As Nethery started down the stairs he heard the man add another word, "Yankee."

At the bottom Nethery emerged into a large room. The first thing he saw was a bar, and behind it dozens of bottles of colored liquid glittering on shelves mounted on a mirrored wall. On either side of the bar were small low stages lit up with colored lights. The room stretched out into dark and spacious corners with numerous semicircular lounge areas along the walls, furnished in red velvet couches and each with a low table. About half were occupied by what looked like businessmen, some alone, some in groups of two or three.

He made his way across the room toward the bar, suddenly fearful of looking to one side or the other. He felt a familiar twinge of nostalgia as memories of pleasant nights spent in bars and clubs flowed back into his mind, overpowering the memories of what came after, the not so pleasant nights that began a few years before, around the time he turned thirty. He sat on a stool and the bartender approached him, a tall man, with shiny black hair, slicked-back with some kind of grease or dressing. This was going to be complicated, Nethery thought, and for a moment he considered having a few drinks simply to avoid confusion. He reminded himself that that would be a bad idea and after some verbal wrangling conveyed to the bartender that he wanted a Coca-Cola.

Bad techno came over the sound system, bombastic bass with a mishmash of electronic squeaks and buzzing. It was incoherent. A dancer came out and took the stage to his left. She looked half asleep. She swayed lazily, her long lithe body out of sync with the music, lit up garishly in reds and yellows. When the song ended she wandered amongst the tables. Nethery didn't know what to do. But then, this was obviously a brothel of sorts. He'd been in them before and they operated under their own language that trumped words of any sort. Another dancer came out and began dancing to a song even more horrid than the previous one, some combination of rap and heavy metal. It was grotesque, and Nethery decided then he would finish his drink and leave.

Backstage, Lily bent down and finished strapping on her sandals. She sat up and applied some of her favorite lipstick, smacked her lips together, then gazed at herself in the mirror, turning her face to one side and then the other. She teased her hair up. She had cut it into a bob after the last club. She'd also changed her name, for the fourth time, or was it the fifth? She couldn't recall. The last year had been a blur of sorts, as she'd made her way from club to club, and it had been so long since she'd used her real name that it almost seemed as if it didn't belong to her anymore. She stared at herself the mirror and said her name aloud, "Agnieszka Bogova." Her neck and face grew warm, as the past rubbed up against the present. She sighed and pushed the feelings away. That was then and this was now, she told herself, and for the first time since the modeling had ended things seemed to be going pretty well. She picked up a lit cigarette from the ashtray, took a drag, careful to not lose too much lipstick, and then set it back down in the ashtray.

She was adjusting her bikini top when Vaclav, the manager of the club, appeared in the doorway.

"Lily? Get out there and shake your ass, bitch," he said in Russian.

"Fuck you," she said, and waited for his inevitable smile.

When it came she smiled back. She watched him leave and close the door behind him. Vaclav had been a bartender at the first club she'd worked and there had always been a kind of unspoken understanding between them, as if they both knew they didn't belong doing what they were doing. She knew one thing—he was a hell of a lot more tolerable than the other club managers she'd worked under. They had all made her fuck them, and Lily just didn't have the built-in forgetter the other girls seemingly had, or had developed. Submitting to the old men had pissed her off infinitely more than the customers ever could. With them it hadn't been about pleasure, or even test-driving the product, an exchange of currency, it had only been about power. They had screwed her simply because they could. They'd known that she'd been a model and had taken a twisted pleasure in showing her the realities of her new life. And even then, if they had just left it there she would have been able to put it out of her mind but they kept coming, sensing her resistance, her strength, intent on teaching her a lesson, breaking her spirit, bringing her into the fold, showing her who was boss, or some fucking thing. Probably all of them. They had a fondness for overkill, for rubbing it in.

Men. How is it these fuckers run the world? Lily thought. Most of them were moronic and juvenile, and they were all so easy to figure out. She could spot their weaknesses a mile away, and they all had them. She found it difficult to not point them out. Sometimes it had been impossible. Something would set her off and with a few well-chosen words she would twist the knife in exactly the right spot, usually some crack about their masculinity, or their appearance. It had gotten her fired and once even a fat lip when one of the managers slapped her around. It did not achieve their desired result. It just made her more angry and determined to outsmart them, so she'd put on an act of being stupid or on drugs until they were convinced she would be a continuous problem, not a moneymaker, and that it was just easier to let her go to another club. And yet this same intelligence and perception that got her in trouble made her very good at what she did. She only had to spend a few seconds with a man to know what sort he was, what sort of woman they wanted her to be, what sort of illusion they wanted her to create. Usually she could tell before they even opened their mouths.

Lily checked herself in the mirror one last time. Someone had once said she looked like a young Charlotte Rampling, and there was a similarity in her thin body, her long fine neck, her hooded, alluring eyes, her small breasts, and the curl of her upper lip. But her career wasn't quite working out like Charlotte's, was it? Her fine features hardened into a kind of determination and she stood, walked out of the dressing room, peeked out through the curtain, and looked around the room. It looked like a slow night. She signaled to the bartender that she was ready. The song that was playing began to fade out and Lily stepped out into the light.

The first saxophone notes of Charlie Mingus's "Goodbye Pork Pie Hat" floated out of the sound system and filled the room. Nethery was halfway to the stairs leading to the door, and it was so different than anything that had come before that he stopped in his tracks and turned around. The stage to the left was dark, the dancer barely lit up in a soft blue spotlight, with a hint of red. She was moving slowly, perfectly in tune with the music. He became very self-conscious for some reason, and realized he must look ridiculous standing there alone in the center of the room and drifted toward the tables off to the left. He sat down and his eyes went straight back to the girl. She seemed to have been trained in some kind of dance, ballet probably, the way every move of her thin body seemed precise and accurate. During the portions of the song where there was a long progression of descending notes, her body seemed to slowly melt into a dark shape on the floor of the stage. Then she would rise again, and it reminded Nethery of the smoke drifting up from the end of a cigarette.

Lily allowed the music to take possession of her body. She had developed a kind of dance that was sensual and hypnotic, a mix of modern with some adagio-type movements. It calmed her down when she was angry, almost like yoga, and helped her to forget the direction her life had taken, and how it had come about. And yet, the transition to hooking hadn't been so bad, not nearly as distasteful as she'd always imagined. But this troubled her at times, and she wondered occasionally why she wasn't more upset about it. Maybe it was something she was telling herself, that it was just another line? It was true she'd crossed many already, most without even knowing. It wasn't so unusual. Many of the models did it on the side, or some varia- tion of it, as modeling just didn't pay enough—unless you were top tier. Some had men to support them, some only did XXX magazines, some did nude videos, some had websites where they fucked their boyfriends, some did only girl-girl, some straight sex but not anal, mandatory condoms . . .

Lily remembered a saying she'd heard somewhere, *Once you've killed five, it's easy to make it six.* She understood what that meant now. Once you've done modeling in bikinis, it's easy to do see-through lingerie. Once you've done that, it's easy to do it naked. Once you've done photo modeling, it's easy to do video. Once you've fucked for free to further your career, it's easy to fuck for money, and before you know it you've crossed ten lines, or they all blur into one, and it becomes harder to go back to the place you were before. A familiar fury began to rise, and she quickly hammered it back down with her pride. Self-pity was one thing that she despised more than anything. Things could have been much worse, in reality. She could have fallen for one of those "job offers" to be a maid or a waitress in Italy, or Greece, and ended up trapped, smuggled into Turkey, without a passport, forced to fuck fat farmers on the floor of a barn in the middle of nowhere. It had happened to a few girls she'd known from Ukraine, the less pretty ones, the more desperate ones, ones with kids or sick family members to support. Some of them managed to find their way back home, eventually. Some didn't.

Lily dragged herself out of her thoughts, before the anger and self-pity congealed and hardened. It was useless to get all worked up about this. Even if she could get her passport back from Claude, what would she do? Go back home and work in her mother's café, maybe dance in the strip clubs for much less than she was making now? Model for a travel brochure once or twice a year? She could hang around the nightclubs, hoping to latch onto some idiotic soccer player or a rich businessman, but she'd already done that, a couple of times. Her mouth had gotten her in trouble there too.

So now, she was letting them touch, instead of just look. Was it so terrible? It was just a body. Flesh and blood. They weren't touching her spirit, her soul. The clients weren't abusive with Sergei around, and the pay wasn't so bad. She had to give the club half of what she made, but it wasn't like having a pimp who beat her up and took everything. This club was better than the previous ones. It was safer than escorting, and there was more money in it here than back home, or the FKK clubs in Germany, even Dubai. But still, sometimes she thought about how close she'd been to that point in a model's career where all these side ventures were unnecessary. All she had wanted to do was work. She'd been a good model, responsible, always showing up on time and ready to go, not hungover or drugged out or throwing tantrums. She'd been serious and ambitious. She had the look and the confidence and the verve. The important people in Milan had been following her career, and had plans for her. It hadn't been enough.

The song ended and it took Lily a moment to notice. She stepped off the stage and walked directly toward the far side of the room to a table of men drinking champagne. The big man from the door was there, and they exchanged a few words, and then she glanced in Nethery's direction. She was there only a few moments, and she stood straight up, pivoted on her heel, and walked straight toward Nethery, her body like a leopard, each foot stabbing out in front of the other. As she reached the center of the room she stopped, looked around, and moved toward a table of three men two booths down. As soon as she approached the two girls who were already there sat up straight, turned their attention away from the men, and glared at her. She slowed and then stopped, and there seemed to be a sort of standoff. One of the men reached out to wave her over. The girl sitting next to him quickly grabbed his arm, pulled it down, and draped herself all over him, saying something in his ear. The other girl continued to glare, then made a motion with her hand for her to go away. Lily took another step toward the table. At that moment a youngish man came over from the bar, put his hands on her shoulders, and turned her away from the table. He smiled a bit as he talked. Lily said something back, waving her arms emphatically. The man put his hands on her shoulders, turned her to where she was facing Nethery, and gave her a gentle push. She resisted and the man said something in her ear and she jerked her head around, said something, and then started toward Nethery's table. She walked up to the end of the couch and put her hands on her hips.

"Sergei tell me you are American," she said, looking down at him.

"Sergei?" Nethery asked, confused. She spoke English, and pretty well. He'd been unprepared for that. He'd been unprepared for any of this.

"Yes, Sergei," she said, pointing, "the doorman."

"Oh, ummm, yes. I am American."

"Well?" she said, standing up straight and pushing her small breasts out slightly. Her hands were still on her hips, the long delicate fingers curled around her jutting hipbones.

"Well . . . what?" Nethery asked, not knowing how this was supposed to proceed.

The girl stepped back from the table and looked away for a second, exasperated. Then she stepped back and stared at Nethery.

"Do you like me?" she asked.

Nethery was speechless. Sensing his confusion the girl spoke. "Is not trick question," she said, a wry smile playing on her lips.

"Yes," Nethery said, smiling back, "I like you."

"Okay then," she said, sitting down on the red velvet couch and sliding next to him, "buy me a drink."

The girl's grammar was a bit off, but her English was very fluent and almost without accent, just a hint of what he guessed was Russian. She flagged over the waitress and ordered a shot of vodka. Nethery ordered a Coca-Cola. The girl looked at him strangely.

"Are you . . . ummm . . . how you say . . . cheapskate?"

"What? No . . ."

"Why you not buy drink?"

"Uhh, well, I used to have a drinking problem."

"Pffft. Everyone have drinking problem. So what?"

It was true about these Russians, Nethery thought. The concept of not drinking was like the concept of not eating to a fat American. The drinks arrived. Nethery paid the waitress. The girl downed the vodka in one gulp.

"You wanna fuck me?" she asked, slamming the glass back down onto the table. She looked at Nethery with the most stunning green eyes he'd ever seen. They were pale grayish-green and had a luminescent quality. Her eyelids seemed to float up and down slightly, fluctuating between intensity and a sleepy seductiveness. They had a hypnotic effect on him and he had a hard time looking away, and even stringing two thoughts together.

"Ummm . . . well," Nethery said, trying desperately to think of how to respond, "I'm at a bit of a loss . . . I hadn't expected to find anyone here that speaks English."

"I speak English. Yes. So what? We go to room. In back. You like?"

"Ummm, well . . . look . . ."

"I say again," she said, slightly irritated, "is not trick question. You want to fuck me?"

Nethery gave up trying to be tactful and just answered her.

"Well, no, actually, not right now."

She seemed unprepared for that, and took a moment to gather herself.

"What hell you do here then?" she shot back.

"I'm not sure," Nethery replied after a moment, looking down at the table.

"I'm looking . . ." and he let the sentence trail off. He saw her shifting around, moving away from him toward the end of the couch.

"I met a man at a café," he said. "He told me about this place. He gave me a card."

"You can drink any place," she said, flipping her hand dismissively at his Coke. "Here we have tits. Here we have pussy. Here we have ass."

Nethery stared at her, unable to think fast enough to keep up with her.

"This what we do," she continued, bluntly. "This what happen here. We have bodies. You no like my body?" she asked, looking at him with a penetrating stare as if daring him to say no.

Shouting from across the room caught her attention and Nethery took the opportunity to get a good look at her. It wasn't that the other girls weren't beautiful, but they had more of a vulgar sexuality about them whereas Lily radiated a supreme refinement, a kind of divine grace. It seemed completely out of place here. He continued looking at her face, and it seemed to change depending on the light and the expression. One moment she looked like a woman, completely without illusions as to what she was doing there, and the next she would look like she was fourteen and knew nothing of the ways of the world.

"Well? You like me?" she said impatiently, turning back to face him.

"Yeah, um . . ."

"I am most beautiful here," she said, matter of fact, the corner of her mouth turned up into a knowing smirk.

"I can see that," Nethery answered, "it's . . ."

"You will not find better. Not here. Not nowhere."

"It's just that . . . uhhh . . ." Nethery left the sentence unfinished and, not knowing what to say, stared at his drink. There were a few moments of uncomfortable silence.

"I think you in wrong place," the girl said sharply, losing patience.

"Yeah, I suppose I am," Nethery muttered, still staring at the condensation running down the sides of the bottle.

Lily slid to the end of the couch and was about to get up when she felt the man grab her wrist. She looked back, about to lose her temper, but there was something in his eyes that stopped her. She paused for a moment. Normally she wouldn't have cared, written him off as another pathetic sucker and let the other girls have him, but for some reason she felt like giving him another chance. She slid back over until she was right up next to him and geared herself up to play the game. It was such a rare occurrence anymore that she'd forgotten to try. Usually the men were so intimidated by her beauty she could push them

around, be blunt and rude, and they just took it. She turned toward him slightly and carefully put her hand on his knee.

"So? What is your name?" she asked, as the waitress brought
another round of drinks.

"My name is James."

"Mmm, James. I like that," Lily said. Downing the shot of vodka,
she sat up straight and let her fingertips slowly trace up his thigh. "So,
James, what do you want?" and then looked up at him.

"The other girls here don't seem to like you very much," he said.

Oh no, Lily thought, he's one of those. They were the most
tedious of all, with their talking and questions. She preferred the
others, they usually had more money and it was simple. They
paid, and she put out. That was the way she liked it, lots of turn-
over. It meant more money, fewer complications, and the time
passed quicker. But despite her suspicions, Lily kept her cool. She
wanted at least to see what this guy had to offer.

"Yes," Lily said, pouting dramatically, "the other girls. They
are very mean."

Her expression of sadness was so exaggerated it made Nethery
chuckle.

"What?" she shouted, losing her temper. "It is not funny."

"Oh, I know. It was just the look on your face."

"They are bitches," she spat. "The men like me more. It is not
my fault," she said angrily. Then she caught herself and calmed
down again.

"Who cares about them?" Lily said, and her voice quiet and
seductive again, "I am here now."

It wouldn't be the first time Nethery had paid for sex. He'd done
his fair share of that in his twenties, when he had a high-paying
job at a bank. At the time it had seemed the thing to do, like
owning a BMW, going clubbing, wearing expensive suits, and

snorting coke. All the other bankers did it. He went along. But there had been a faint and sordid emptiness about the whole thing that had always bothered him. It wasn't that it seemed wrong, exactly, only that it seemed vapid, shallow. Like there was more to it, or should have been. The drugs and booze had helped alleviate these feelings, but still it had been uncomfortable and he had no reason to think that this would be any different. Still, there was something about her, and even if he didn't know what it was at the moment, he knew that he would need to communicate to her in a way she would understand or risk her getting angry and leaving or maybe having him thrown out.

"Well, um, I wanna fuck you," Nethery said, the words coming out quietly.

"Yes," Lily said, smiling, "everybody does. It is not cheap," she said, testing him.

"Oh, yeah," he said, "I'm sure it's not. But I don't care. I have money."

"Okay then," Lily said, "we go to room."

She slid to the end of the couch, stood up, and held out her hand. It was thin and delicate and cold. She was tall, but probably couldn't have weighed more than a hundred pounds. He stood and let her tow him across the room and when they reached the far corner they passed through a doorway covered with red velvet curtains. She continued to pull him down a long narrow hallway. The walls were covered in thick and sloppy dark gray paint and it was chipped in places. There were pipes running along the ceiling. They passed another girl in the corridor and she stared straight ahead and didn't even acknowledge Lily as she passed, but then she smiled seductively at Nethery. Eventually they came to a door.

Lily opened the door, pulled him inside, and gestured for him to sit down on the bed. She grabbed a bottle of vodka from a small bar along the wall, next to a large hamper overflowing with bedsheets. She took a slug straight from the bottle and noticed Nethery was fidgeting. She took another slug of the vodka and watched him out of the corner of her eye. Usually by this point the man had tipped his hand in some way, and Lily would effortlessly morph into what he wanted, do the job, and get him out of there. Even though the men that came to see her were wealthy and sometimes powerful businessmen, sports stars, trust fund babies, local politicians, musicians, she was still able to intimidate them and twist them around her finger because she was always so aloof. It made her seem unattainable, even to them, even when they were fucking her. They may have bought her, but they did not own her. She even occasionally exuded a bit of contempt for her clients, and they hardly ever complained. She took another slug from the bottle of vodka, angry about being turned away from the table of men after she danced. They were regulars and always spent a lot. She set the bottle on a night table and lit a cigarette. She took a deep breath and attempted to focus on the task at hand. It was too late. Her anger had solidified above ground, shining a light on everything negative; how she'd ended up here, the other girls, Claude, and those Japanese businessmen. The grudges and resentments multiplied. Lily heard the man say something.

"Yes?"

"You seem a little . . . distracted," the man said.

"Yes," she replied, "I am distracted. So what? Take clothes off."

Lily stood up and untied her bikini bottom and let it fall to the floor. She turned to Nethery and he was still dressed.

"You want me to help you?" she asked, seductively, moving next to him on the bed and reaching for his belt.

"Umm, look . . . Lily?"

"Yes?"

"I really want to see you . . . just not here."

Lily rolled her eyes and drew a breath. Here we go. He wants to play games. She began to lose her temper.

"You want to fuck me, you don't want to fuck me. Why you waste my time?" Lily reached down to pick up her bikini bottom. She began to put it back on.

"Here," Nethery said, holding out five hundred euros, "this is for right now."

Lily was about to say something insulting, but then she looked at him and once again, she hesitated. She took the five hundred euros, folded the bills, and slipped them inside her top.

"Can we meet somewhere?" Nethery asked.

Lily took another good long look at him, sizing him up.

"It is possible," she said, "but you must not tell club. It is not allowed for me to see men outside."

"Oh, sure. Of course. I understand."

"We must wait to go back out," she said.

Lily drank vodka from the bottle on the night table. She asked him where he was from, but then obviously wasn't paying attention when he replied. He asked her the same, and he had to repeat the question three times and even then she did not answer, but looked at him curiously as if she were examining something under a microscope.

"It is safe now. We can go back," Lily finally said, after they'd been in the room for about fifteen minutes.

"Would you like to dance?" Nethery asked.

"Dance? There is no music."

"Let's just pretend," Nethery said smiling, standing up from the bed and holding out his hand. "Come on, just for a minute," Nethery said.

"You are strange man," Lily said and she chuckled and stood up. Nethery put one arm around her waist and with the other he took her hand. They slowly swayed together and he buried his face in her hair. It smelled of flowers.

A t the top of the stairs was a glaring hole of light, and Nethery fished his sunglasses out of his pocket and quickly put them on. Dozens of people followed him up the stairs, their footsteps bouncing off the concrete walls, and for a brief moment he felt as though he were being pursued. When he reached the surface he was immediately assaulted by the sun. Even with the sunglasses the glare was intense. He moved off to the side and looked back at the Metro exit and watched as people poured out of the earth. There was a small newspaper stand nearby and he bought a copy of *Le Monde*, then walked to a bench and sat down in the shade of the trees that lined the esplanade. It was very warm for May, and the air was remarkably crisp and clean and the grass fields around the Esplanade des Invalides were a vivid green as if the rains of the previous night had washed a kind of filth off the entire city. He removed his leather jacket and slung it over the back of the bench. A couple of young mothers leisurely strolled past pushing baby carriages. Children played on the grass behind him, and out on the field in the center of the esplanade some students were kicking a soccer ball around.

On the front page of *Le Monde* was news from home, some kind of attack on the Chase Tower in Chicago. There were pictures. A dump truck had crashed through the revolving doors, smoke poured out of holes in the lower floors, and a pair of rocket launchers were lying on the sidewalk. Nethery set the paper down, leaned back on the bench and he saw her, coming off the Pont Alexandre III. She looked different, but he immediately knew it was her. She was wearing jeans and sneakers, with some kind of scarf wrapped around her head and big dark sunglasses, like she was trying to hide her identity. She walked with a kind of spring in her step, on the balls of her feet, as if she was unused to flat shoes. She casually strolled up to the bench and sat down beside him.

"Hello," Nethery said, staring straight ahead.

"Hello."

"It's a nice day."

"Yes. You have money?" she asked, bluntly.

"Here," Nethery said, handing her an envelope with a thousand euros in hundreds. "Is that enough?"

"Maybe," she said, counting the bills. "What you want to do?"

"I thought we might take a walk."

She looked over at him curiously for a moment, her head tipped forward so she could see over her glasses.

"A walk?" she asked.

"Yeah. Get some sandwiches, take a walk along the quay," Nethery said, continuing to stare straight ahead. She said nothing, but after a moment she tucked the money into her bag.

They found a boulangerie not far away and Nethery bought two ham-and-cheese sandwiches and cans of Orangina. They made their way back to the bridge and found a flight of cement steps that led down to the quay and followed the river's edge a short way toward the Eiffel Tower until they came upon a sunny spot. They sat down on the edge of the quay, dangling their legs over the river. Glass-topped boats sailed past, filled with tourists, snapping photos and pointing. They ate in silence, and Nethery stared off toward the Eiffel Tower. Now that he was here, and she was here, he didn't know what to do or say, as if his attraction to her was not earthly desire or something similarly mundane but some unfathomable and incomprehensible thing. Something supernatural. When they were finished eating he lit up two cigarettes and passed one to her, and as they smoked he noticed that she was staring at him.

"What?" he asked.

"Why you no talk?" Lily asked.

"Talk?"

"Yes. Ask questions?"

"Questions? Like what?"

"The men that don't want to fuck want to talk."

"Oh, really? What do they want to talk about?"

"They want to find out things."

"What's a nice girl like you doing in a place like this? That sort of thing?"

"Yes. They want to tell me things."

"Really? Like what?"

"They think I should be something else."

"Something else?"

"Yes."

"You can't be something else?"

"No."

"Why?"

"You have seen me," she interrupted. "I have this body. I have this face. They have more value than anything else. *Much* more value."

Even though she'd tried to cover up by wearing casual clothes and the scarf, she was one of those women who are so beautiful it was difficult for him to imagine her doing what ordinary people do. He tried to envision her working in a clothes shop or an office, but it ended in a totally absurd picture, and for a brief moment, Nethery thought there was something fundamentally wrong in that, but he forgot about it quickly.

"I used to be model," Lily said quietly, looking down, "on magazine."

"But not anymore?"

"No."

"Why not?"

"I will not talk about that."

"Why not?"

"What good it do? This what I am now."

"That's a little bit cynical, isn't it?" Nethery said.

"Cynical?" Lily asked, not understanding the word.

"Yeah, umm, negative."

"Oh, yes, No. Not cynical."

"No?"

"It is truth. People say everyone is the same. It is not true."

There was a short silence while Nethery thought about what she said.

"I did not make this situation," she said, defensively.

"No, but . . ."

"What good it do? What good it do to pretend that this," she said, pointing to her head, "or this," pointing at her flexed bicep, "have value."

"Yeah, but . . ." Nethery began, but she cut him off.

"What good it do to pretend that this," she said, cupping her small breasts, "is not for sale?"

"Well . . ."

"I am supposed to be waitress back in Kiev? Clean house? Nurse?"

She had suddenly become very animated.

"This what men want me to be," she continued, a quiet resignation in her voice. "This what world want me to be. This what has value. This is future. I am supposed to fight these things?" she asked.

"Not if you don't want to," Nethery said.

"World has chosen," she said, and closed her eyes. "Do not mistake me. I do not complain. I have seen the other way. I have seen the Communist way. It is very much worse. Much worse. You are not one of those . . . those . . . people who are dreaming about some paradise, are you? Where everyone is the same and there are no problems?"

"No . . ."

"This is real world. Not some . . . idea . . . in the sky. You think I could have done something more? Something different?" she blurted out.

"No, no . . ." Nethery said, emphatically, shaking his head.

"Gisele Bündchen is whore. I am whore. She sell body, I sell body. What the difference?"

"Ummm . . . well, she's just a model. She's not letting people touch."

Through her sunglasses Nethery saw her eyes narrow and her lips draw tight.

"There are many ways of touching," she said, and then she opened her mouth to continue but nothing came out. "She was lucky. I was not. That is all." A pained expression came over her face and she turned away. Then she looked at him again and there was fire in her eyes.

"You American," she said, a touch of anger in her voice. "You like to play with words, don't you? Make people think one thing is happen when it is something totally other."

"Huh?"

"Come, let's have *party*," she said sarcastically. "Escort, prostitute, model, whore, date . . . is all same thing."

"You're from Kiev?" Nethery asked, not understanding and trying to change the subject.

"I will not answer questions," she said, sharply.

"Okay," Nethery said, letting it go.

There was a moment of silence. Lily turned back and stared at him, not comprehending his silence.

"I do not understand you," she said, looking puzzled.

"What?"

"You don't want ask questions?" she asked.

"Well, I tried," Nethery said, "but . . ."

"I will talk," she said, looking at him curiously.

"It's cool," Nethery replied. "None of that shit really matters, does it? How you got here, how I got here. The why? It doesn't make a goddamned bit of difference."

"I have not met man like you."

"Oh, sure you have. I'm no different than the men you meet in the club. I'm just as creepy, just as lonely. It's just that . . . right now anyway . . . talking and fucking don't mean anything to me. That's all."

"What you doing here?" Lily asked, shaking her head. Nethery shrugged.

"You do not know much, do you?" Lily said.

Nethery looked down at the ground and for some reason he was not insulted, but found it hilarious. He began laughing and he laughed so hard that Lily laughed as well. After a few moments the laughter subsided and he reached into the paper bag and handed her a can of Orangina.

"Why you choose me?" Lily asked, taking a sip from the can.

"Does it matter?"

"I don't know. Maybe."

"You're . . . different . . . than the others."

"Yes. I am different. So what?"

Nethery stared at the ground.

There were a few moments of silence, and then Lily spoke again.

"I am sorry," she said, "I am not normally so plain speaking."

"It's okay," Nethery said. "You're right. I don't know why the fuck I came here. I guess I thought I might find something . . ."

"World is what world is," she said.

"Yeah," Nethery sighed, and there were a few moments of silence.

"Why you not go back home?" Lily asked.

"Home?"

"Yes."

"I was dying back there."

"Dying? Are you sick?"

"No, no. Not like that. I just . . . couldn't breathe . . . I couldn't . . ."

"You are fine looking man. You could find nice girl."

"You're not a nice girl?"

"No," she said chuckling, ". . . I am . . . how you say . . . ruined."

"You don't look ruined to me."

"Everyone is ruined," she said, matter of fact.

"What?"

"Everyone is . . . they . . . how you say . . . have hole inside. They buy. Or they sell. They fuck. Or they are fucked. There is nothing else."

"Yeah."

"It is good for business," she said casually as if stating a well-known fact.

Nethery looked at her, and there were a few moments of silence again, as they both stared into the distance. He felt a vague sense that their time together on this day was coming to an end.

"I would like to see you again," Nethery said.

"Yes?"

"Yeah. I think so."

"Why you choose me? Others better maybe."

"I like you."

"Nothing will happen. This is not movie."

"I know."

"What will we do?"

"Oh, I dunno. Kill time."

"Very well," she said, grinning and nodding her head slightly. "I will kill time with you."

Nethery smiled and looked over at her, and then she smiled, and then he laughed and she joined in and she was surprised. She was actually having a good time. It was a first for her, when meeting a man outside the club. She decided to bring the situation back down to earth.

"It will cost much money," she said.

"I know," Nethery said, as if he'd known she would say that.

"You won't ask questions? You won't try to make me quit job? Follow me to club and make trouble?"

"No."

"Why?"

"That's none of my business."

"Yes," Lily said nodding, looking at the ground, "it is true."

"Can I ask you one question?" Nethery asked.

"Maybe," she replied.

"How do you speak English so well?"

"With my mouth."

Nethery looked over at her. She was grinning and he chuckled.

"I see," he said, "you're a smartass."

"Yes. I am smartass. This is problem?"

"No. In fact, I kind of like it."

They sat there and smoked another cigarette. The tourist boats had disappeared and it had become very quiet. Neither of them spoke yet there wasn't a rising tension driving an impulse to begin talking again. The sun had moved to a different place in the sky, and they were no longer sitting in the sun. Nethery gathered up their trash and threw it into a garbage bin. They walked back to the Esplanade des Invalides in silence. When they got to the bench, they arranged to meet again in two days. Nethery leaned forward and kissed both her cheeks, as he assumed he was supposed to, and when he did, he felt her arms begin to reach around him, but they stopped as he responded, and in the end they shared an awkward half embrace. He sat down on the bench and watched her walk toward the bridge.

Nethery woke the next morning in a state of confusion. He thought about exploring the city, like he'd been doing every day, but his thoughts kept drifting back to Lily. Images of her kept floating in front of whatever he was thinking about, particularly her pale grayish-green eyes and the way they would change, from sleepy and seductive to innocent and bright. He puttered around the apartment, trying to settle on a museum or tourist attraction to visit, but he found himself unable to come to a decision, the image of her face superimposed over his thoughts.

Eventually he forced himself to go out and get some coffee and croissants from the rotonde on Avenue St. Ouen. Not knowing what else to do he'd gone directly back to the flat. He drank the coffee and ate the croissant, went into the bedroom and opened the French windows and looked out into the courtyard. A breeze came in and blew the long sheer white drapes around him. He sat on the window ledge and smoked a cigarette, tipping the ashes into a soda can he had placed in the planter that sat in a tiny wrought iron balcony mounted below the window. After, he went into the kitchen, looking for something to do, and his eyes were drawn to the bottle of wine on the counter. The woman he'd rented the place from had left it as a welcome gift. He hadn't told her about his drinking problem. He stared at the bottle, and a nervous tension crept into his stomach. He took a Coke from the fridge and sat down on the couch. He turned on the television but the only thing on that he could understand was the news. Eventually he turned the television off, put his feet up on the coffee table, and fell asleep.

He awoke at around 8 p.m. Very quickly he became angry with himself for wasting an entire day. He went to the sink to get a glass of water, and his eyes were once again drawn to the wine, the magnetic pull starting to play tricks on his mind, rationalizations and justifications floating around in his head, looking for a crack in his defenses. He figured he'd better get out of there and do something. Anything. He put on his leather jacket and pork pie hat, made sure he had cigarettes and his map of the Paris Metro, and left.

Outside the night seemed darker than usual, and the city was very quiet. He walked down Rue Carpeaux to Place Jacques Froment and sat down at the bar of Le Petit Caboulot. He ordered a coffee, but very quickly became restless and knew that a trip half a block to the café was not going to be enough. He finished the coffee, walked back down past his flat, turned down Rue Etex, and headed toward Avenue St. Ouen. When he got there he descended the steps to the Guy Môquet station and bought a ticket from a machine. There were only a few people on the platform. The train arrived within minutes and he took a seat near the door. Across from him an old woman sat reading a book. After two stops a young girl not more than fourteen boarded towing an old beat-up grocery cart that had been altered into a sort of dolly. On it were stacked a car battery and what looked like a mixing board and a speaker. When the train got moving she turned on some hip-hop music and strolled up and down the aisle rapping through a wireless microphone to the music blaring from her contraption.

At Invalides station he got off, followed the passageways, and climbed the steps until he emerged from underground. He felt like he'd been in a tight and closed space, and he took a few deep breaths and looked around. The area was very quiet. The bench where he'd met Lily sat empty and the newspaper stand had its flaps down. The Pont Alexandre III, just off to the left, was lit up like a movie set by Art Nouveau lamps that lined each side. It was magnificent, the most beautiful infrastructure he'd ever seen. Nethery stepped onto the bridge, passing between two tall pedestals with winged horses mounted atop. He continued walking until he was near the center, next to a cherub of hammered copper that leaned out over the river. He set his elbows on the elaborate railing and gazed off at the Eiffel Tower, the lights forming an arrow pointing at the sky. They're right, Nethery thought, this is the City of Light.

He removed the passport from the inside pocket of his jacket. In the glow of the overhead lamp, he stared at the photo. He didn't recognize that person anymore, the wry smile, the smug look. What a punk, he thought. Entitled, arrogant. He stared for a moment longer, and then scrunched up the pages of the passport, one by one. He removed his Zippo lighter, flipped open the lid, and spun the wheel. He held the flame under the passport and eventually it caught fire. Turning it in his hand, it burned slowly, the gentle breeze not enough to put it out. He watched the flame change colors from yellow to orange and then blue as it slowly crept across the photo. Eventually pieces of ash began to fall away, down into the blackness. When nothing remained but the spine, he let it fall from his fingers. He leaned over the rail, looked down, and there was nothing, the river silently flowing beneath a surface of black.

His cell phone rang and he became immediately irritated. He jerked the phone from his pocket, but he simply held it in his hand and let it ring. He put the phone back into his pocket and stood there, slumped on the railing, mesmerized by the lights flickering on the surface of the water. Black and shiny, like a river of oil. He lit a cigarette, smoked it until it was done, and flipped it out over the edge. He began to walk, took about ten steps, and stopped. He removed his cell phone from his pocket, walked over to the railing, and grunted as he hurled the phone as hard as he could into the darkness.

He left the bridge and began wandering the Left Bank. He walked and kept walking, not paying attention to where he was going. The image of Lily's eyes kept flashing in his mind and as he walked he wondered what she was doing at that moment and then he knew, and it bothered him a little and he felt a twinge of jealousy. He wondered if he was becoming obsessed with her. But it was more than her outward beauty that attracted him, and continued to attract him. Or perhaps he was just telling himself that. Maybe he did only want to use her and then throw her away and was making up all this so he wouldn't feel so bad about it.

Lost in thought, he almost walked into traffic. He looked around and found he was on the Boulevard St. Germain. It began to rain. He started walking again and eventually turned off the boulevard onto a side street. He had no idea where he was but he didn't much care. His clothes were beginning to soak through but he ignored it and followed a few back streets and found himself on a street corner and realized he was hungry and tired. He walked past numerous cafés but they were French and he couldn't face the language barrier at the moment. Eventually he came upon a place called The Moose that he guessed was a Canadian bar from the sign, a large red maple leaf. He stood there for a few minutes, perplexed, wondering what a Canadian bar was doing in Paris, but he began to grow cold and walked inside. There were moose heads mounted on the walls, and a crowd of English-speaking people were watching

BBC World News on a television above the bar. He made his way through them up to the bar, took a peek at a menu, and ordered a cheeseburger from the bartender. He found a table near the corner, next to a smaller television mounted on the wall.

There was a man at the next table. He had a bunch of papers spread out covering the entire table except for a small area for his glass of beer and plate of food. Nethery looked over, and the man was smiling at him.

"*Bonsoir*," the man said, cheerfully.

"*Bonsoir*," Nethery replied, hoping the man would leave him be.

"English?" the man asked, discerning Nethery's accent.

"*Américain*," he replied, trying to pronounce it the way the French did.

"Ah!" the man exclaimed. "What are you doing here in Paris?" he asked, in fluent English.

Nethery thought for a moment and chewed on his lip, but said nothing.

"Are you here on business?" the man asked.

"Uhhh," Nethery replied, "I don't really know what that word means, *business*."

The man looked at Nethery strangely and then continued.

"Are you here for work?"

"No, no . . ." Nethery answered, and it occurred to him that he didn't know what that word meant anymore either.

"What is it you *do*?" the man asked.

"Well, I don't really *do* anything," he replied, chuckling, "not anymore. And you know," Nethery said, staring off into space, "I'm not sure I ever have."

"So, you are on vacation?" the man asked, responding to Nethery's confusion.

"I came here to get away from there," Nethery said, blurting out the truth in the simplest way he could.

"Ahhh, yes," the man said, nodding. "Why Paris?" the man asked.

"Oh," Nethery said, shrugging his shoulders, "I just had to get out of there. The place is goin' down the drain."

"Yes," the man said, "we are living in strange times."

"At least America is strange, and sick."

"Bravo," the man said. "It is true, empires come and go, but Europe remains. But I must warn you. Paris is not much better."

A waitress brought Nethery's cheeseburger and the man at the next table went back to savagely attacking the steak on his plate. Nethery began to eat, and as he chewed he was overcome with a feeling that eating was the most tedious and disgusting activity on earth. The way his jaw moved up and down, mechanically, the incredible violence of his teeth breaking the food into tiny pieces, the sickening and out-of-control way his mouth produced saliva, and the repulsive way his throat convulsed when it shoved the lump of food down his throat. He couldn't even bear to imagine what happened to the food once it was down in his stomach. He set the burger down on his plate and stared at it. He took a drink from the glass of water and swilled it around to try and wash the sickening taste out of his mouth.

Nethery heard shouting from the men at the bar and saw that they were staring at the television. He turned his attention to the television near his table and there was a banner across the screen: *BBC Special Report*. After a few moments a man appeared on the screen holding a microphone. He appeared to be standing on a beach, and the wind was blowing his hair around.

> *This is Joshua Coleman of the BBC, reporting from Nassau in the Bahamas. Ben Chandler, CEO of Brighton Holdings, one of the largest hedge funds in the world, has been assassinated, apparently by the People's Mafia. His wife and three bodyguards were*

also killed. Their headless bodies were discovered outside the smoldering ruins of Chandler's thirty-million-dollar mansion. The heads were later found as part of some kind of mobile, assembled from bamboo poles and fishing line, hanging from a palm tree on the beach. Attached to the tongue of each was a length of fishing line, dangling from which were the words "This-Is-What-We-Do." Reports suggest that last week Mr. Chandler received a threat of some nature at his office on Wall Street, and had reported it to the FBI. Apparently, he had decided to come here while it was investigated . . .

Everything was going to hell. These attacks, if that's what you chose to call them, had been happening for a while. Nethery's thoughts drifted back to how the whole thing had begun, about a year before. He'd been at work. His coworkers had been gathered around a computer, watching a video. It was night. A house filled the screen, the camera placed in the front yard. A man stepped in front of the camera. He looked to be about thirty-five, and he gazed at the camera for a moment, as if he was about to say something, but then he turned and walked toward the house. He was carrying an old-style red steel gas can in one hand, and in the other a bouquet of roses. He set the flowers on the doorstep and poured gas over the front door, the porch, and all along the front of the house. He then kissed the door and set fire to it, took a few steps back, threw the bouquet of roses into the flames and watched. Within one minute the entire front of the house was ablaze and he had to keep taking steps back from the heat. He then turned and walked back toward the camera, his face getting closer and closer and until there was nothing but his face filling the screen, surrounded by an eerie glow. He grinned and said, "*This is what we do.*" And then he walked off screen, a gunshot was heard, and the video ended.

The video went viral. The man, Paul Delaney, had automated the video to flood the internet after he killed himself. Media reports stated he had lost his job, had financial problems, and his wife had died. It would have been a footnote but three days after that the FBI cornered a man named Donovan Brand in a bank in Cleveland. He had taken hostages, and there was a tense standoff that went on for hours, broadcast live by the major news networks. At one point Brand emerged from the bank and, reminiscent of Al Pacino in *Dog Day Afternoon*, he strutted up and down the sidewalk waving a towel and screaming, "We are the People's Mafia! Yeah, baby! That's right! We are the People's Mafia!" to cheering crowds. Shortly after he released the hostages and detonated a bomb, killing himself and destroying part of the bank.

Because they were both suicides, and seemingly trying to convey some kind of message, the media speculated that Delaney and Brand were part of some organized revolt. It seemed absurd to Nethery, but the story acquired a kind of momentum that failed to dissipate and actually triggered an escalation. It was as if the phrase "*This is what we do*" had been slipped into people's minds when they were sleeping, fueling an epidemic of crime including a rash of bank and armored car robberies and all of them marked the scenes of the crimes with the phrase, *This is what we do*. Within a month the phrase was everywhere, in cities spray-painted on walls and buildings and on cleverly altered billboards, and in the country, spelled out like a crop circle in a field of wheat, painted on the sides of barns and grain silos. Trucks carrying goods across the nation had it painted on their trailers. Nethery had even seen on the news where some schoolchildren, after being busted for skipping class, responded by saying, *This is what we do*.

The man at the next table laughed, and it pulled Nethery out of his thoughts. On the television they were having a White

House press conference. A government official appeared at the podium and said that no expense would be spared tracking down these criminals and bringing them to justice. A reporter asked about the People's Mafia, and the official responded that there was no such thing, that these were crazed loners and lunatics. The reporter then asked why, if there was no such group, private security forces had been brought in to protect Wall Street. The man at the next table laughed again, and Nethery looked over at him. The man wildly cut off a piece of steak, stabbed it with a fork, wiped it through the bloody juice on his plate, placed it into his mouth, and then looked over at Nethery and grinned as he chewed on the meat.

She double-checked her makeup in the mirror. Over the last couple of years she had grown ambivalent about her face. She no longer meticulously spent hours applying her makeup. It was more out of habit. She had the products that she trusted, and that was all, she no longer got excited about trying out every new product that came on the market. In fact, it now seemed like an enormous waste of time. What used to be two hours in front of the mirror was now fifteen minutes. How many hours had she wasted sitting in makeup chairs or gazing into a reflective piece of glass? How many hours had she wasted looking into the bottomless pit, searching for the end of the abyss?

It had been two days since her date with Nethery, and strangely Lily had found herself thinking about him. He kept surfacing in her mind, buoyed by the fact that he was something more than merely a source of cash. She couldn't quite put her finger on what it was that interested her, his placid sort of nihilism, his pragmatism. It was very different from the other Americans she had met. He seemed more European.

Lily bumped her elbow on the medicine cabinet and cursed. The bathroom was tiny, the apartment as well. She still hadn't adjusted. When she'd arrived in Paris, Claude had set her up in an apartment in the Marais, large and airy with high ceilings and a spacious bathroom. Entirely another world from the one she now inhabited. The future had seemed so bright, for a time. That was over. Claude had seen to that. Even before she'd been blacklisted her career as a model had begun to fall apart, like pieces flying off a world spinning too fast. It wasn't she that had changed, it was a gradual narrowing as her access to certain people shifted. It was like the decay of a living thing. If you stood there and watched, it appeared that nothing was happening.

She stepped into the hallway, locked the door of her apartment. And there it was: the quagmire of self-pity, the thing that she despised almost more than anything else, in herself and everyone else. She drove it away before she began to sink and focused on the task at hand, meeting Nethery, and getting his money. At least it wasn't awkward, being with him. He was even a little bit funny. More often than not spending time with the ones that wanted to talk ended up being unbearable, so tedious and uncomfortable it was almost not worth it. There were many times when it had taken a supreme effort to just not be a bitch, but it was different with this one. She didn't feel compelled to belittle or insult him, and at the moment she didn't know why.

She started down the hallway and as she passed #203 music assaulted her from within the apartment. This time, some kind of heavy metal with a pounding bass. It was so loud it was as if the door wasn't even there, and seemed to drive her all the way over to the railing. She had only seen the tenant once, in the hall, screaming at his girlfriend. When he saw Lily he had pulled out a large bag of cocaine and tried to lure her into the apartment, right there in front of his girlfriend. Lily had ignored him and kept walking and he had called her a bitch. She had also caught a glimpse of his apartment through the open door. While most of the apartments in the building were tiny studios and one bedrooms, his was a futuristic space seemingly made up entirely of chrome and stainless steel. Henri down in #102 had told her his

father owned the building, and was some sort of business tycoon, chairman of a bank. Lily despised him, and the girl. They
had driven her friend Jeanette in the apartment next to theirs to
tears on numerous occasions, keeping her awake for days on end
with the music.

It was raining, and Lily stepped outside of her building and
opened her umbrella. Nethery had wanted to meet at Deux Ma-
gots, only a few blocks from her flat. It wasn't cold but the rain
looked as if it would get worse, and there were dark clouds covering the entire sky. She walked the short distance to the café and
found Nethery already there, sitting under the awning, sipping
on a café crème.

"Hello," he said, "sit down and have a coffee."

"Thank you," she said, shaking and then closing her umbrella. She sat down and ordered a shot of espresso. Nethery slid
an envelope containing the money across the table. Lily put it in
her purse without looking at it.

"What we do today?" she asked.

"I thought we might just walk around," Nethery said, looking across the street at the church, Saint-Germain-des-Prés.

"But . . . it is raining," Lily replied. "We will be wet."

"It won't kill us."

Lily grinned and dug around in her bag, and then cursed in
Ukrainian.

"What?" Nethery asked.

"I have forgotten my mobile."

Lily felt safe enough to suggest that they walk to her flat together to pick up her phone, and after their coffee they set out.
The rain had gotten worse and Lily suggested Nethery walk next
to her in order to get under her umbrella.

"Since we aren't gonna . . . you know . . . get involved . . .
can I ask you a few questions?" Nethery asked, while they were
stopped at a crosswalk.

"Oh. Very well . . ."

"Why aren't you modeling anymore?"

"That is long story," she said.

"I have time."

The light changed and they started across the street.

"I came to Paris with man named Claude. When I am sixteen," Lily said. "He is manager of models. He discover me in Kiev. He bring me to Paris, get me jobs."

"And?"

"For long time it is good. I am rising star. I am doing runway show, photo shoot for magazine. Milan, London, Madrid, Barcelona."

"Uh-huh."

They had reached the other side of the street and Lily angled off until she was under an awning. Nethery followed. When they were out of the rain she turned and looked up at him with a serious face.

"I was on cover of magazine many times. I was on television, advertisement. But . . . I . . . when I am twenty years old . . . I am not so popular."

"Really?"

"Yes. I had some . . . problem . . . with photographers . . . some of them . . . they want to play games. I only want to work. I do not like games," she said, looking hard up at Nethery as if issuing a warning.

"So the jobs . . . they do not come so much. It is not so unusual. Many models are only popular for one years, two years. Unless you get to top."

"I see."

"But there are other things. To make money. Private show, go on dates. Claude has friends," she said, raising her eyebrows and looking up at him.

"You do not *have* to do these things. But I was . . . not happy that I was not so popular."

"I see," Nethery said.

"It is fine. I understand. It is the way. The men, they just want to *party*," she said, sarcastically. "But it is okay. I say I don't want do something, they hear me. But one time, I am model for big shots of makeup company. From Japan. Business friends of Claude. I do it before. It is okay. They are strange. They want me to lay naked on table and eat sushi from my body. I do this two times, no problem. Ten thousand euro. Is good money. I understand, they are silly men. They want to play games. What I care? It is good money. But then last time, one man . . . he was big boss, from Tokyo . . . he was . . . how you say . . . he have that look. He was bad man. I can tell," she said nodding. Then she looked up at Nethery and continued, speaking slowly and with a quiet intensity.

"He get drunk, he get close, he look down at me . . . in the eyes. No smile. Then he push my legs open, he push rice into my pussy. Put chopstick in ass. I do nothing. It is okay. What I care? But then he . . . oh, what it called . . . the green . . . ?" she said, rubbing her thumb and forefinger together.

"Wasabi?"

"Yes. Wasabi. He rub wasabi onto my pussy. It burns and . . . and . . . and . . . I go crazy. I grab chopstick and try to stab him in eye. I miss, but his ear cut up, start bleeding. I was . . . broken," she said, shaking her head, ". . . I was so angry . . . the other men. I scratch them and kick them in balls. They are scared. They run into bathroom and lock the door."

"Wow."

"Yes."

"So what happened?"

"They say to Claude, she must be punished. She must not be allowed to work. No more jobs."

"Fuck."

"Yes. Fuck."

"That really sucks ass."

"Yes."

"You couldn't find another manager?"

"No. Claude know everyone. In many countries. If I start work somewhere, he get trouble. So he tell everyone."

"That's how you ended up at the club?" Nethery asked.

"Yes . . . I did not know what to do . . . I could not go home . . . Claude had passport . . . and I was . . . going to parties and being drunk and taking many drugs . . . and one of the models, she work at club sometime . . . and so . . ." she shrugged, "I was there too."

There were a few moments of silence, and then Lily continued.

"I wanted to be model, still," she said, looking up at Nethery, wincing, her voice dripping with regret. "I was good model. Not like most. Most are only good at one thing, walking runway, face model, bikini. I do everything. I was never drunk, I never take drugs, never complain . . ." she said. Nethery could see the pain, the disappointment as she remembered. It was written on her face, and her shoulders sagged as if she was trying to curl up in a ball while still standing.

Nethery didn't know what to say, and he stood there, searching for words. Eventually she looked up at him. She was standing straight again, and had obviously placed it all into a compartment and shoved it away. She forced a smile, turned, and began walking. He caught up until he was walking beside her. She stared at a point on the sidewalk ahead of her and very quickly they were at the door or Lily's building. She shook the rain from her umbrella and closed it up.

"You come," she said, and Nethery followed her through the door.

They reached the top of the staircase and there was an old woman, slumped against the wall, next to the door to #203.

"Jeanette!" Lily exclaimed, and ran over to her. She put her arm around the woman, helped her up and began to lead her down the hall. They exchanged some words in broken English. As they neared an open door toward the end of the hall the old woman saw that Nethery was there. She perked up, wiped the tears from her face and said something to Lily. She walked over to Nethery, put her hands on his shoulders, gazed up into his face and smiled, then turned back to Lily and began talking. Lily managed to usher her through the open door of her apartment. They spoke for a minute longer, out of earshot, but Nethery could see that the old woman had cheered up slightly. Eventually Lily said goodbye to her and Nethery followed Lily farther down the hall to the door of her apartment. She unlocked it and Nethery waited in the narrow alcove as Lily retrieved her mobile phone from the kitchen table.

They walked down to the Seine and caught the RER to the Eiffel Tower. On the train they chatted about this and that but after they arrived, they were walking together under her umbrella and his curiosity got the better of him.

"What was going on with that old lady?"

"Oh," Lily said, "that is Jeanette. She is sweet old lady."

"Were you talking about me?"

"Yes," Lily replied, grinning. "She was very excited to see me with man."

"Oh?"

"Yes. She has been after me for months to get boyfriend," Lily said, chuckling. "She say you are good man."

"Her judgement leaves something to be desired," he said, and then he laughed.

"What? You are not good man?" Lily asked, grinning.

Nethery seemed to be thinking for a moment.

"Why was she upset?" he asked.

"The man in apartment next to her? He is piece of shit. They are always with the music. She cannot sleep. She call police, she call apartment people? They do nothing. She go to talk to them, and man, he piss on her! In hallway!"

"What? You mean he . . . ?" Nethery said, pointing at his crotch.

"Yes! He follow her down hallway!" she exclaimed, holding her hands before her pelvis, gesturing like she was spraying a hose.

They had lunch in a café, and afterward they talked and smoked and laughed. Lily's bag was on the ground between their chairs, one of those large stiff rectangular black patent leather bags. He glanced down and something caught his eye. It was a handgun, sitting atop her wallet and other things. It looked like a Walther PPK, a model he'd used at the gun range years before. Nethery stopped smiling and looked up.

"What's the gun for?" he asked carefully, nodding down toward her bag. Lily paused for a moment, took a drag of her cigarette, and then blew the smoke out slowly, looking him straight in the eye.

"Men," she replied, quietly.

Nethery looked back at her apprehensively, not knowing what to say.

"I know," Lily sighed, "I am prostitute. You think I should let people do what they want?"

"Nooo . . ." Nethery replied, shaking his head.

"They pay and they do what I let them do," Lily continued, staring hard at Nethery, suddenly very upset, her voice beginning to rise. "They do not pay and do what they want. There are some girls who do not care. There are some girls who turn off. There are some who take drugs. They do not care. They let men do what they want. I understand this. But not me! I am the one who say what happens."

"I thought maybe it was for me."

"For you?" she said, and laughed. "You think I have gun for you? No," she said, still laughing and shaking her head. "Not for you."

They spent the rest of the afternoon walking around the parks near the Eiffel Tower. It continued to rain, and Nethery jokingly would wander out from under Lily's umbrella. She would pretend to be irritated and he would pretend to reluctantly join her again under the umbrella. They had stopped in the center of a grassy field and she handed the umbrella to Nethery in order to light a cigarette. Nethery tore the umbrella to pieces.

"Now we both have to be wet," he said, handing the broken umbrella back to her. Lily stood there, the rain running down her face in little streams. She threw away her soggy cigarette and stared hard at Nethery. It seemed like she was going to throw a fit for a moment, but then she relaxed, smiled, and raised the useless umbrella over their heads. They both laughed. They continued walking and Nethery would drift out from under the imaginary cover of the umbrella and she would chase him around trying to get him back under it. Eventually they were soaked through to the skin and they made their way to a café. Nethery ordered coffee for both of them.

"What you do before you come here?" Lily asked.

"Oh Christ."

"Tell. I want to know."

"Well, I worked for a cell phone company."

"Yes?"

"It was a good job, I suppose . . . I mean . . . it paid well, but . . ."

"Yes?"

"It was what we call back in the States soul-destroying."

"What that?"

"That's where you don't create anything, you don't build anything, you spend hours, days, months, years on end, just sitting there, staring at a screen, just moving numbers around, not really doing anything . . .

"I didn't really hate it, exactly . . . and I kept wondering why I didn't hate it, because it was pointless. I kept finding myself asking why I was doing it, why I didn't quit, and I could never come up with a good answer."

Lily obviously didn't understand, but got the gist and made an ugly face.

"That sound bad," she said.

"Yeah well. People do it their entire lives. It's no wonder they're so fucked up."

"But that wasn't what made me quit. It was something else. Something happened . . . and I just couldn't stand it anymore."

"What happen?"

"The girl in the next cubicle . . . she started bringing her dog to work."

"Dog?"

"Yeah. It was against the rules. But she bothered and bothered the office manager. He always said no. Then she went to the bosses, they said no too, and eventually she threatened to sue the company if she wasn't allowed to bring her dog to work with her. She tried to claim it was some kind of service animal, and she couldn't function without it. They gave in. Don't ask me why. There was nothing wrong with her. So she brought her dog to work. It lay under her desk and made yelping noises and threw up all the time."

"It is stupid," Lily said, looking at him.

"You got that right. Everyone complained, but since they had given in they said they couldn't do anything. But I should actually thank her, really. It was the last straw. That fuckin' place," Nethery said, shaking his head and starting to laugh. "I'd been thinking about quitting for years, but I had never been able to do anything about it until that woman brought that damned dog around."

Nethery was leaned over the stove in his flat, glancing at directions he'd scrawled onto a piece of paper. He'd always been a terrible cook and he wanted to get this right. A week had passed since the Eiffel Tower and he and Lily had seen each other almost every day, and most nights when Lily wasn't at the club. They'd been to obscure movies in far corners of the city, had dinner in tiny cafés, took long walks through parks and cemeteries. Lily had agreed on a price of one thousand euros for each date regardless of time spent. It had been an awkward conversation and Nethery had noticed that Lily had stopped asking him for the money. She displayed some reticence when taking it but Nethery was happy to keep giving it to her. A couple days before, Lily had asked him over to her flat for dinner; they were joined by Jeanette, who appeared to be the only friend Lily had in Paris. Jeanette spoke passable English, and was very talkative. She had a sister who lived down on the south coast of France. The only thing that ruined the evening was the noise from #203. They hadn't even been able to converse without shouting. Eventually Nethery went down the hall and banged on the door. The man appeared, stinking of booze, his bloated face dripping with sweat, and wearing a Brown University T-shirt with food stains all over it. He hurled a few obscenities, and slammed the door in Nethery's face.

The fish was done cooking, or he guessed it was, and he turned the stove down to warm and checked the table settings. He'd gone down to the market at St. Ouen earlier in the day and bought some fresh fish and vegetables, candles for the dinner table, and some flowers to put in a vase. It was strange, trying to impress a woman. It wasn't something he'd done before. They had just come and gone and he hadn't felt anything for any of them except a fleeting desire, not love, not even obsession. He'd begun to wonder if there was something wrong with him, that he lacked some fundamental human quality. For the longest time he didn't give this a second thought, but meeting Lily had brought it sharply into focus, and he vaguely felt compelled to try and do things differently with her if he had the chance.

He was also aware that a physical attraction had developed between them. Nothing had happened yet, and since it hadn't, the normal sequence of events had been off course and he wasn't quite sure how to get them back on track. And even if he did, was he was falling in love with her or was it simply desire? Had he been in love before? Love, desire, lust, he was unable to tell them apart with any precision. Somehow, he felt that knowing the difference was essential before proceeding, so every time he felt like grabbing her and kissing her he held back, partly because of that and partly because their friendship seemed to be going along so smoothly he didn't want to risk ruining it. There was a certain sense that what he had stumbled upon was something so delicate, and so rare, that he was treading very carefully so as not to break it.

"I think I am going to go see Claude," Lily said after they had eaten, smoking on the window ledge of his bedroom. She was staring out the window.

"Really?"

"Yes . . . I . . . he has passport."

"He'll just give it back to you?"

"No," she said, chuckling, and turning back to face him. "I will have to do something."

"Like what?"

"I am not sure. Porno, maybe."

"Claude does porno?"

"No, he would never be seen with these people. But he knows them. I have met them. With him. You have problem with this?"

"No, I don't care. I just . . . can't you just give him some money?"

"You do not understand," she said and she laughed. "Claude, he has money. No, he will want me to do something. Something I do not want to do."

After dinner they were walking down Rue Etex when Lily slowed, took a few unsteady steps and put her hand on a car to lean against it. He hadn't flinched when she mentioned the porno. He hadn't reacted with disgust, hadn't even looked at her differently. The full meaning hadn't crystallized, or possibly she had also been deliberately ignoring it, but now it hit her like a brick. She hadn't really had any friends in many years, not really since grade school it seemed, when she'd been an awkward, gangly kid. Of course she had found that many people wanted to be around her when she was modeling, but her exceptional beauty had alienated her from most of her peers and the less pretty girls she had been a bitch to. At any rate they had all vanished as soon as Claude blacklisted her. She wasn't so dim that it surprised her, but she had been saddened the way every single one of them had abandoned her. And now she had a friend, possibly even something more, the implications of the latter she refused to even consider. She looked over at him. It was true, he was absolutely free of judgement. Even though Nethery was good-looking he was not the kind of man she would have dated when she was riding high, and yet she didn't feel the need to condescend or display the arrogant and bitchy aloofness she had so many times with men like him.

Nethery saw something was wrong, came over, and took her arm.

"Are you okay?" he asked.

"Yes. I am fine," she lied, trying to stamp down her emotions, embarrassed at her reaction.

Lily gathered herself, raised her head, took a couple of deep breaths, smiled half-heartedly, and then pulled herself together. She hooked her arm through Nethery's and they continued on to the Metro station.

Nethery followed her through the turnstile and onto the platform. As they waited for the train to arrive Lily thought about how over the last week their goodbyes had grown increasingly awkward. What had begun as a simple hug had become a tense and complicated affair as she felt a kind of vacuum, as if the moment was lacking something. She was certain he felt it too. When the train was close enough they could hear it coming. Lily looked deeply into Nethery's eyes, brushed his hair away from his face, got up on her tiptoes, and kissed his cheek softly for a few seconds. Nethery stood there, stunned, and was going to hold her and kiss her back, but before he could do anything she turned, walked toward the train and through the open doors. As the train pulled away she looked back at him through the window.

The Place de la Bastille was terribly noisy, and there was a seemingly endless stream of honking cars circling the July Column. Nethery sat on the bench and chewed slowly on a baguette. Lily was sitting next to him, energetically devouring her sandwich, occasionally looking over at him and grinning, her mouth full of food. She had surprised him by coming over first thing in the morning. She'd been very excited, and told him something good was going to happen today and that she wanted to see some museums. He'd asked her what it was about but she had merely smiled. Nethery hadn't slept much and would have rather done something relaxing, but he went along and followed her first to the Rodin, then the Orsay, until they ended up nearby at the Picasso Museum. She had been checking her watch all day and earlier mentioned something about needing to be in this neighborhood.

Nethery finished his sandwich, lit a cigarette, and looked over at her. She was leaning back on the bench with her eyes closed and her face tilted up toward the sun. He could see now why she'd been such a versatile model. She had an unusual quality, an ability to transform her appearance without the assistance of makeup or lighting. Normally she looked like an incredibly pretty young woman, but with a slight shift in posture and facial expression she could go from that to a seductress who screamed sex or an innocent teenage waif who knew nothing of the ways of the world. This quality seemed to extend to her physically as well; some of the time she appeared voluptuous and curvy but right now she looked like a skinny young girl. Lily's cell phone rang and it brought her out of her reverie. She answered the call and had a brief conversation.

"I have to see Claude," Lily said cheerfully after she hung up.

"Oh?"

"Yes."

"Right now?"

"Yes."

"You gonna get your passport back?"

"Yes," she said, smiling. "Come with me. Is not far."

They set off, walking along the median of Boulevard Richard Lenoir. After a couple of blocks Lily stopped, grabbed Nethery's arm, and looked up at him seriously.

"You know that . . . this thing . . . it cannot . . ." she said, glancing down at the ground. Nethery looked at her, not understanding.

"This thing? It will not go forever," she said, looking up. "You will run out of money and go home," she continued, "I will go work somewhere else. Germany maybe, where is legal."

"Isn't there something else you could do?" Nethery asked. There was a pause, and she seemed to be thinking.

"I could do website," Lily said, looking up at him.

"Website?"

"Yes. What some models do. They have website for strip show. For fucking boyfriend."

"But you would need a boyfriend."

"You could do," she said, grinning.

Nethery was surprised and didn't know what to say.

"It is okay," Lily said. "If you still here after money gone I will see you. Maybe, I pay you to see me," she said and then she laughed, twirled once, and skipped a few steps ahead. Nethery caught up to her and they continued walking along the median. After a few blocks they crossed the street and arrived at an apartment building.

"This will not take long," Lily said, pushing a code into a keypad by the door. "You can wait here. Claude does not allow cigarettes."

There was a tiny market next door, and Nethery bought a Coca-Cola, walked out to the median of the boulevard, and sat on a bench in the shade of some trees. The sun was preparing to disappear somewhere behind him and he could feel the beginnings of a slight chill in the air. He watched as the shadows before him grew longer and longer as the night worked to finish what it started.

Lily climbed the stairs up to the second floor, and as she walked down the hallway she remarked that somehow it seemed much longer than before. She came to the door, hesitated for a moment, and then knocked. There was music coming from inside and after a moment the door swung open.

"Agnieszka!" Claude exclaimed, overdoing it in that artificially happy way that Lily knew so well. Lily stepped inside the apartment and Claude gently pushed the door closed.

"Let me take your coat," Claude said. She removed her bag from her shoulder and set it at the foot of the coatrack. Claude helped her remove her coat and hung it up.

"Come in, come in," Claude said and led the way out of the hallway and across the living room to a table by the windows. Off to the side Lily noticed two men sitting on a couch in the corner of the living room with their backs to her, playing some kind of video game. Claude sat on one side of the table and Lily the other.

"How are things going at the club?" Claude asked, smugly. Lily paused for a minute, wondering how he'd known about that.

"The club is fine," she said, trying not to sound surprised.

"Ohh, Agnieszka," Claude said, sighing and staring at her, "you are as beautiful as ever. Your new haircut is . . . very sexy."

"I not use that name anymore."

"Oh? And what shall I call you?"

"Call me Lily."

"Lily?"

"Yes. I change club, I change name."

"I see. That is smart. You always were, and you always were . . . very . . . spirited. And so? What do you want to talk about?" Claude asked, a slight smirk on his face.

He knows damned well what I want to talk about, Lily thought, but she kept her cool.

"I need passport back, Claude."

"Of course my dear. I had forgotten. It's here somewhere, I think."

Lily could tell he was playing games so she continued.

"I've been thinking about the porno," she said.

"Yes, well, we can probably work something out," Claude said, folding his hands on the table in front of him. The way he said it irritated her.

"But it cannot just be anything," Lily continued. "It cannot be some cheap shit. It must be good movies, top class. Private, or something," she said.

"Of course, of course," Claude said, "I will make some phone calls. We will get you started."

The ease at which he agreed made her nervous, and she looked at him closely to see if she could discern what he was thinking, but as usual his face gave away nothing. It remained pleasant and calm. It was a lie, and she knew it. Claude never outwardly expressed anything, but she had seen how vindictive and cruel he could be, and the pleasure he took from it. He stood up and walked around the table until he was directly behind Lily. He put his hands on her shoulders and she tensed up.

"Lily, my dear. You know that you cost me a lot of money," Claude said, rubbing her shoulders slowly.

"I'm sorry, Claude," Lily said, alarm bells going off inside her. "They should not have . . ."

"I know, my dear," Claude said, soothingly.

"They were . . ."

"Shhhh. It is okay. You can make it up to me."

Lily faintly sensed that something bad was going to happen, and became slightly frightened, but told herself that she was imagining things and pushed it back inside her. Claude had moved around to the other side of the table again, sat on the stool, and was looking at her.

"If we are to do this," Claude said, "I have to make certain that you are suited for it."

"What?"

"I have to know that there will not be a repeat of what happened before. I have to know that you can do this."

"Of course I can do it," Lily said, indignantly.

"Yes, but . . . I have to *know*."

The two men had gotten up from the couch and were walking toward them. They were well built, Spanish-looking. Models probably.

"Claude? What are you doing?"

"We are going to see if you are suited to do porno," he said, casually.

"You fuck," Lily spat.

"Now, now, Agnieszka . . . or Lily . . . or whatever you want to call yourself. Do not be upset. Think of this as a test. A screen test."

"I do not need this. I do not need test," Lily said, angrily.

She stood up from the table, but realized that the two men had moved to a position between her and the way out.

"This can be easy, or not so easy, my dear. Either way, you *will* be tested."

"You fuck!" Lily shouted. She grabbed a glass vase from the table and hurled it at Claude. He ducked and it crashed through the window behind him and fell to the street below. The two men had come up behind her and grabbed her arms. She managed to get out the beginnings of a scream and then a hand clamped over her mouth.

Nethery heard breaking glass behind him and he turned to look. Something had fallen into the street and shattered. He looked up and saw a hole in a second-floor window. He got up and began to walk across the street. He thought he heard a woman scream, briefly, just for a second, and he continued to the door. It was locked. He walked back out into the street, looked up at the window, and stood there for a minute. Nothing more happened, but he had a bad feeling in his gut. He noticed a woman coming out of the building and he ran over and caught the door before it closed. She gave him a dirty look, but he ignored her and walked in and climbed the staircase to the second-floor landing.

One of the men was behind Lily, one hand over her mouth and one arm around her waist. The other ripped her shirt from her body. He tore it to pieces and used one of the sleeves to gag her, tying it behind her head. The other man pulled her pants off. She tried to fight them, but they were much stronger. They dragged her over to the table and forced her over it facedown. One of them was on the window side and he used another remnant of her shirt to tie one of her arms to the table leg. The other was behind her, holding her down on the table and trying to avoid her flailing legs. Claude walked over to the corner of the room and retrieved a video camera and tripod. He set it up behind and off to the side of her. He walked around to the window side of the table to where Lily could see him, bent down, and looked her in the face.

"My friends will now give you the test," he said, as if it was the most ordinary thing in the world. She stared back at him, hatred in her eyes. Claude stood up and disappeared out of her vision. Lily struggled for a few more minutes until she realized it was hopeless, and then she went limp. She wasn't about to give them the satisfaction. She would just check out, imagine that she was with a tedious client. She would let them play their games. Eventually it would be over. And then she remembered a magazine spread she'd done for Carl & Carlos in Milan. It had appeared in ads and billboards all across Europe. She'd been wearing black lingerie, and was being held facedown on a table by a bare-chested male model while two other bare-chested male models looked on.

"Claude?" one of the men said, "I think she has passed out."

Claude walked back over in front of her, took a fistful of her hair and yanked her head up. Her eyes were wide open, boiling over with hatred and rage.

"But of course," Claude said, smiling, "you have become accustomed to being fucked, haven't you my dear? Well I must inform you that *this* . . ." he said, letting the word hang in the air, "will be much more than fucking," he said, and laughed. Then he let go of her hair, stood up, and disappeared again.

"You two?" Claude said to the men, "put on the masks I gave you. And you? Roll down your sleeves, cover up those tattoos."

Claude walked over in front of Lily again and bent down so he was close to her face. He spoke slowly and calmly.

"I have decided to not do the test. Instead, I think we will make a movie."

He stood up again, but stayed directly in front of Lily so she could see what he was doing. He removed a black satin mask from his pocket and pulled it over his head. It had holes for his mouth and eyes and that was all. He knew that the mask would terrify her. BDSM, pain, and power games were something she was not into. She had even refused to model if the job had been one of those gigs, with vinyl corsets and latex stockings and the like.

"I think this will be enjoyable," Claude said, after he had the mask on and had adjusted it. He moved out of Lily's view and across the room. Then she heard his voice again.

"I know many people who will enjoy seeing this. People will enjoy seeing someone so . . . beautiful . . . and young . . . suffer. I am going to start the camera now. You two," he said to the men, "keep your mouths shut."

Claude removed the camera from the tripod and turned it on. He carried it over to the table and for a few minutes shot close-ups of Lily, documenting every aspect, her legs kicking, her back muscles clenching and unclenching. He finished by shooting her face. She tried to close her eyes and turn away, but Claude grabbed her by the hair again and yanked her head up. He made sure to get a long shot of the fear in her eyes. Then he replaced the camera on the tripod.

Nethery put his ear up to the door but all he could hear was music playing. He recognized it as Dusty Springfield's "The Look of Love" and after a few moments he heard a loud crack coming at regular intervals. At first he was perplexed but after hearing it a few times he recognized it as the sound of a whip. He felt a jolt of adrenaline course through his body, and his hand automatically moved toward the door. He pushed down on the lever. It was locked, but the door hadn't latched completely and he was able to push it open. He stepped inside and found himself in a long vestibule. He saw Lily's coat hanging on a coatrack and her bag on the floor. He quietly walked to the end of the hallway and peered around the corner into the main room. He stood there for a few moments, trying to come to grips with what he saw. Lily was bent over the table. One man was fucking her from behind. Another was off to the side, whipping her back. A third was on the other side of the table holding her down.

The sheer ugliness of what he saw seemed to push him away and quietly he backed into the hallway, out of sight, until he found himself up against the wall. He retched. When he opened his eyes he was bent over, staring down into Lily's bag. He reached down. His fingers curled around the butt of the gun. He pulled it out of the bag and stood up. He released the catch and slid the magazine out of the butt and seeing it was full, he slid it carefully back in and then pushed hard on it with the heel of his hand. He then pulled the slide back and let it go forward slowly, watching through the ejection port as a cartridge was fed into the chamber. He made sure the safety was off. The sound of the whip cracked at regular intervals like the second hand of a giant, slowed-down clock. His heart beat normally, and his breathing was measured and calm, possessed by a stillness borne of an infinite rage.

He calmly walked up to the man who was screwing Lily from behind, put the gun to the back of his head and pulled the trigger. The sound was so loud that he would hear nothing but ringing in his ears for the next few minutes, which seemed to happen very slowly. The man's forehead blew apart and a spray of blood and brain matter splashed across Lily's back and formed a pink mist in the air. His body went limp and he slumped to the floor. The man across the table let go of Lily's arms and stood up straight. A bullet hit him square in the chest and knocked him back against the wall below the window. The man with the whip backed up a step and pulled the mask from his head. He took a few more steps back, stumbled and fell. He let go of the whip.

Nethery turned his attention to Lily, in a heap at the foot of the table. He gently shook her shoulder but she was unresponsive. He tried talking to her and he could only faintly hear his own voice. There were severe welts all over Lily's back. Nethery was filled with a warm energy that made him feel nauseous and yet terribly powerful. He covered her with his jacket and removed her gag. Out of the corner of his eye the last man was trying to get to his feet. He was angling to make a run for the door and Nethery stood up and moved to block his way. The man fell to his knees when he saw his path blocked and began crawling toward Nethery, saying something in a shrieking and irritating voice. He tried to reach for Nethery's pants leg and Nethery stepped back. The shrieking voice became louder and Nethery wanted it to stop.

"Shhhhhh," Nethery said, holding the barrel of the gun up to his lips like a finger. The man saw the gesture and stopped, but only for a moment, and then he started up again, more frantically than before and crawling forward trying to grab his legs. Nethery had backed up to a couch and could not retreat any farther. The man was looking up at him from his knees, still making all kinds of noise and had gotten hold of one of his legs. Nethery calmly raised the gun. The man managed to get out the beginnings of a scream before the bullet hit him in the forehead. Nethery stepped back and looked at the dead man for a moment. He felt nothing, and for the briefest of moments he thought it strange, almost as if he'd been standing off to the side, directing someone else to do what had been done. He walked over to the stereo and turned it off, then walked back over to Lily, who had curled into a ball under the jacket.

"Lily?" he said. She was still lying on her side on the hardwood floor and he tried to gently turn her onto her back, but her limbs were frozen. Her face was expressionless, her eyes were smeared with makeup and she had a thousand-yard stare.

"Lily come on, we have to get out of here."

"No, no," she mumbled. Nethery retrieved her pants and shoes, and with some coaxing he got her to relax to the point that he could move her arms and legs and he dressed her. He put his jacket on her last, as gently as he could and looking for signs of pain, but she was apparently not feeling anything. He managed to get her to her feet. She was unsteady but he managed to escort her toward the door. It was then he noticed the video camera and saw the red light, indicating it was running. He left Lily leaning against the wall of the entrance hall, retrieved the camera and put it and the gun into Lily's bag. Nethery returned to Lily and helped her out of the apartment, down the stairs and across the street to the median where he sat her down on a bench.

"Lily?" he asked, hoping for some kind of response. She looked up at him with a blank stare.

"I'm going to get us a taxi," he said, and then he stood. Lily's arm darted out and she grabbed his arm tightly.

"No, no," she said, looking up, her eyes distraught and panic-stricken.

Nethery kneeled down in front of her. He placed his hand on her knee and looked at her. What had been done to her overwhelmed the beauty of her features, and even drowned out the life and spirit he'd seen emerging from her the last few days. It seemed to Nethery to be the most sick and wrong thing he had ever witnessed and it was made even worse because as he began to think of what to do next he looked around and somehow everything else at the moment seemed very vivid and beautiful, the green grass of the median, the twilight coming down through the trees. Nethery tried to keep a calm demeanor and squeezed her shoulder and then leaned over and hugged her gently.

"It's going to be okay," he said. He put his hands on her shoulders and pushed her back so she could see him.

"Lily? Look at me."

She raised her head, looked him and Nethery sensed the beginnings of recognition in her eyes, but it was very faint as if she wasn't sure she wanted to grasp that thread and pull herself back into the present.

"I'm just going for a minute," he said, "to get us a taxi. Okay? Don't worry. I'll be right back. I *will not* leave you."

She didn't say anything and stared at him with bloodshot eyes that seemed bigger than ever. Her eyes softened very slightly, indicating understanding of what he'd said on some level, and she nodded once.

Nethery ran across the street to get a taxi. He waited right in front of the apartment building, which he knew was unwise, but the other side of the boulevard was too far away and he wanted to keep an eye on her. He waited for five minutes, and it seemed like much longer. He flagged down a taxi, gave him a twenty-euro note, told him to wait. He ran back out to the median, retrieved Lily from the bench, helped her to the taxi, and carefully bundled her into the back seat.

"Montmartre," Nethery said, and the driver pushed some buttons on the meter and began driving. Nethery wanted to keep Lily out of the rearview mirror, and he gently tried to get her to slouch down in the corner of the back seat. Occasionally Lily let out little moaning sounds. Nethery gently laid his arm around her shoulders, hoping to provide a modicum of comfort, and began to gather his thoughts. He was unsure of what to do next. He uncurled his arm from Lily and leaned over to speak to the driver.

"Take me to St. Denis instead," he said, "by the Stade de France."

Nethery was surprisingly calm and composed. He emptied

his mind and watched the city scroll by out the side window. He derived a kind of calm from the motion of the taxi and the hum of its engine. It relaxed him. Time seemed to be moving much slower and the city suddenly seemed like a fascinating and interesting place. He would see a light on in a third-floor apartment, or a young couple crossing the street and he became acutely aware of the raucous vitality of the city, of the millions of stories going on all around them at that very moment. It was odd that he'd been unable to feel or see this before, and that it had all seemed utterly mundane. There was something else that was new and different: since he'd met Lily, he hadn't been dwelling on the existential question that had tormented him for so long. In fact, it hadn't even crossed his mind, not once. He tried to bring his thoughts back to the present. Their situation was serious and dire and while he recognized it, and it began to sink in, it seemed unable to touch him emotionally. It simply did not register in that way. He was no longer wandering through a fog of stagnation and it made him feel alive and strong as if mild and pleasant electrical currents were running throughout his body. It also allowed him to focus with crystal clarity, and it only took him a moment to conclude that they would need to get away, run, somewhere, and as soon as the idea formed in his mind he felt a kind of exhilaration borne of having a firm direction. Lily had begun quietly whimpering in the corner, and he opened his eyes and put his arm around her again and leaned into her gently.

The ride took about twenty minutes and the driver pulled over to a curb. The Stade de France was a dark mass off to the right. Nethery paid, carefully helped Lily out of the taxi, and they walked a short distance to a small square with benches under some bare trees.

"We need to wait here for a few minutes," Nethery said, "then we'll take a taxi to my place. We'll be safe there."

Lily looked up at him as he spoke. Her eyes were vacant,

except for the pain, and occasionally a tear would fall from one of her eyes.

"It's okay. I'm going to take care of you," he said, trying to smile.

He soon flagged down another taxi. When they got to his flat he ushered her inside and put her on the couch. Now that he had gotten her here he didn't know what to do. He backed away from her and stood in the center of the room. He looked around, searching for something to trigger an idea, but then it became clear on its own, organically.

"Lily? I'm going to run you a shower. We need to get you cleaned up," he said. She had pulled her knees up to her chest and was slowly rocking, staring straight ahead into space. She looked up at him but didn't say anything. The tears seemed to have lessened and were possibly petering out.

Nethery went into the bathroom and turned on the shower. The hot water was still not working, as he had discovered days before, and he used the trick he'd learned and turned on the hot water in the sink in order to get it flowing in the shower. He then adjusted the temperature a little cooler than normal, then went back out to the living room. Lily was completely docile and let him undress her. There were streaks of blood and a few small pieces of human tissue smeared across her back. She seemed to still be completely oblivious to pain. He examined his jacket for a moment, and then seeing it was ruined, flung it over near the trash can.

Nethery took her hands and pulled her to her feet, put his arm around her gently and led her into the bathroom. She looked curiously for a moment at the water running in the sink. She stepped into the shower and winced. Nethery wetted a soft sponge and, urging her to slowly turn around, he gently brushed the blood and pieces of tissue from her back. With his hands he guided her head under the water and encouraged her to stay there, hoping the water would help wash away some of the ugliness. Then she suddenly tensed up and Nethery felt that the water had gone cold.

He fiddled with the tap in the sink to no avail. Lily had backed into the corner of the shower stall and she stood there, hugging herself, her entire body stiff and shivering. There was a flimsy aluminum access panel screwed into the wall under the sink, and Nethery had always suspected the problem lay behind it amongst the pipes. He grabbed the edge of the sink and kicked the panel as hard as he could. A corner of it was now bent up and he got down on one knee and ripped the panel away from the wall. There were some things packed in there, a big cloth bag, and a couple of pink plastic boxes. He reached into the wall, pulled them out, and threw them aside. A couple of flexible hoses had been pinched and twisted. He straightened them out and after a minute of fiddling with the taps he got the shower working properly again.

Nethery gently urged her back under the spray. Going by the reactions of her body and the expressions on her face he adjusted the temperature of the water, and eventually he saw her body begin to relax. She was still unable to function and he used the sponge to scrub her as gently as he could. When it was done he retrieved his terry cloth robe, wrapped her in it and escorted her to the bed. He found some salve and bandages in the bathroom, and had Lily lie facedown. There were dozens of raised welts and in a couple of places the whip had broken the skin. He applied the salve to the welts and tried to dress the wounds as best he knew. He felt her body tense up, but she said nothing. When he finished he turned her over, made her as comfortable as he could and went into the kitchen to make some tea. It seemed to take forever for the water to boil and when he glanced in to check on her she was sitting up against the headboard under the covers, her knees pulled up to her chest and her eyes were glazed over. She stared straight ahead.

He brought the tea and she drank it quickly. He sat on the edge of the bed and watched her and after five minutes she began to get agitated, looking around the room, as if searching for a way out. He remembered the bottle of wine, jumped up, and retrieved it from the kitchen. He helped her drink three glasses. The alcohol seemed to soothe her, and she finally turned onto her side under the sheet. Nethery sat on the window ledge smoking cigarettes and watched her. After about thirty minutes he checked on her. She had fallen asleep.

Nethery was soaked from the shower, and put on fresh clothes from his suitcase, then went out to the living room and sat on the couch. He lit up a cigarette, taking long drags and tipping the ashes into a saucer. He tried to clear his head and evaluate his options. His gut told him to run away with her, but maybe he should he turn himself in? He had the tape. It would be proof that Lily had been raped. But would that even make a difference? Was it the same here as the States? If it was, he was fucked. He had no connections or a rich family. He was unable to come to a decision and finished the cigarette, went into the bathroom and as he was pissing he saw the things he'd pulled out of the wall, scattered on the floor.

When he was finished he squatted down and looked at the items. There was a handmade bag with yellow, red, and green stripes stitched onto it and two pink plastic Hello Kitty lunchboxes. He opened one of the lunchboxes and a large package of white powder fell out, wrapped in thick clear plastic. The other lunchbox contained a package as well, and the African bag contained four. Each package was at least a kilo, he guessed.

Nethery leaned back on his haunches until he was against the wall, slid down the short distance to the floor until he was sitting and after a few moments, began to groan. He closed his eyes and hung his head, exhausted and angry. After a few moments he pulled himself together, dug his keys out of his pocket, and stuck a tiny hole in one of the packages. He extracted a tiny bit of the powder and touched it to his tongue. It was unmistakable, the bitter numbing. Cocaine. He sat there for a few minutes, the implications whirling about in his mind.

Eventually he got up and took the packages out to the living room and placed them in his duffel bag. He then sat on the couch and had another smoke. Being so close to the cocaine had triggered a physical reaction. His palms grew sweaty, and there was a nervous tension in his stomach. He rubbed his hands on his pants. His mind had lost focus and gone haywire, and terrible and cold fantasies began to fill his mind; leaving this place right then, holing up somewhere, using until the drugs were gone. He pushed these thoughts away, but a familiar and awful nervous tension had swept throughout his entire being. He felt like he had to go to the bathroom. He thought of the wine, craving a drink just to calm down.

He went into the bedroom and checked on Lily, hoping to get his mind back on track. She was sleeping peacefully, and his eyes were drawn to the bottle sitting on the night table. It wouldn't be the first time he'd drank himself into unconsciousness. He sat on the window ledge and had another cigarette instead. Directly across the courtyard he could see people moving behind the curtains. On one of the upper floors, someone was having a party, and voices bounced around the walls of the courtyard. He finished the smoke, and lay down next to Lily on top of the bed and eventually drifted off into a restless sleep.

Nethery awoke the next morning, and the first thing he felt was a sense of relief. He had half expected that he would wake up in jail. Lily was not next to him but there was nothing but a wonderful smell coming from the other room. The weight of the previous day began to make itself felt, and through sheer obstinance and force of will he batted it away like a pest. He heard a noise from the kitchen, climbed out of bed, and went to the doorway. She was standing at the kitchen counter, pouring hot water into the French press. He grunted and she turned to look at him.

"It will be ready in few minutes," she said, smiling, indicating the coffee. Nethery didn't know what to say and he opened the French windows, sat on the ledge, and lit up a cigarette. He hadn't expected to see her like that. She seemed fine, calm, moving with coordination and purpose. A far cry from the utterly shattered and crushed girl of the previous night. It appeared that she had come back from it, but come too far, and was pretending that nothing had happened. He marveled at the strength it must have taken to box that up and shove it away. This was a problem, Nethery thought, because in order to have a conversation about what to do next, what had happened would have to be acknowledged. She would have to face it. And he had no idea how to break it to her without destroying her once again. Maybe she could handle it, maybe she couldn't. He didn't know. Lily walked into the bedroom carrying a tray and set it down on the bed.

"Come," she said. Nethery flipped his smoke out the window and sat on the bed.

"Cream and sugar, yes?" she said.

"Yeah," Nethery replied. She fixed his coffee and handed him the cup. He took a drink.

"It is good?"

"Yeah, it's good." Nethery decided to broach the subject right away.

"Lily?"

"Yes."

"How is your back?"

"My back is fine," she said, as if it were nothing, setting down her coffee. But then she became visibly tense and her face darkened. She stood up and walked over to the window and looked out for a minute. Then she turned to him.

"You should not have done that."

"What?"

"You should not have killed them."

Nethery was stunned into silence for a few moments, but he recognized that at least she hadn't buried the event somewhere completely as he'd assumed.

"Yeah well . . . I'm . . . I had to stop them. It . . ."

"I would have lived."

Lily was looking down at the floor. Then she raised her head and spoke.

"I am . . . happy they are dead. Do not think that . . . do not think . . . that I am not thanking you . . . but now . . . now there will be trouble. For you. And for me."

She sat down on the bed beside him and winced, then buried her face in her hands.

"I could turn myself in," Nethery said. "We have the tape."

"No," she said, looking up. "I am not trusting police. My visa no good, my passport gone, you are not from here. That is not good idea."

"I don't care. I'll do it anyway," Nethery said.

"You do not understand," Lily said. "Claude has many friends. In police, out of police. They not care about tape. You will go to jail. I will go to jail."

"Well then, we have to get out of here."

"I do not have passport," Lily said, "I not get back from Claude."

"Shit," Nethery spat. He stood, paced around the bedroom for a minute, and then he stopped and looked toward the window.

"I have an idea," he said, the vaguest of plans coming together in his mind.

Lily was feeling cornered and it made her unable to think.

"I . . . idea?" she finally managed to say.

"Yeah, but we've got to get out of Paris."

Lily was unable to process what he said. Nethery stood there, waiting for her to respond, but she continued to gaze straight ahead and there was no expression on her face. Nethery walked over and stood before her. She didn't register his presence, and he squatted down. He placed his hand on her knee.

"Come on," he said, "we have to go."

Her face was blank, her eyes empty, staring at nothing. He squeezed her knee and he saw her eyes come into focus and gradually meet his, but she clearly didn't understand what he'd said.

"Come on, we have to go," he said as gently as he could.

"Go?" she said, eventually.

"Yeah, we have to get out of town," he said.

She seemed to be thinking about what he'd said, but she had a confused expression on her face, and then she appeared to give up.

"I must . . . get clothes . . . from my flat," she said robotically. Nethery helped her get dressed in what was left of her clothes from the previous night and one of his shirts. He led her out to the kitchen. Nethery quickly put a couple changes of clothes into his duffel bag. He put the gun in his jacket pocket, made sure the camera and the drugs were in his shoulder bag, and then slung both his bags over his shoulder.

It was late morning and the Metro was not very crowded. They sat next to each other, and Nethery wanted to talk to her but she stared out the window. She was obviously not interested in talking. He sensed a barely contained fury, most likely directed at him. He gave up trying to engage her, hoping they'd be able to discuss it later. He revisited the events of the previous night, trying to sort through exactly what had happened, trying to gain some understanding. He was slightly in awe of what he'd done, and at the same time, confused. It had been very out of character. He'd always been one to stay out of trouble, to avoid conflict, at least if he wasn't drunk or doing drugs. He could have threatened them with the gun, made them stop, and possibly called the cops, but none of those would have come close to balancing out the scales of justice, as if they had been pushed too far and were broken. The great emptiness inside him, the void that was new and unknown, had called out in a primal voice for true force. He had followed it out of the fog and answered. And he had made no attempt to stop it.

They transferred at Montparnasse and arrived at the Saint-Germain-des-Prés station. As they neared her apartment Nethery wanted to try to talk to her again but the vacant look on her face had been replaced with a scowl. She refused to look at him. They reached her flat, went inside and Lily stood in the center of the room for a minute, looking around, as if she didn't know what to do. Nethery was about to tell her to get moving, but stopped himself. He stood there, fidgeting, waiting for her to get herself together but she continued to stand there and say nothing. After what seemed like a long time she eventually walked over to a dresser, jerked a drawer open, and began yanking clothes out and throwing items onto the floor. Occasionally she stopped, examined an article of clothing, and threw it onto the bed. This went on for minutes, as she went through drawer after drawer until she froze, grunted, and flung an armful of clothes wildly into the corner of the room. She turned to face Nethery, her face screwed up into a kind of grimace.

"Why?" she asked, tipping her head forward and glaring at him.

"What?"

"You . . . why did you kill them?"

"I told you."

"Everything was fine," she said calmly, but the rest of her body was wound tight. "I only want to make money and go back home. And now . . . it is all . . . finished."

"Whoa whoa, what did you say?" Nethery asked. "I thought you wanted to go to Germany."

"This is huge mess!" she screamed. "What we do!?" she screamed. The controlled rage gave way and Lily reached down to the floor, picked up a shoe and hurled it at Nethery as hard as she could. He ducked and she threw another. She bent down for another but there were only clothes and she stood up straight and glared at him, a crazed look in her huge eyes. Her mouth opened to say something, but nothing came out and he could see the energy drain out of her.

"You want to go home?" Nethery asked once again, and then her shoulders sagged and she stumbled back a step and sat on the edge of the bed.

"Yes. No. Maybe. Oh, I do not know . . . it is impossible now. What good it do to . . ."

"I told you . . . I think I know how to fix this," he interrupted.

"This cannot be fixed," she said.

"I know how to get some money," Nethery said, trying to keep things moving.

"What you talking about?" she asked, quietly.

"There's no time to explain now. I have a little money left to get us someplace, and I know how to get a lot more. It will be enough to get you home."

Lily looked up for a moment, and Nethery could see that she was completely and totally defeated. She then turned and stared out the window. He spoke to set things in motion again.

"It's gonna be okay," he said, bluffing. "Just get ready to go, okay? I'm gonna go down to the boulangerie and get some sand-wiches and some cigarettes. Just finish packing, so we can go when I get back," he urged. She said nothing. He moved toward her, but she turned her face away and after a moment stood and began mechanically digging through the dresser again, flinging clothes left and right. Nethery backed up and stood in the center of the room. Eventually he left the apartment and quietly closed the door behind him. Jeanette was sitting on the floor halfway down the hall, leaning against the wall. She appeared to be sob-bing. He hurried over, knelt down, and touched her shoulder. She looked up, tears streaking her face.

"What's the matter?" he asked, but she couldn't hear him; the music from the British place was so loud it seemed to be out in the hallway.

"What is wrong?" Nethery shouted, and then he leaned close.

"Those people," she wailed, "I try . . . I try to talk to them. But they do not care," she said, totally distraught.

"Lily is home," Nethery said, helping her to her feet, "why don't you go down and see her?"

"*Oui*," she said, and Nethery escorted her to Lily's door. When she was safely inside he said he'd be right back. The noise from the apartment was deafening, and it made him want to run to get past it as quickly as possible.

Outside the sun was trying to break through the clouds. He walked to the boulangerie, picked up four ham and cheese baguettes and then made his way to the rotonde on the corner. As the clerk was getting his cigarettes Nethery noticed a newspaper on the counter, and on the front page was a photo of Claude's apartment building, a headline in huge letters, three words and an exclamation point. He looked closer at the photo, probably taken by a traffic camera, of Nethery helping Lily across the street. It was too grainy to see their faces, but Nethery's hat was recognizable. The same hat he was wearing right then. The clerk seemed to take forever. Finally he paid for the cigarettes and a copy of the newspaper, and turned around, expecting everyone in the place to be staring at him. But they weren't. Most had the newspaper open and were chatting excitedly and gesturing at the headline. He found that he didn't want to leave immediately and moved to the bar and ordered a coffee. He sat there for around ten minutes, watching them read the newspapers and talk about him. It was exhilarating.

He wanted to stay longer, but he finished his coffee and started back to Lily's flat. The sun had broken through the clouds and as he walked he was overcome with a feeling similar to the one he'd gotten in the taxi right after Claude's, a kind of energizing euphoria, the same and yet different than before. It had grown out of the exhilaration from the café. Everyday things that had always seemed mundane and utterly boring, the everyday stuff of life—the sights, sounds, and smells of the city and the most basic physical exertion of walking—had suddenly become intensely pleasant. The world seemed terribly colorful and vivid. He noticed dozens of things happening all around him, and they all seemed very interesting as if they had taken on new meaning.

He entered Lily's building and strode to the foot of the staircase and began to bound up it two steps at a time. He was halfway up when the noise hit him and he stopped. He looked down at his feet. The staircase was old and wooden, and he should have been able to hear the creaking of the wood, but the music totally drowned it out. He started up again, climbing the stairs slowly, looking down, testing each step, and rocking on his feet. When he got to the top he walked over to the door of the apartment, the noise washing away his pleasant feeling and making him increasingly nauseous. He removed the gun from his jacket pocket and put it in the waistband of his pants, in front, and carefully set the bag of sandwiches down on the floor against the wall. He tried the door handle but it was locked. He stood there for a moment, staring at the door, and then he stepped back and kicked the door right next to the handle. It gave way and the door swung open. He walked into the vestibule and down a long hall until he came out into a living room. The man and his girlfriend were sitting on the couch, and when they saw him they stared with their mouths open. On the glass coffee table before them were half devoured take-out boxes of food, some glasses, a bottle of whiskey, and a pile of cocaine on a large rectangular mirror.

The look of surprise slowly turned into a look of anger and the man began to get up, but the couch was so soft and deep and he was so heavy that he sat there flailing his arms, as if he were doing a breast stroke. Nethery took aim with the pistol and shot the coffee table. It shattered almost soundlessly, everything on it collapsed to the floor, and the man stopped trying to get up. He looked up at Nethery, and then he became enraged again and made a move once more to get up. Nethery smiled, slowly shook his head *no* and the man gave up. The woman had a terrified look on her face. Nethery looked around the room and found the stereo against the wall right behind him. He turned it down to where he could be heard.

"What's this all about, mate?" the man asked.

Nethery stood there, not knowing what to say.

"What do you want? Money?"

Nethery thought for a moment. It would be nice, he supposed, to help Lily, but it wasn't why he'd kicked the door down. But then, he wasn't sure why he'd done it, exactly. The man on the couch sensed Nethery's indecision and took it as a sign of weakness.

"You don't know the shit you're in now, you . . . you fucker," he said, emboldened. "Do you know who my father is?"

He was going to continue talking but Nethery raised his finger to his lips.

"What do you want? Huh?" the man shouted again.

"I want you to be quiet," Nethery said softly.

"What? Listen you fucker . . ."

"I wanna talk to you," Nethery said, pointing the gun at him.

"So talk then, you shit."

"So this is it, huh?" Nethery asked, making a sweeping gesture around the room with the gun hand, "booze and drugs and shitty music?"

"Listen, you American piece of shyte . . ." and Nethery burst out laughing.

"What's so funny?"

"You really should be careful what you say. We Americans are violent. Haven't you heard?"

"You don't scare me," the man said, and Nethery grinned for a moment, and then became serious.

"I'm here about Jeanette."

"Eh? Who's that?"

"The old lady next door."

"That old bat!? Fuck her!"

"Oh come on now. She just wants some peace."

"I do what I want!" the man screamed.

"Yeah, I can see that. That's the problem, isn't it? You do what you want, and there's no one to stop you."

"Sod off you shit!"

"Shut up!" Nethery shouted, pointing the gun. It shocked the man into silence. Nethery turned to the window for a second, rolled his eyes, shook his head, sighed, and then smiled and looked at the couple on the couch.

"So this is it, huh? This is what you're gonna do?"

"I do what I want!"

"All right," Nethery sighed. "It'll make an interesting headstone, I suppose. Here lies so-'n'-so, who died for being an idiot. It's not much of a mission in life, I have to say," Nethery continued.

"Fuck you mate!" the man yelled, losing his temper again.

Nethery laughed.

"From the moment I heard about you I wanted to do this," Nethery continued, tapping the barrel of the pistol gently against his head. "I thought up a million reasons. A million rationalizations and justifications . . . you know, the world would be a better place without you, that sort of thing. But you know what? They're all bullshit. I'm gonna kill you," Nethery said, shaking his head, "for one reason and one reason only . . . because I don't like you."

The man took a few moments to digest this and finally realized he was in trouble.

"Wait wait," he pleaded, "you don't have to do this. I can get you whatever you want. Money, drugs . . ."

"I've met hundreds of people like you . . . thousands probably . . . just oblivious that there are other people in the world that matter as much as you do. That level of ignorance is just . . . I don't know. It's not something to be proud of, you know."

"Oh yeah? What makes you so special, mate?" the man yelled, losing control again. "Eh!? What have you ever done that's so fucking great?"

Nethery chuckled.

"You should have asked me that a week ago. I wouldn't have had an answer."

"But now you do?" the man asked.

"Yeah," Nethery said in a kind of sigh, as if he regretted the answer. "Now I do," he said, and he looked at the ground and grinned.

"Well? What is it, you wanker?"

"This," Nethery said quietly, and he raised his head and looked at the man. He lifted the gun and shot the man twice in the chest.

The woman tried to get up but he shot her as well. The bullet knocked her back and she tipped onto her side and her body seemed to lose all definition and become a featureless blob of flesh. It oozed off the couch and spilled onto the floor. He had wanted to shoot her twice as well but there had only been one bullet left and the slide of the gun was in its retracted position. Nethery held the gun up before his face, looked at it, released the catch and let the slide go forward. He stood there for a few moments and looked at the dead bodies, and his mind drifted back to a car accident he'd witnessed years before, where a person had died, and he remembered the profound sadness he had felt upon seeing the dead body. This was nothing like that.

He stuck the gun into his waistband, turned up the stereo again, not as loud as it had been but just so it would seem someone was home, and walked to the door. The doorjamb was shattered, but he got down on one knee and tried to make it look as normal as possible, throwing some splinters that didn't seem to fit anywhere back into the apartment. He closed the door carefully, picked up his bag of sandwiches, and headed down the hall. He only had a moment to think about what he'd done before he got to Lily's door.

Inside the apartment Lily and Jeanette were sitting at the tiny kitchen table. Lily appeared to be in a better mood. Nethery stood in the center of the room for a moment, not knowing what to say or do, and then he stepped over to the window. He put his hands on the windowsill, leaned forward and hung his head.

"What is the matter?" Jeanette asked, but Nethery was so lost in thought he did not hear her. Not getting his attention, Jeanette looked at Lily, questioningly.

"James!" Lily shouted, and Nethery stood up straight and faced them.

"Huh?" he said, still halfway caught up in the thoughts whirling in his mind.

"What is the matter?" Jeanette asked again.

"Oh. Um . . . Lily and I . . . we need to get out of Paris for a while. That's all. It's too fucking crazy here. Pardon my French."

This statement hung in the air for a moment, and then Jeanette brightened up.

"Come with me!" she exclaimed.

"Huh?" Nethery replied.

"I am going to sister's house," Jeanette said. "In Cassis. Not far from Marseille. There is small guesthouse. It is empty. Oh yes! You must," she exclaimed, and then she looked at Lily to see how well the idea was being received.

Lily managed a small smile and looked at Nethery to see what he thought of it. He looked at Jeanette, and then back to Lily, concerned that Lily had told Jeanette what had happened. He gestured that he wanted to talk to her and when she stood he pulled her aside.

"You didn't tell her what happened? Did you?" Nethery whispered urgently when they were out of range of Jeanette.

"I am not stupid," Lily said, trying to wrest her arm free. Nethery let go, and they both went back and sat down at the kitchen table.

"The guesthouse. It has been empty for many years," Jeanette said. "It is right on water. It is perfect place for you. Oh, yes! You will like. It is so beautiful there."

Nethery's mind was racing. They had to go somewhere, before the cops began watching the train stations or whatever they did when they were looking for a killer. He sat there, thinking through the possibilities, while Jeanette and Lily talked, and it was only then it began to dawn on him what a huge mistake he'd made shooting the people next door. It had been very foolish. And yet somehow he didn't care, and wasn't overly concerned, almost as if there were some divine force guiding him. It was utterly bizarre. He didn't have a sense of his future narrowing, of being closed in, but rather a strange and inexplicable feeling that his fortunes had turned and that more opportunities would present themselves. He wanted to think about it further, analyze it, but there was no time.

"Pardon . . ." Nethery said to Jeanette, ". . . um, one minute," and then he pulled Lily out of the chair and drew her aside again.

"What do you think?" he whispered.

"I think is okay," Lily answered, shrugging her shoulders.

"Okay," Nethery agreed, "we'll do it. But don't tell her anything. Okay?"

"You think I am stupid?" Lily asked.

"No, goddamnit. Of course not. Look, I'm just trying to figure this out. I have some ideas, but I just think we . . ."

"What idea?"

"I'll tell you later."

"Tell now," Lily said, standing there, hands on her hips. Nethery sighed.

"There's no time, Lily. I don't even know if it's gonna work."

"You do not know? Damn you . . . you fool."

"Lily, come on. If we stay here we have no chance. None. I know that much."

"Pfft," Lily said, and then she sat back down at the kitchen table.

Nethery remained where he was and watched them talking, and eventually his mind gravitated back to the immediate problem. The bodies next door would probably be found soon, and then the cops would question everyone in the building, and then . . . *and then*, he thought, as he played out scenarios where they would be caught. But there wasn't anything he could do. He couldn't very well take the time to dispose of them. He wouldn't even know where to begin. Drag the corpses down to the basement and hack them to pieces? Feed the pieces to pigeons? He may have had no issue with killing them, but the thought of disposing of the bodies was very distasteful. He would just have to hope that they weren't discovered for a while.

Nethery drove the disturbing images from his head, sat on the windowsill, and turned his attention back to the women. He overheard Jeanette say she was leaving in two days. Nethery interrupted to say that he and Lily had to leave Paris immediately. This provoked a strange look from Jeanette and she seemed to be thinking for a moment but she merely shook her head, smiled, and said she would call her sister to let her know they were coming. She then got very excited again, telling Lily about how much fun it was going to be and all the things they could do around Cassis, how beautiful it was there. She made a comment about how wonderful it was to be able to talk, without shouting, as the music from the neighbor's apartment had been turned down.

"Yes, it is very strange," Lily remarked.

"Maybe they have finally come to their senses," Nethery blurted out, which provoked a strange look from both Jeanette and Lily.

"It's possible," Nethery said, and shrugged.

Eventually Jeanette went back to her apartment to phone her sister. Lily got up and began going through her clothes again, picking out items to bring and throwing them onto the bed next to her suitcase. Nethery sat at the kitchen table, took off his hat, and threw it like a Frisbee into the corner of the room.

"What you do that for?" Lily asked, "I like hat."

"Look," Nethery said, showing her the newspaper he'd brought with him from the rotonde. "That's us, outside Claude's apartment." Lily snatched the paper out of his hands, sat down at the table and stared at it.

She began trembling.

"Come on," Nethery urged her eventually, "it's gonna be okay. Just finish packing."

Lily pulled herself together and began sorting through the clothes scattered on her bed. She picked out a pair of jeans, a tailored shirt that buttoned up the front and some high-heeled sandals, and changed into them. She didn't even acknowledge Nethery's presence when she stripped. When she was ready they caught a taxi to the Gare de Lyon. Nethery found a bench inside and told Lily to wait. He found a ticket window and bought two first-class tickets on the TGV to Marseille and the connection to Cassis. It took about fifteen minutes and when he returned Lily was gone. He climbed up on the bench and turned slowly, scanning the cavernous hall. There were hundreds of people. He thought about shouting her name but it would have been useless. He continued looking for a couple of minutes, and then gave up. She had left. He carefully climbed down from the bench, sat down, and stared at the floor.

Lily towed her suitcase into the bathroom stall and closed the door. When she was finished she stood, pulled up her jeans, suddenly felt light-headed, and leaned against the partition of the stall. She saw spots, as if she'd stood too quickly and grew dizzy. She sat on the toilet again. Images of the incident at Claude's surfaced in her mind, gradually taking shape, and with them the totality of what had happened. The floodgates were now open and she buried her face in her hands. She began shaking and sobbing from a combination of sadness, rage, regret, and shame that hit her all at once. It devastated her, and she was also angry with herself for allowing it to hurt her, and for allowing her life to reach this point.

Nethery sat on the bench, looking at the shoes of people who walked by. She has decided to go off on her own. Could he blame her? Not really. She probably stood as good a chance of getting home on her own as she did with him. They'd only known each other for less than two weeks. Maybe she was frightened of him? He couldn't blame her for that either. He was being selfish, wanting her to stay, and for the first time in quite a while he felt very alone. He sensed someone sit down on the bench beside him. He opened his eyes and it was Lily, trying to hide her face with her hands.

"Where'd you go?" he asked.

"I go to bathroom," she said, without looking up.

"Goddamnit!"

"What is matter with you?" Lily said, and she raised her head and looked at him.

Her mascara and eye shadow were smeared all around her eyes, forming black trails that streaked down her face.

PART II
THE EDGE OF THE SEA

The TGV swayed slightly as it sped down the track, and as Lily walked the passageway she occasionally reached her hand out to the wall to steady herself. She dipped her head for a moment in order to look out the window. The landscape was a blur of green and gray and brown. At the end of the passageway was the entrance to the lounge car and she noticed her reflection in the polished glass door as she approached, her hips swaying, feet stabbing out precisely one in front of the other and she wondered for a moment how long it would take to stop walking the way she did, to unwind years of training. She was wearing ridiculous shoes for traveling, she thought, Gucci high-heeled sandals.

She came to the door, reached out to push it open, then hesitated and took a step back. She wanted a good look, see if she had changed at all. Her jeans were so tight they were pulled up into her crotch and her nipples were hard and poking out from behind her thin white shirt. She tipped her head this way and that, looking at herself like some kind of curiosity. She lingered over the reflection of her face, and as she looked closer there was something in her eyes, something she'd never seen before, a dark sort of vacancy. It wasn't surprising, after all that had happened, but the blank look was unexpected, and slightly disconcerting. She assumed she'd have looked haggard or worn out from the events of the last couple days, but there was only the expression-less, frozen beauty of her face. She tried to smile, to see if she could make the blank stare go away, but it only left her with a grotesque expression. She shrugged, shook her head slightly, and pushed through the door.

She entered the lounge and sat down on a stool in the center of the bar. The bartender was chatting with a man a few stools down. They noticed her enter the lounge, stopped talking, and stared for a few moments. They quietly exchanged a few more words, casting glances her way. The bartender walked over to stand before her. She ordered a shot of vodka. The bartender brought the drink and she drank it, ordered another, and drank it too. He was looking at her in a way she'd seen far too many times. The man from two stools down appeared on the stool next to her. He and the bartender exchanged a smirk. He was well dressed in an expensive suit and when he placed his hand on the bar she noticed the wedding ring on his finger. Any minute now, she said to herself. She spun around on the stool and glanced around the lounge. There were three other men, sitting alone at tables. She spun back to face the bar and ordered another shot. The man next to her said something to her in French.

"I do not speak French," she said sharply in English. She did, fairly well even, but she preferred English and she was feeling obstinate. She stared straight ahead, and the bartender set the drink on the bar before her.

"Oh," the man said, "I speak English, a little."

She drank the shot and ordered yet another. The bartender hesitated for a moment and then nodded. She was starting to feel the vodka and it soothed her nerves, but it also removed bricks in the wall inside her, exposing the intense fury that lived there. The bartender set the shot in front of her, and then walked down the bar and began washing glasses, possibly in an attempt to slow her down.

"Are you Russian?" the man next to her asked, guessing her accent.

She said nothing.

"Can I buy you a drink?" the man asked.

He's not going to give up, she thought, and she sighed.

"I have drink," she replied, quietly, looking straight ahead.

"Would you like another?" the man asked.

She remained silent, stared at her drink, and a few more bricks of her self-control fell away. She picked up the shot glass and noticed her hand was shaking, the vodka threatening to spill. She leaned forward and downed the vodka quickly.

"You are very beautiful," the man said in a low seductive voice.

She sat up straight, closed her eyes, took a deep breath, and then let it out slowly and turned on the barstool to face the man.

"You like me?" she asked, staring at him with half-closed eyes, the corner of her mouth turned up into the beginnings of a smile. "You want me?"

"*Oui,*" the man said.

"Thousand euro," she replied matter-of-factly, then spun back around and stared at her empty shot glass on the bar. There was a moment of silence, and she raised the shot glass, trying to signal to the bartender for another drink, but he was still washing glasses and had his back turned.

"Uhhh," the man said. She spun back to face him.

"Thousand euro and you can fuck me," she said, ultra-casually. "Right here. Now. On . . . this table right here," she said, pointing.

The man suddenly couldn't look her in the eyes.

She snorted, stepped off the barstool, moved out to the center of the room and turned to the man. He hadn't moved.

"What? It is too much? You think it is not worth it? Look at me!" she said to his back, twirling around, posing. She then turned and addressed the other men.

"Look at this face! Look at small tits! I am like little girl!!"

The men were staring at her intently, with the same look as the bartender, and the man, and her bosses at the clubs, and Claude . . .

"Look at me!" she screamed, and then she smiled an absurd smile and pushed her forefingers into her cheeks. "You can make like you be fucking your daughters!"

The bartender had been leaning on the bar, watching with amusement but now he was beginning to get alarmed.

"Come on!" she shouted, looking at each of the men at the tables in turn. "I know you! You want me! Thousand euro!"

The bartender had walked out from behind the bar. He grabbed her slender arm and held it in a viselike grip.

Nethery wasn't sure what to do. The way Lily stormed off concerned him. "I go to get drink," she'd said, and then left before Nethery could try to talk her out of it. She'd been quiet but restless most of the day and he sensed that she was on the edge of losing it. The way her eyes would dart around and then stare blankly, the way she fidgeted, as if she was trying desperately to control herself. He moved to get up and go after her, but then remembered, and opened the travel bag on the seat next to him. His eyes roamed the compartment for a few seconds, and then he pulled his other travel bag down from the overhead, removed a couple of his shirts, and stuffed them on top of the cocaine. He zipped the bag closed again and put it in the overhead compartment behind the other bag. He stood and made his way quickly down the passageway. He raised his hand up to push open the glass door of the lounge and saw Lily, standing in the center of the lounge struggling with the bartender.

"*Madame! Calme*," the bartender said to her, trying to get hold of her other arm.

She flung herself back and tried to twist free of his grasp.

"Pardon," Nethery said to him, "what's the problem?"

The bartender stopped and looked at Nethery for a second, surprised by the English.

"Drunk! She is drunk!" he spat, and then mumbled some words in French.

Nethery put his arm around Lily's waist. She was consumed by rage and oblivious to Nethery. She twisted and turned, struggling to get free.

"Come on!" she screamed, ripping her shirt open with her free hand, spraying buttons everywhere and exposing her small breasts. "Look at me!"

Nethery grabbed her by the shoulders. He pulled her free of the bartender and turned her to face him.

"Lily?" he said, looking her in the face, "Stop." She recognized him and quit struggling.

The bartender had taken a step back, and was shouting in French.

"I will take care of her," Nethery said to him. Lily tried to pull free and go after the bartender but Nethery put his arms around her and hugged her.

"Shhhhh," Nethery said into her ear. "Come on, Lily. Let's go back to the cabin."

"Noooo," Lily said quietly.

"She crazy!" the man who'd been sitting at the bar shouted. Lily's body stiffened and she tried to turn and confront him but Nethery hugged her tighter and kept her from moving. Over her shoulder he glared at the man, who quickly turned his attention back to his drink. Lily was still struggling but Nethery had her in his arms.

"No, no," he whispered into her ear. "Come on. Let's go back to the cabin."

Lily struggled for a moment longer and then stopped. Nethery leaned back to see her face and it was expressionless. She looked sleepy. He pulled her shirt together to cover her breasts as best he could and escorted her out of the lounge and down the passageway, one hand holding her shirt together and the other on the small of her back, gently urging her forward. She toppled in her heels and he put his arm around her waist. When they got back to the cabin he set her down. Her shirt had fallen open again and he pulled it back together. He took off his jacket, covered her with it and then sat down across from her. He didn't know what else to do. She tucked her legs under her, and stared at the floor. After a few moments, she lifted her head and looked at Nethery.

"I am . . . scared," she said quietly, her voice trembling, trying to maintain her composure. Nethery got up and moved across the compartment to the seat next to her and put his arm around her. She threw her arms around his neck, laid her head on his chest and began sobbing, quietly.

Lily slept for over two hours. Nethery stayed where he was so as not to wake her. He had never been the protector of a woman, or responsible for one either. He had always shunned such things, and kept his distance in order to avoid such entanglements. He viewed it as a nuisance, and unnecessary. He was surprised how it made him feel. He would have expected to feel weighed down by the burden, and want to divest himself of it immediately but instead it made him feel proud, and strong. It also sharpened his thinking and with diamond clarity he could see the immediate steps that he needed to take. He let Lily sleep as long as he could and woke her only when the conductor indicated they were twenty minutes out of Marseille. She got up, rubbed her eyes, and managed a bit of a smile. She seemed to be more composed, sobered up, and she went mechanically about gathering her things and getting ready.

The train pulled into the St. Charles station. They had a short wait and then transferred to another train. They got their bags stowed and the train accelerated very quietly and was soon going full speed, the landscape flashing by outside the window. Lily sat across from him, thinking about something. Then she seemed to gather her composure, and looked him in the eyes.

"What you doing?" she asked, quietly, her eyes narrowing.

"Uh . . . what? What do you mean?"

"Why you help me? You can go home," she said, shaking her head. "You have passport. Just get on plane and go. I am not problem for you."

"I'm not going back there."

"What?"

"Look," Nethery sighed, "I don't know if you can understand this . . . it's just . . . I don't know . . . that place . . . where I'm from, it's not my home. It never really was . . . and this thing . . . it's made me feel alive again . . . and . . . I had forgotten what that felt like."

Lily shook her head, unable to understand, and then she remembered what he'd said earlier.

"Tell me about *big plan*," she said sarcastically, and then she sniffled.

Nethery reached up, grabbed the small duffel from the overhead, and pulled it into his lap.

"Take a look at this," he said, unzipping the top of the bag, pulling aside the shirts and tipping the bag in her direction.

"What is that?"

"Cocaine."

"Cocaine?" Lily asked, rolling her eyes. "What good that do?"

"I found it at my flat. When you were taking a shower."

"I say again. What good that do?"

"I can sell it. Get us some new papers and get you home."

Lily took a moment to try and digest this, but began to get angry.

"This is solution?" she asked, shaking her head. "More crime? You know someone in Marseille?"

"No, but it shouldn't be that hard."

"This is . . . damn crazy."

"Yeah well, that's probably true," he said, "but do you have a better idea? You want to hitchhike back to Kiev?"

Lily went silent. She didn't have a choice. Or did she? She knew how to make men do what she wanted, and this was the south coast after all. Cannes and Monaco weren't far away. There were rich men with money to burn and maybe the connections to get her home. She would just have to hit the clubs, and then one thing would lead to another, just like when Claude had discovered her. But she realized that in a way she didn't want to go down that path again. In fact, she wasn't certain that she even *could* anymore, and it was more than simply not wanting to. She looked over at Nethery, her eyes full of apprehension and fear. She was about to say something when the conductor appeared in the doorway, and she turned away and tried to hide her face.

Nethery fumbled in his jacket pocket, found the tickets, and handed them over. The conductor processed their tickets and left. He looked at her. She was obviously upset, but he didn't know what to say. There was nothing *to* say and the phrase *be careful what you wish for* popped into his mind. This was what he had wanted, wasn't it? He'd come to Paris with some half-baked idea of forcing a new direction in his life, but really, he hadn't expected anything to come of it. But something had. Something had changed. His life had always carried a kind of weight, a dense and dark mass of energy precariously perched, and his entire life it seemed had been spent running around frantically trying to keep it from moving, afraid of what would happen if it did. Now he would find out. The weight had been cut loose and it felt as if a great machine had been set in motion, one that was far greater and more infinite than he would ever understand. Intuitively he knew there was nothing to do but stand back and get out of its way.

Lily stared out the window, half watching the countryside streak past, allowing the blurred images to lull her into a relaxed state. But whenever her eyes began to get heavy the powerlessness of her situation brought her back, gnawing at her, causing a kind of tightness in the pit of her stomach. She got tired of looking out the window. She had no desire at the moment to talk to Nethery, and she sat there curled up on the seat until the train arrived in Cassis. The trip had only taken about twenty minutes.

The station was an old building slightly larger than a house. They walked in one side, out the other and into the blinding sun. Lily immediately put on some big sunglasses, but Nethery didn't have any, and he squinted until his eyes adjusted to the brightness. They made their way to a semicircular drive outside the front of the station where there was a small taxi stand, chose one, and climbed into the back. Nethery handed the driver the slip of paper with the address on it. After about five minutes of driving through low hills along a two-lane highway they reached a curve on the side of a hill facing the sea. The town came into view off to the left, a picturesque little seaside village sitting at the innermost point of a bay. The road continued to wind its way down in the general direction of the sea. They followed it until they reached the center of the town and turned onto a broad boulevard that ran along the waterfront. Nethery could see a small harbor filled with colorful wooden boats, local fishing craft, a few sailboats, and powerboats. To the right appeared to be a man-made spit with a small lighthouse at the outer tip. On the far side of the spit a long white sand beach stretched away from the town. The driver headed away from town and took them along a series of narrow winding roads that vaguely followed the shoreline. Nethery became so engrossed in the scenery that they were at the house before he knew it. He paid the driver, and he and Lily carried their bags to a gate in a wooden fence that surrounded the house. Nethery pushed a button next to the gate and after a minute an old woman appeared.

"*Bonjour, bonjour,*" she said cheerfully, following that with something else in French. Lily and Nethery looked at her, not having a clue what she said.

"My English is not so good, but I know a little. I am Fanny," she said, bowing slightly. "Welcome to my home. Jeanette call me and say you come. It is good," she said, smiling. She then beckoned them to follow her. She was a short woman, and old, but she walked quickly and with purpose. They followed her along a walkway made of flat stones that curved around the house. As they emerged on the other side the sea was spread out before them, wide and blue and glittering. A small guesthouse sat a little ways down the path and beyond that there was a cliff. They had to pick up their bags as they descended a curving stone staircase that led down to the guesthouse. When they arrived Fanny took some keys, opened the door, and ushered them inside.

"When I was young," she said, "Jeanette and I bring friends here. In summer. For vacation."

"It's very nice," Nethery said, smiling.

"You must be Lily," Fanny said, moving in front of her, "let me see you. Oh, *mon dieu*, you are pretty. Jeanette has told me much about you. I do not know why she stays in Paris," she said, shaking her head. "She has no friends there, but for you. She likes you very much."

Lily smiled uncomfortably, not knowing what to say.

"I do not know why she does not come live here, with me. That city? The noise? The English next door? *Merde*. She has told me." Fanny handed the keys to Nethery.

"Here," Nethery said, holding out a thousand euros in hundreds.

"Oh! *Mon dieu*. I cannot take money."

"I insist," Nethery said firmly.

Fanny eventually took the money and then stood there, as if she didn't know what to do or say. Finally she spoke, and told them that Jeanette would be arriving in a couple of days and if they needed anything to just come up to her house and ask. She mentioned that she was going into the town the next day to do some shopping and invited them to come along. Then she excused herself and left.

Lily had only brought one suitcase, and she lifted it onto the couch. She made a move to open it, then stopped and after staring at the case for a moment, walked out the door without a word. Nethery watched her curiously. He thought about following her, but she still seemed to be angry. He took a quick look around the place. It was not unlike the apartment he'd been renting in Paris—a kitchen/living room combo, a small bathroom, and a spacious bedroom. The place was a little dusty. He looked in the refrigerator. It was empty. He threw his jacket down onto the couch and went outside.

Lily had followed the stone walkway to a bench that was perched on a small bluff near the edge of the cliff. Nethery sat next to her. She was staring out at the sea. Nethery was going to say something, but any of the words that came to mind seemed incapable of conveying what he wanted. After sitting there for a few minutes Lily spoke, continuing to stare straight ahead out at the shimmering sea. Nethery answered, without looking at her. They talked for a few more minutes. He would say something and then she would, things that had already been said, sentences that included the words what, why, how. They never turned to look at each other, as if they weren't even talking to each other, but rather to the great expanse of space that lay spread out before them.

Nethery woke the next morning on the couch. He threw the blanket off, sat up and groaned. His head hurt. Lily was in the kitchen looking through the cabinets, and she heard him waking up.

"There is nothing here. No coffee . . . nothing," she said, throwing her hands up.

"Yeah. Well, I'll give you some money. You can go into Cassis today and get some stuff."

Nethery's head throbbed, and he rubbed his temples. Lily was only wearing panties and a T-shirt and she looked terribly desirable. Despite all the other things going on at that moment he wanted her, in a new and more powerful way.

"This is how people get in trouble," he mumbled to himself, "get a grip on yourself."

There was a knock at the door. Nethery got up and opened it. Fanny marched through the doorway carrying a tray.

"Oh *bien*. Good good, you are awake. There is no food here. I bring coffee and croissants."

She marched across the room and set the tray down on the small kitchen table.

"You will have to forgive me. I should have gone to town and buy some things for you."

Nethery thanked her, then sat at the table and began eating a croissant. Fanny and Lily made plans to go into Cassis that day, speaking in broken English.

"You will not be coming with us?" Fanny asked.

"No, I have to take care of some business in Marseille," Nethery replied.

"Oh! *Mon dieu!* That city! You must be careful. There are drugs in Marseille."

"I'll be careful," Nethery said, grinning. He gobbled down a croissant and washed it down with coffee. Lily nibbled on one and chatted with Fanny. They seemed to be getting on well.

"Is there a way to get down to the beach?" Nethery asked Fanny as she was standing in the doorway, preparing to leave.

"*Oui oui*, you can walk down to Port-Miou," she said pointing along the shoreline, "on the road, or there is a path down right here. It is difficult, but you are young."

After Fanny had gone Lily stared at the wall. Mechanically she raised a croissant to her mouth, tore off small pieces with her teeth and chewed slowly.

"Let's go down to the beach," Nethery said, trying to bring her out of it. Lily stopped chewing, and looked at him for a moment.

"Very well," she sighed, "we go to beach."

The path descended a short distance past the bench and then required them to scramble down sections of the limestone cliff. Nethery moved slowly and helped her down the steep sections. Finally they reached the shore, the beach just a tiny stretch of sand about thirty feet across. On either side, limestone outcroppings jutted out into the sea. Nethery led the way in the direction Fanny had pointed, toward Port-Miou. They had to wade out into waist-deep water to get around the outcropping and on the other side there was a slightly larger section of beach, about a hundred feet across, with a much larger headland at the far end of the beach that extended about thirty yards out into the sea.

Nethery walked ashore and stood there, looking around. The beach was untouched and almost inaccessible. It was long and narrow, and there was only about twenty feet between the water's edge and the face of the limestone cliff. In order to get here one would have to scramble down the cliff as they had or come ashore by boat. Lily followed him ashore and sat down on the sand a few feet away, looking out at the horizon. Nethery turned away from the cliff and walked into the sea until it was up to his waist. The sea was mesmerizing, a clear aquamarine, like the glass of an old bottle. It had a calming effect on him, and his mind went down through the gears until it was moving very slowly. The sky was clear and blue and endless. If only this were the entire world, he thought, this stretch of beach with a beginning and an end, a world where one could see what was coming next, where the sun rose and fell, and the tide came and went, every day the same, where things were simple and easy to understand. But there was all the rest, the Mediterranean before him, the horizon beyond, and the other world behind him, which he knew all too well, filled with people and all the stupidity and madness that came with them. He had to go back there, and this simple fact conspired with the gravity of his situation and he suddenly felt devastated. He stumbled ashore and sat down at the water's edge. The waves washed over his feet. Lily came and sat down next to him.

"What is matter?" she said.

"Nothing," Nethery lied. "Look at this water," he said, trying to change the subject.

"Yes. It is beautiful," Lily said, softly.

"If something happens to me," Nethery said, "if I don't come back, I want you to ask Jeanette and Fanny for help."

"I knew it! You leave me here!"

"No, I'm not. I'm just saying. If something happens, I think they will help you."

"You are crazy. Marseille is tough town. You will be killed."

"I've been around drugs. It's not as dangerous as people make out."

Lily looked at him, and then buried her face in her hands. Nethery wasn't sure what to do. She seemed to have lost something in the assault, a barrier, because she'd been crying quite a bit, something he'd never seen her do before. She had seemed so tough before, so determined not to play the victim. The epitome of the icy cold and aloof fashion model. But everyone has a breaking point, and he assumed she had been pushed far past hers. She gripped his hand tightly. Nethery put his arm around her and looked out at the sea.

He wasn't particularly looking forward to leaving this place, going out into the world again, but it had to be done. If they stayed they would eventually be found. It was in motion now, and he had to see this thing through to the end. It had to run its course. It made no sense to stop at this point. He wasn't frightened, in fact the sense of purpose it gave him just added fuel to his determination. He imagined the world outside the beach, and the image that came to mind was of a highway where all the cars were going as fast as their engines would allow. He admonished himself. It was useless to think about how unpleasant it would be, or to worry about all the things that could go wrong. Marseille was a city, like any other. He closed his eyes, and focused only on the repeating and regular sound of the small waves gently washing over his feet.

Nethery made his way outside the main hall of St. Charles station. He walked across a plaza until he stood at the top of a broad marble staircase that looked out over the city. It was a clear day and he could see the Old Port in the distance. He examined the map in his guidebook, and between that and following the majority of people he descended the staircase onto the Boulevard d'Athènes. He followed that to the Canebière, and then headed for the Old Port. Along the way he stopped at Centre Bourse, a shopping complex, a block off the Canebière. After a brief search he found a boutique and bought the first suit he found that fit, a Hugo Boss. He also picked out a shirt. From there he made his way to another boutique and bought an expensive pair of Persol sunglasses and at a third shop he picked up some black dress shoes and some socks. As he went from place to place he discarded his old clothes.

On his way out of the mall he stopped and looked at himself in a wall of large mirrors. He looked good, even stylish. He looked like money, like he'd just rolled into town from Monaco with a suitcase full of cash. He left the mall and stopped at a small corner store and bought some plastic bags, then found a phone store and got a prepaid cell. All together the shopping had taken almost two hours and he walked the few blocks to the harbor and had a coffee at La Samaritaine.

After resting for a bit he went to the bathroom and locked himself in a stall. He'd taken approximately three ounces of coke with him and he eyeballed one ounce into each plastic bag. It was in large chunks, and had a pinkish tone, the crystals flaking apart and shining almost like mother of pearl. He'd seen this type of cocaine before, many years ago in Seattle. It was called 'Bubble Gum' because of the color and was processed with ether instead of acetone. It was very rare and potent. As he was bagging the coke he got some on his fingertips and he stuck them in his mouth. The taste made his entire body stiffen and his hands became sweaty. He scolded himself for tasting it.

He wandered around the Old Port aimlessly, as if he was trying to avoid what he had to do. The few clouds he'd seen as he exited the train had vanished, and the day was becoming very warm. Marseille was an extremely noisy city. Everyone seemed to be yelling and car horns honked continuously. It didn't take long for him to figure out he wouldn't get far in this part of town. There were only nice restaurants and upscale bars and the people looked like tourists and rich businessmen. He examined the guidebook and decided to venture up into Le Panier, a very old neighborhood. It was situated on a hill to the north of the port, a maze of extremely skinny streets, narrow passageways, traverses, and steep winding staircases. He buckled down and began hiking up the hill. After twenty minutes, he neared the top, looked around, and realized he was lost. Between buildings he would occasionally catch a glimpse of the Old Port and regain his bearings and then head back in that direction, but there was no direct route and he kept ending up having no idea where he was. But he kept on, and after two hours he began to get discouraged, and wondered if he'd overestimated how easy this was going to be.

The bars he'd come across were the right type, small and inconspicuous, but the bartenders weren't what he was looking for. He sat down at the top of a winding staircase and had a cigarette. An old woman dressed in black walked past him and descended the stairs. She was towing a small cart with a bag of groceries strapped onto it and as she climbed down it clattered behind her. He sat there for about fifteen minutes until he felt slightly reenergized and he set off again, heading back in the general direction he had come but taking different streets. The afternoon sun was hot. He began to sweat and he took off his jacket and slung it over his shoulder.

Lily stood on the sidewalk and looked out at the harbor. She thought it was strange that so many of the boats remained tied up. There were only a couple of empty slips. And it was a beautiful day. Why weren't they out sailing? She turned around and looked to see if Fanny had come out of the flower shop. She was not there. Lily sat down on a bench that faced the sea. The morning had been interesting, or at least it had kept her mind off things. At the grocery Lily had tried to pick up a few things, but Fanny had put them back on the shelf and chose another brand, or another bunch of bananas, claiming it was better.

Lily bought food enough for a few days, knowing she would need something to keep her busy. Even though she knew very little about it, cooking had been the only thing that had come to mind to pass the time while she waited. She wasn't used to waiting. She was used to people waiting for her. But now she had no control. The idea did not please her at all. Nethery's plan was ludicrous, wasn't it? He was probably not coming back. It would go haywire, he'd get arrested or killed. Or he would take the money and leave her hanging. As the day wore on these negative scenarios spiraled out of control. Despite the sun warming her skin she began to get cold inside. She stared out into the harbor, not looking at anything in particular, and her eyes were drawn to a large expensive yacht, all by itself, tied up to a small cement dock out by the mouth of the harbor. She had been on boats like it, many times, and she wondered who owned it. The idea of walking out there to see if they wanted some company entered her mind.

She turned and faced the town. Across the street was the flower shop. Cafés and quaint little restaurants lined the rest of the waterfront. There must be some nightclubs here somewhere, she thought. There was definitely money in this town. Maybe not as much as Monaco and Cannes, but the villas she'd seen and the yachts in the harbor indicated that it was here. All she would have to do is find it, find the men who had it, and then make them do what she wanted. Fanny appeared across the street, smiling, with her arms full of parcels. She crossed the street and Lily relieved her of a few items. They made their way to a nearby taxi stand and caught a ride back to the house.

Nethery had passed so many bars in the last three hours they all began to blend together. It mattered very little whether they were nice upscale bars or down and dirty dives. The bartenders were the key. Some were too clean cut and would likely call the police, some were too young and wouldn't know the right people, and some were just plain arrogant looking. He was looking for a particular type, someone who'd been around the block a few times—hard, but not crazy. They weren't too hard to spot. He'd met some back in Seattle, usually ex-cons who had grown older and wiser and no longer looked for trouble. Many owned bars. And he had to find one that spoke passable English.

Eventually he came across a couple possibilities. At the first, when he'd brought out the cocaine the bartender had flipped out and reached for the phone, presumably to call the police. It could have just been a bluff but as soon as he reached for the phone Nethery had walked out, leaving the drugs behind. At the second, the bartender had merely given him a hard stare, thrown the drugs into the trash and pointed to the door.

Nethery was beginning to get tired. He managed to make his way back down to the Old Port by following some traverses and staircases on the edge of Le Panier. He sat down at La Samaritaine, had a coffee and read a copy of *The London Times* he'd picked up from a newsstand. On page three there was an article about Claude. People from the fashion industry were going on and on about what a great man he was and how much he will be missed.

"What a crock of shit," Nethery thought. "They wouldn't be saying that crap if they saw the tape." The French police were investigating. The man in charge said it was a cold-blooded murder and that he would not rest until the perpetrators were caught.

He sat in the sun for a good half-hour and then set off again, this time on the other side of the harbor. He wandered up and down side streets a few blocks removed from the Old Port. After checking out about ten more bars without finding a suitable one he began to wonder if this was a futile mission, and ponder other ways to get new passports. There were none, and he knew it. He stopped on the street and lit a cigarette, frustrated by the way things had seemingly ground to a halt. For the first time in his life events had begun to unfold by themselves, as if propelled by a natural force. The way things had played out to this point had a feel of inevitability to them, and because of that he had not questioned it. And logically he had assumed it would continue, but now it seemed like everything had stopped, and he didn't understand why. He gave up for the day, made his way back to the Canebière, and began to walk in the direction of the train station.

The sidewalks of the Canebière were crammed with people yelling. The street was choked with buses and cars, engines revving, horns honking for no apparent reason. The noise began to grate on his nerves. He knew the general direction of St. Charles station and detoured off onto a side street. He turned onto another narrow street that paralleled the Canebière and kept walking until he realized it was quiet and stopped to rest. He leaned up against a wall, lit a cigarette, and noticed that he was outside a small bar, so inconspicuous a person wouldn't even notice it unless they were right in front. There were a couple of faded posters in the window and no sign outside. Nethery peered in through the dirty window. It was a tiny little place, narrow, with a row of tables along one wall and the bar along the other. The bartender was behind the bar, talking on the phone. He was about fifty, and looked like a man who'd seen his fair share and could handle himself, but was very neat and clean.

Nethery finished his cigarette, walked in, and sat down at the bar. The man glanced in his direction, then turned back and continued to talk on the phone for a few minutes. This was another good sign, Nethery thought. This bar probably doesn't make jack shit for money, and the man clearly doesn't care, which could mean that the bar is a front for something. Finally the man got off the phone and strolled over.

"*Bonjour,*" he said.

"*Bonjour,*" Nethery replied. "*Parlez-vous anglais?*"

"Yes, I speak English," the man said, his eyes narrowing slightly. He had some kind of accent that Nethery couldn't pinpoint. German possibly.

"Can I have a Coca-Cola?" Nethery asked. The man didn't answer, and seemed slightly perturbed but went about getting the drink slowly and deliberately and when he was done he nonchalantly flipped a coaster onto the bar before him, and set the drink on it. Nethery lifted the glass and took a drink. It was cold and washed away the stale muck coating the inside of his mouth. Nethery discreetly watched the bartender and he could sense that the man was sizing him up.

"What's your name?" Nethery finally asked, setting the glass down on the coaster.

"Klaus," the man replied.

"James," Nethery replied, offering his hand across the bar. Klaus took his hand and Nethery looked him in the eye.

"That accent," Nethery said, "where's it from?"

"Germany."

"Germany, huh?"

"Yes."

"Never been there." Nethery took another long drink of the soda. "What's a German guy doing running a bar in Marseille?" he asked.

"You ask a lot of questions," Klaus said. "What is an American man doing here in Marseille?"

"I'm just passing through."

"Marseille is not exactly a town that one *passes through*," Klaus said, eyeing Nethery with a bit of suspicion.

"Oh?" Nethery remarked, raising his eyebrows.

"Yes," Klaus said, seeming to drift off into thought.

"Why's that?" Nethery asked.

"It has a way of . . . capturing a person," Klaus replied, searching for words.

"Really?"

"Yes."

"Did it capture you?" Nethery asked.

"Yes. Is this so strange?" Klaus asked.

"Well. It's just . . . you look like a man who would be difficult to capture, that's all," Nethery said and smiled.

Klaus grinned slightly, and then he looked off to the side.

"Can I buy you a drink?" Nethery asked, slapping a hundred-euro note onto the bar.

"Yes. Thank you," Klaus said, and then he poured himself a shot of Jack Daniel's.

"This is a nice little place," Nethery said.

"It is not so nice, but . . ." Klaus said, leaving the sentence unfinished.

"But it's yours. Right?" Nethery said, and then he indicated Klaus should have another drink.

"Yes. It is mine," Klaus said, seemingly thinking about something. He poured himself another shot.

"Is that how you got captured?" Nethery asked as calmly as he could, trying to lure the bartender into a conversation.

"Oh. In a way, yes. I came here as a boy. I joined the Foreign Legion," he said, pointing to a photo hanging on the wall behind him of about ten soldiers. "Twenty years ago I was finished with that, and I wanted to go home . . . to Germany . . . but . . . it never happened."

"Why's that?"

"Well," he said, "I . . . became distracted."

"You found work?"

"Yes, you could say that."

"It's a cool city," Nethery said.

"Cool?" Klaus replied, and he chuckled. "Maybe."

"I spent all day wandering Le Panier," Nethery said.

"Le Panier? What were you doing there?"

"I was . . . looking for something," Nethery replied, and then he intuitively felt it was time to roll the dice.

"I'd like to talk to you about something," Nethery said, looking at Klaus in a way that he would know it was something important.

"Oh?" Klaus replied, cautiously.

"Yeah. I'm looking to do a spot of business. The kind of business that . . . well . . . the police would not approve of," Nethery said and grinned, watching Klaus closely to see how he would respond. A spark of interest flashed across his eyes, and then it vanished.

"What kind of business?" Klaus asked.

"This kind," Nethery said, pulling the last bag of coke out of his pocket and placing it on the bar. The room seemed to grow quieter. Klaus looked at the bag for a moment as if he was trying to decide what to do, and then he relaxed, picked it up, and examined it. Before he could respond Nethery continued.

"If you like that sort of thing, you can have it. Or, if you have friends who like it, give it to them."

"Maybe I will just call the police," Klaus said, feeling Nethery out.

"Well, yeah, you could do that. But then you would miss out on all the money to be made. I have six kilos like that," Nethery said, "and I will give you a price you won't believe."

Klaus opened the bag, touched his pinky to his tongue, stuck it into the coke and then onto his tongue again. He stepped back, crossed his arms and looked at Nethery.

"And why are you telling me this? You think you can just walk into a bar in a strange town and start selling drugs?"

"Yeah," Nethery said, laughing, "I think I can." It was an infectious laugh and he saw Klaus smile, but only barely, and only for a second.

"Look, sometimes things happen. Sometimes we get lucky. I'm sure as a soldier you can understand that."

Klaus was about to throw him out when he paused. A memory floated up from the past and he fingered the silver coin hanging from a chain around his neck. His mind replayed the incident, for the thousandth time. He'd been with the Legion in the Congo, 1978, with the 2nd Parachute Regiment. They had dropped and were on their way toward Kolwezi, where some European and Zairian hostages were being held by a group of rebels. He was on point, and should have been focused on the terrain ahead, the windows and doorways of the empty buildings, but for some reason his eyes kept drifting toward the ground at his feet, as if a part of him had known something would be there. And eventually there was, a silver coin, sitting there in the mud, blood, and shit. It shone like a solitary star in a night sky. Klaus bent down to pick it up and at that instant a sniper's bullet whizzed through the space he had just been occupying and struck another soldier who had been following in his footsteps.

"Klaus?" Nethery asked, seeing that he was lost in thought.
"Uhhh. Yes?"

"Well? What do you think?"

Klaus shut off the memories and gathered his thoughts.

"It is a very dangerous game you are playing," he said.

Nethery laughed again. "You think I just went down to the Old Port and put up a cardboard sign?"

Klaus grinned for a moment.

"No, but . . . there is a way of going about these things," Klaus said.

"I know that," Nethery said, "but I don't have that luxury. I don't know anyone in Marseille and I don't have a lot of time. That's what I was doing in Le Panier, checking out some bars."

"Bars?"

"Bartenders know what's going on in a town more than anyone else, the cops or the crooks. You know that," Nethery said and he smiled.

"Yes. That is true," Klaus said, grinning slightly.

"Look, I just don't know anyone here. And you look like the kind of man who . . . knows things."

Klaus rubbed his chin for a moment. Given his history, this could quite possibly be a setup, despite the fact that he hadn't been involved in anything since he got out of prison. That'd been eight years now. But still, his name could have come up in some investigation, the cops would look into it, they would see he was running this quiet bar that was often empty, assume he was involved with something again, and decide to take a run at him. That kind of thing happens all the time. They always assume once you've been mixed up in the underworld at one point, you always are—and while it was true that getting out was easier said than done—getting to the periphery was doable, it just required some lifestyle changes and some sacrifices.

Klaus stood there, looking at the coke on the bar and then

at Nethery. He began imagining what he could do with a pile of money. He could ask Lauren to marry him. They could take a vacation. He could upgrade the bar, make it classy . . . and then he snapped out of it. Some stranger walks into my bar and wants to sell kilos of coke? That's crazy, and I'm crazy for even considering it. He walked over to the bar, picked up the bag of coke, held it up in the air over the trash bin, and slowly and deliberately dropped it, watching it fall into the can. He then looked up at Nethery without saying a word, and the look on his face left no doubt. Nethery grinned. He'd known it was a long shot. He climbed down from the barstool, put on his jacket and his sunglasses, thanked Klaus for the Coca-Cola and headed for the door.

Klaus watched Nethery walking for the door and then it hit him. This couldn't be a setup. There was no way. The Marseille cops would never have a foreigner working for them, especially an American. He knew enough to know that they would never, ever contemplate such a thing. They were extremely territorial and fanatically proud. They even ran Interpol out of town whenever they came around, even if they knew where to find whom they were looking for. He glanced down at the bag of cocaine in the trash. Instantly the wheels began to turn, in that old familiar way. Nethery was almost to the door when Klaus called out to him.

"Wait."

Nethery stopped, and turned.

"Yes?"

"How good of a price?"

Nethery made his way back to the bar.

"Well, what's the going rate on a kilo? About ten thousand euros?" Nethery asked. He guessed it was a bit more actually, especially quality stuff, but he didn't want to push it.

"It's more like six," Klaus said.

"I think it's *more* than ten thousand actually," Nethery said smiling. "But the price doesn't really matter to me. I'm only here for a few days, and there's something I need, besides the money, so if you can get it for me I will sell them for five thousand. Each."

Klaus looked hard at Nethery, looking for red flags, for the slightest look, word, gesture, that would set off the alarm. But there was nothing. Nethery seemed genuine, and sincere, and Klaus was a very good judge.

"This thing you need?" Klaus asked. "What is it?"

"Some papers. I need a new passport for me, and another person."

There were another few moments of awkward silence, and the tension in the air was so thick it was like mud. But strangely Nethery was as relaxed as he'd ever felt, having given himself over to this new thing, and feeling good that events had begun moving again.

"And I tell you what," Nethery continued, "if you can get me the papers I will give you a kilo. Free."

Nethery stood there, waiting for Klaus to say something, but it appeared he was waiting for Nethery to make the next move. Nethery removed a pen from his jacket, checked his new cell phone for the number, flipped the coaster over, and scrawled the number down onto it.

"I just want to do some business," Nethery said when he was finished, looking Klaus square in the eye, "the way business is supposed to be done. I get something, you get something. We both come out ahead. No rip-off, no scam, no bullshit," Nethery continued, shaking his head, "just business. That's my number. If you're interested, give me a call," he said, pushing the coaster across the bar. "But don't take too long. If nothing happens, I might clear out in a couple of days."

On the train ride back to Cassis, Nethery thought about what had transpired. He had doubts that anything would come of it. Klaus had seemed somewhat interested, but getting from interest to the point of doing a deal was still quite a ways to travel. Bridging the final distance would require some trust, and that was a rare commodity even when you knew someone. And then there was always the possibility Klaus would call the cops and wait for Nethery to show up with the dope. But his intuition was telling him that Klaus would either do a deal, or forget about him. And if he did the latter, what other options were there? Nethery stopped himself. Why did he keep looking for alternatives? There were none. This was it. It would either happen, or it wouldn't. He just had to wait. It was, in his estimation, his only chance. He couldn't keep going back into Marseille, prowling the bars. The bartenders had probably already put word out on the street that some stranger was in town selling top-drawer cocaine. The people who owned the drugs were certain to be on the warpath as soon as they found out their dope was gone. They would talk to the girl who'd rented him the place, and they would have his name and a description. Not much to go on. But they were sure to have ears on the street, even this far away.

He arrived back at the guesthouse shortly after 10 p.m. He was exhausted. He opened the door, stepped inside, and something didn't seem right. The place had been transformed. It was spotless and the few pieces of furniture had been arranged. There were flowers in a vase on the kitchen table and also in glasses on the window ledges. Lily came out of the bedroom. She looked surprised at first, and then smiled.

"You come back," she said, trying not to appear overly relieved.

"Of course I did," Nethery said, grinning. "Did you think I was just gonna ditch you?"

"Ditch? What is ditch?" Lily asked.

"Leave. You thought I was going to leave you?"

"Yes. I thought maybe . . ."

Nethery hung up his new jacket on a coatrack, turned to face her and smiled.

"I might be a lot of things, but I'm not a liar."

Lily appeared confused, and was looking him up and down.

"What is it?" Nethery asked.

"The clothes," she said, "they are . . . very nice."

"Oh yeah, the clothes. I needed some. I can't very well hope to interest someone in a big drug deal looking like some disco reject, now can I?"

Lily looked at him, clearly not understanding.

"What I mean is I have to look like I have money."

"Ohh, yes, I understand. It is good, the clothes. It look like money, yes. What happen?"

"I talked to a few people, bartenders. One guy seemed interested. I picked up a cell phone and gave him the number. I think he's gonna call," Nethery said, trying to reassure her. "What's this all about?" he asked, sweeping his arm around the room.

"I was . . . bored. I go to town with Fanny. We buy food. And flowers. She is very nice."

"You want food?" Lily asked.

"Yeah, that'd be great."

"Okay. Sit, sit," Lily said.

Nethery sat down at the table and lit a cigarette. He watched as Lily moved around the kitchen. She was wearing nothing but boy shorts and a tank top, without a bra. There was a part of her that was oblivious to the effect she had on men, and Nethery took this to mean that she still retained some of her innocence. It surprised him, after all she'd been through. She brought him a sliced baguette with ham and provolone. Nethery suddenly realized he was very hungry and devoured the sandwich quickly, ignoring his cigarette. It burned down slowly in the ashtray as he ate. Lily watched him, occasionally picking up the cigarette and taking a drag.

Nethery swung his legs off the couch, leaned forward and rubbed the sleep out of his eyes. He'd fallen asleep almost immediately after eating the night before. His clothes were slung over the end of the couch and he fumbled around in his jacket for a cigarette. Finally he found one, lit it, and swung his legs back up onto the couch. He took long drags and when he exhaled the smoke got caught in the morning light coming in the window, billowing like clouds in fast-motion. He tipped the ashes into a saucer on the floor.

Lily came out of the bedroom and cheerfully went about putting on some coffee. When it was ready they ate croissants and coffee at the kitchen table, drinking out of bowls, occasionally looking across the table and smiling at each other, their mouths full of food. After breakfast, Nethery turned on the television and found the BBC channel. There was more news about Claude. Nethery changed the channel immediately, but Lily had seen it and made him change it back. Her good mood vanished, and she became very tense and quiet. She sat cross-legged on the floor, directly in front of the television, and stared at the screen, not even blinking her eyes. The same police commander Nethery had read about in the paper was on, repeating what he'd said before, that they would not rest until the killer was caught.

Lily watched in silence. When it was over she hung her head and looked at the floor.

"Let's go down to the beach and have a swim," Nethery suggested. Lily slowly turned and stared at him, her mouth open as if to say something, but no words came out.

"Come on. It'll be fun. There's nothing else for us to do. We just have to wait. That guy in Marseille is gonna call. I know it."

Nethery made sure he had his phone and they left the guesthouse. They negotiated their way down the cliff and when they reached the bottom they crossed the tiny beach, took off their clothes, and holding them high over their heads waded out into waist-deep water, rounded the small promontory, and walked ashore at the larger beach. Nethery put his clothes down on the white sand and then walked to the edge of the sea and sat down at the water's edge. The sun was directly overhead. There was something about the tiny waves, the softness, the regularity, that transfixed him, and he felt the same calming effect as the last time. Eventually he looked out at the horizon. Lily sat down next to him. He looked over at her. She seemed to get more beautiful each day, more vital, as they ventured further and further from the worlds they had both inhabited for so long. Nethery gazed out at the horizon. This entire experience seemed to amplify reality. He felt the warmth of the sun on his hands, the sea washing over his feet, the fresh air filling his lungs, the sound of an occasional bird behind them on the cliffs. It was all intensely pleasant. He suddenly felt an urgent desire for her at that moment, more strongly than ever before. He reached out and took her hand. She lowered her head, opened her eyes and looked at him. He wasn't sure what he was going to say, the exact words, but he knew what it would be about and felt a twinge of that familiar trepidation but it was quickly lost in who he used to be, which was fading with every passing day, dissipating like smoke.

"Lily?"

"Yes?" she asked, looking at him. He couldn't hold her gaze and stared down at the sand.

"I . . ." he said, trying to stop himself, "I think I am falling in love with you." There was a moment of silence and Lily continued to look at him, waiting for him to do or say something more. But Nethery just stared at the sand. She gave up waiting and looked out at the horizon and she saw out of the corner of her eye that Nethery had raised his head and was looking at her. But she continued to stare straight ahead, and then without saying a word she stood and walked out into the sea.

She waded until the water was at her waist, dove and began to swim, slow strokes, her arms darting out before her. She swam out for about fifty yards and then turned back to the shore, treading water. She floated on her back and stared up, and the limitless blue of the sky and the weightlessness combined to give her a form of vertigo—something akin to the spins from drinking too much, minus the nausea. She tipped her head up occasionally to get a view of the shore and make the feeling go away. The water was warm on her skin, and she focused on this. She twisted her body and began treading water. The sea was so clear she could see light sand on the bottom. She'd been a swimmer in school and it felt good, stretching her long body, working her lean muscles. It had been a long time since she'd engaged in any sort of physical activity besides fucking. She saw Nethery get up and walk into the sea and then saw his arms flashing one after the other as he swam out toward her.

Nethery stopped swimming and treaded water for a moment. He scanned the sea where he'd last seen Lily. She'd swum a distance down, parallel to the shore, and then turned back toward the beach in order to avoid running into him. He swam after her. When he got to the beach she was already there, sitting on a towel. He walked out of the water, shook his head, and sat down on a corner of the towel. He waited for a minute before saying anything, looking for signs she'd heard what he said, but she just sat there looking out at the sea, a pleasant look on her face.

"Didn't you hear what I said?" Nethery asked, looking at her.

"Yes. I hear you," she said, still gazing out at the horizon.

"Well?"

"Well what?"

"Don't you have anything to say?"

"We do not have time for . . . stupid games," Lily said, dismissively.

Nethery felt the blood rush to his head, and he fumbled around in his pants pockets looking for a cigarette.

"Fuck," he said, pulling out his cell, unable to find his pack of smokes. He was going to say something, but he couldn't find the words and out of frustration he opened the phone. Someone had called. He knew it must be Klaus, and he pushed the return dial button and choked back his anger. He continued to search for his smokes while the phone rang.

"*Oui?*"

"Hello? Klaus?"

"Yes."

"It's James. You called?"

"Yes."

"What's up?"

"I think we may be able to . . . do some business."

"Okay. What do you have in mind?"

"I can help you with the papers."

"Okay . . ."

"I will need some photos."

"Of course. How about tomorrow? Around, say, three? I need time to get them."

"Yes. That is fine. I will need a down payment."

"Well . . . I dunno."

"This person . . . he is professional. I require something, you understand. In case you disappear, I will still have to pay him."

"Okay, sure," Nethery replied, "how about half a kilo tomorrow, half on delivery of the papers?"

"Yes. That will be fine."

"How long will it take?"

"I am not sure. The man said two weeks."

"Shit!" Nethery cursed.

"Is this a problem?"

"No," Nethery replied, realizing he didn't have much choice, "I was just hoping it would go faster."

"These things take time."

"Yeah . . . yeah. Are you gonna want to do some other business while we are waiting?"

"Yes. Most surely."

"About that? I only want to deal with you. No one else."

"Of course."

"Okay, great. Tomorrow at three. At the bar?"

"Yes."

"Okay. See you there."

"*Au revoir.*"

Nethery shut the phone. He had found his cigarettes while he was talking and lit one.

"What happen?" Lily asked. She had scooted over next to him.

"I can get us some passports. We need to go into Marseille tomorrow, get some photos and give them to him," he said without emotion. "It'll take two weeks."

"I cannot believe . . . it is happen."

"Well it hasn't happened yet," Nethery said, partly to keep her expectations realistic, but mostly to cool her off because he was still angry.

Lily looked at him, puzzled.

"These things can go sideways very easily," Nethery said.

"Sss . . . sideways?"

"Yeah. You know, haywire," Nethery said, but he could see that she still didn't understand.

"They can fuck up."

Concern spread across her face.

"But don't worry," he said, reassuring her. "I have a good feeling about it."

"Let's go into Cassis tonight," Nethery said, trying to change the subject. "Have dinner somewhere, maybe check out a club."

"Yes," Lily replied after a moment.

They gathered their things and climbed back up the cliff to the guesthouse. Nethery expected her to say something, some kind of acknowledgement or reaction to what he'd said on the beach. She was acting as if it were irrelevant and meant nothing. In the past, he wouldn't have let it go. He'd have gone back to it immediately, trying to force the issue, in the hope that it would change how the woman felt or to make her feel bad. But he held his tongue, and oddly it wasn't that difficult. It wasn't that he didn't care that she hadn't responded, but rather a strange new form of acceptance.

Nethery turned on the television. All the stations were covering breaking news from America. A pair of former government officials who were now lobbyists for the insurance industry had been discovered in their offices on Wall Street, decapitated, and missing their hands. The perpetrators had somehow smuggled in and assembled a guillotine right in their office on the thirty-sixth floor. One of the heads had been positioned against the wall, and a speech balloon was drawn in blood on the wall to make it appear the head was saying "I got another tax cut." They'd used the rest of the blood to spell out their message, and photos showed a trail of words down the concrete walls of the stairwell: *this is what we do this is what we do this is what we do . . .*

The news was calling it an "Attack on the United States" but apparently, most people weren't seeing it that way. A reporter asked a man on the street what he thought and he said, "Of course it's a terrible tragedy, but they kind of had it coming. Didn't they?" There was speculation on how the perpetrators had gotten past the private security firms guarding Wall Street, and some of the firm's employees were being investigated. A government official came on and said that these terrorist acts were threatening the stability of the economic system.

Nethery sighed. He was really getting tired of the media. It was all a bunch of lies, hyperbole, and fearmongering, playing on his sympathy, urging him to care about floods in Thailand and earthquakes in Venezuela, impending doom, slippery slopes, wars and the national debt and genocide here and there and everywhere. Abandoned pets and cleft palates and starving children in Central America. Who could possibly care about so many things at once? There were limits to empathy, weren't there? It was as if they were trying to overwhelm people, drain them of energy. Reduce them to passive zombies. He turned to BBC International to see if there was any more news about Claude but there was only a commercial for some investment firm using a talking baby. Nethery sat there with his mouth open, not believing what he was seeing. So now they're using babies to do their lying for them?

He was about to turn off the television when photos of a building came on the screen and he recognized it as the place he'd stayed at in Paris, and then there was a photo of the woman who'd rented him the apartment. A female reporter appeared on the screen.

"French authorities are concerned that 'the People's Mafia' may have crossed the Atlantic and come to France. Yesterday a woman was found murdered in a Paris apartment and 'the People's Mafia's' enigmatic message was left at the scene. The Ministry of the Interior has ordered the French National Police to form a task force to investigate . . ."

"Shit," Nethery hissed, under his breath. He heard the shower turn off and forced himself to shut off the television. He leaned forward, put his head in his hands. He resisted the urge to scream "Fuck!" and just groaned. So much for them not discovering the drugs are gone, he thought. These people wanted their dope back. And they wanted it back very badly. Nethery stood up and paced around the room. He lit a cigarette and noticed that his hand was shaking. After only a couple of drags, he walked to the open door of the guesthouse, stepped outside, and flung the smoke as hard as he could at the ground.

"Goddamnit!" he yelled under his breath. "Get a grip," he muttered. He was well aware if he showed any fear whatsoever Lily would know something was up. He was a poor liar and she would eventually figure out what it was. She emerged from the bathroom and went into the bedroom. He pulled himself together and tried to calm down. He shaved and combed his hair. He put on his new suit and sat on the couch and smoked. After about ten minutes Lily emerged from the bedroom and stood in front of him, but she seemed unable to meet his eyes, and kept looking down at the floor. All that arrogance and attitude he'd first seen at the club had totally vanished, and she stood there, waiting for his approval. She was wearing a red cheongsam with black and gold patterns stitched onto it. The dress went down to just above her knees and fitted her slim body perfectly. Nethery tried to say something, but none of the words seemed to be good enough.

"Well?" she said, twirling before him. "You like?"

"My God," Nethery said, when he could finally talk, and this response seemed to please her.

It was a warm night, and they walked into town. A pleasant breeze was blowing in from the sea. Lily undid a few buttons at the bottom of the dress in order for her legs to move and she took off her heels and dangled them from her finger. The moon was full, and the light reflected off the satin of her dress. It clung to her body like a second skin. At one point she walked a few steps ahead and Nethery watched her. She was like a cat, the way her body moved. Her shoulder blades showed through the thin and shiny fabric and the way they moved under the fabric gave him the impression there was an animal under her skin, trying to get out.

They entered the town and walked onto a bustling promenade that ran the waterfront, lined with outdoor cafés and restaurants painted all sorts of pastel colors. They looked like a row of those airy mints that melt in your mouth. Fanny had suggested Restaurant Le Bonaparte, somewhere near the center of town and after a bit of searching they found it. They took a seat in the corner. After they ordered, a jolly fat man came out to greet them. His English was good. He must have been the owner. He described the menu items and brought their seafood out and showed it to them before sending it to be prepared.

The meal was fantastic. It allowed Nethery to briefly forget everything else that was going on. After, they made their way back to the waterfront. Dozens of people and couples were out walking and enjoying the warm night. They strolled along the promenade, losing themselves in the crowd. There was a slight breeze coming in off the water, and Nethery could taste the salt in the air. They walked for a while and sat down at a bench on the Quai des Baux, near the water, under a palm tree that swayed gently in the night wind. Nethery looked around with a sense of wonderment. Everything seemed terribly beautiful, almost alien, the moonlight reflecting off the water, the pastel-colored buildings, the quiet creak of the boats tied up in the harbor. A sensory overload, but intensely pleasant. Lily had closed her eyes and had her head tipped up slightly as if smelling the air. The lights lit up the edge of her face with a colored glow, and the rest remained in shadow, like a charcoal drawing. Nethery forced himself to look away, but his eyes kept finding their way back to her face, and the outside world seemed to dissolve away. He wanted to kiss her, badly.

If they sat there any longer he would have, so he suggested they go in search of a nightclub. The restaurant owner had given them some vague directions to a place called Club Santos and they found it a few blocks from the waterfront. It looked a bit out of place amongst the faded pastel and old brick buildings, all shiny steel and neon. There was a giant bouncer outside, and they paid and climbed the staircase to the second floor where there was a bar and dance club. It was still fairly early, and the place was almost empty. Nethery found a table and asked Lily what she wanted to drink. He ordered vodka for her and was about to order a Perrier for himself when he hesitated. It wasn't even that he craved a drink so much, more an intense curiosity about what would happen. He ordered another vodka and carried the drinks back to the table. As he approached he saw three men at the table next to theirs, staring at Lily and talking amongst themselves. Nothing unusual in that, he thought. She's the most beautiful girl here, probably in the entire south of France.

Nethery handed Lily her drink and sat down. She stared at him with a quizzical expression on her face.

"You have drink," she said.

"Yeah," Nethery replied, grinning.

"What about drinking problem?" Lily asked. Nethery shrugged. Lily raised her glass and they downed the shots. Nethery waited for some kind of reaction to the alcohol but there was none. He wanted to ask her to dance but all they were playing was droning techno. He walked over to the DJ booth and bribed him into playing "Svefn-g-englar" by Sigur Rós. When it came on he stood and took Lily's hand and led her to the dance floor. Upon hearing the song, it had emptied and they danced alone, slowly turning circles, Lily's head on his chest and his arm around her waist. He closed his eyes. He became completely lost in the moment. He felt nothing but the warmth of her body, the smell of her hair, the feel of the silk. He opened his eyes and it was as if they weren't moving at all but that the room and the entire world beyond were slowly revolving around them.

The song ended. The club had begun to fill up. He excused himself, and went to the restroom. As he made his way back to the table he noticed a man had pulled a chair next to Lily's. She was looking straight ahead and he was leaning across the table so he could face her. She was obviously trying to ignore him, but he kept speaking and gesturing with one hand.

"Hello?" Nethery said, leaning on the back of her chair. The man looked up. Nethery recognized that he was one of the men from the next table who'd been staring at Lily. He was older, about fifty. He was going bald and had a bad comb-over, weighed down with grease. The other two men from his table were looking over.

"Can I help you?" Nethery asked.

"I am asking the young lady a question," the man said in English with a Russian accent.

"It looks to me like she doesn't want to talk to you."

"This is not your business," the man said, standing up as straight as he could.

"It's not?" Nethery said, "Hmmm, I thought it was."

"No. It is her business."

"Looks like she's not interested," Nethery repeated.

"I will tell you again. This is not your business," the man said, clearly irritated.

"Well guess what, fat man? I'm making it my business."

The man glared at Nethery, his eyes narrowing.

"Do you know what she is?" the man asked, pointing at Lily,

who had gotten up and was standing next to Nethery. "She is a whore."

"What's your point?" Nethery asked, shaking his head. The man had clearly expected this to shock Nethery, but when it didn't he got confused.

"I want to . . . use . . . her," the man said, haltingly.

"Maybe it's her day off," Nethery said.

"Whores do not have day off," the man said, smiling darkly. Nethery felt a rush of adrenaline, something that used to frighten him.

"Maybe she just doesn't like you," Nethery said, smiling back.

"Whores do not get to choose," the man said.

"James, come," Lily said, tugging on his arm.

"Ten thousand euros," the man said to Lily, "for one night."

"James . . ." Lily said, more urgently, still tugging.

"She's not interested," Nethery said, still smiling.

"Why does *she* not tell me?"

"James . . ." Lily pleaded.

"Some other time, fat man," Nethery said, finally relenting and allowing Lily to pull him toward the exit. She seemed very distraught, and when they got outside she continued towing Nethery toward the waterfront.

"What was that about?" Nethery asked finally, forcing her to stop.

"I see him, at club. In Paris."

"Yeah? When?"

"Many months ago."

"So what?"

"I . . ."

"He doesn't know any of those people, does he? From the club?" Nethery asked, looking at the ground, for a moment.

"No . . . I do not think so."

"Well then, I repeat: who gives a shit?"

"I . . . I . . . thought to go with him. The money . . ."

"Well, why didn't you?"

"I thought . . ."

"You thought what?"

"We were on . . . date."

"I suppose we were," Nethery said, grinning. Lily smiled, leaned her head on his chest, and held him tightly. When she finally let go she stepped back, and smiled again. She hooked her arm in his and leaned her head on his shoulder. They set off for the waterfront again, Lily clinging to his side. When they reached Quai des Baux they found a taxi. When they arrived at the guesthouse Lily went into the bathroom. Nethery sat down at the kitchen table. He expected her to come out quickly and when she didn't, he began to think about the meeting in Marseille the next day. Was he prepared? He felt an urgent need to do something.

He retrieved the gun from under the couch cushion, checked the magazine to see how many rounds were left. Lily came out of the bathroom, and before she could make it to the bedroom he asked her if she had any more ammunition. She hesitated for a moment, surprised and confused, but eventually she gave him two full magazines from her bag. She then stood there and looked at him with a puzzled expression on her face, but said nothing. When Nethery realized she was standing there, he reassured her that it was just a precaution. She stood for a moment longer, waiting for him to say something more and when he didn't, she vanished into the bedroom. Nethery put a full magazine into the gun and then put the gun back and stood in the center of the room, thinking. He retrieved one of the kilos from the cupboard where he'd put them and set it down on the kitchen table. He found some plastic bags and a couple of utensils in a drawer.

Five minutes later Nethery had the package split open completely and was using a wooden spoon to try to make two equal piles, but it wasn't going very well. The spoon was useless for scooping and he had taken a card out of his wallet and was using the spoon to push the coke onto the card and then shovel it into the bags. He had gotten drugs all over his fingers and hands and the table and even spilled some onto his lap.

"What are you doing?" he heard Lily say. He hadn't noticed her come out of the bedroom, totally obsessed with the task at hand. He looked up, and immediately knew he had fucked up. Lily was standing there wearing nothing but sheer black panties and a lace bra.

"I . . . um . . . I . . . we have to have this ready," he stammered. He had fucked up. The pleasant vibe of the evening had been broken, irreparably, as if the air had turned cold. He desperately tried to think of a way to set things back on their previous course, but he was at a loss. Lily stood there, looking around the room for a few awkward moments.

"I . . . ah . . . have to finish splitting this up. We have a big day tomorrow."

"I go to sleep," she said abruptly, and then disappeared into the bedroom. Nethery hung his head and sighed. "Goddamnit," he muttered, kicking the leg of the table. He thought about leaving the coke and going after her, but Fanny or Jeanette would come round first thing in the morning, like they had every day. For them to see a mountain of coke on the kitchen table would not be good. He finished splitting and wrapping the packages as quickly as he could, but it still took fifteen minutes and by then he knew it was hopeless. She was probably already asleep and on top of that she had looked pissed off. He placed one half-kilo in an old vinyl SAS airline bag and set it down next to the couch. He threw himself down on the couch, put his feet up, turned on the television at low volume, and fell asleep.

Nethery put on some coffee, and while he waited he went outside and sat on the bench. A layer of morning fog covered the sea and it drifted around the cliff's edge like smoke from a burning world. He lit a cigarette and as he smoked he remembered the previous night and felt like an idiot all over again. He became very nervous about facing Lily. He heard a noise from inside the guesthouse, flipped his smoke over the cliff, and walked to the doorway. Lily was placing the coffee and a basket of croissants on the table. She looked at him, grinned, and gestured for him to sit down. As they had breakfast it became clear that she had forgotten about his gaffe. All she could talk about was going into Marseille.

They took a taxi to the station and caught the 9 a.m. train. Once in Marseille they walked down to the Old Port and found a place to get the passport photos taken. It would take two hours and they had croissants and coffee at La Samaritaine. After, they explored Le Panier, stopping occasionally to rest and admire the view of the city. Around 2 p.m., they took a taxi back to the train station and he saw Lily off back to Cassis. He had time to kill before the meeting and he wandered the Canebière, looking in shop windows. At a quarter to three he found Rue Vincent Scotto, walked to a corner down from the café, found a good vantage point in a doorway and stood there and smoked. People walked past but paid him no attention. When the coast was clear, he removed the Walther from his jacket pocket and stuck it down the back of his pants. He peered out from the doorway once more, looking for anything out of the ordinary. Eventually he began walking toward the bar, casually scanning side to side and up toward the windows and rooftops. He came to the bar and strolled in as casually as he could, noticing that there were no patrons. Klaus stood behind the bar, drying glasses. Nethery sat down at a stool and placed the SAS bag on the counter. Klaus heard the bag hit the bar and turned.

"Hello, Klaus," Nethery said.

"Hello," Klaus replied, smiling faintly. "Would you like something to drink?"

"Sure."

"What would you like?"

"A Coke is fine."

"You do not want something stronger?"

"No," Nethery said, chuckling, "that probably wouldn't be such a good idea."

"Oh?"

"Yeah. I can get a bit out of control when I drink."

"Ah, I see."

Klaus got Nethery the Coke, and set it down carefully on a coaster. Nethery took a drink, then reached into the side pocket of the bag and removed the passport photos.

"Here are the photos," he said, handing them over.

"She is very pretty," Klaus said, looking at the photo of Lily.

"Yeah."

"You have the other?" Klaus asked.

"Right here," Nethery said, pushing the bag across the bar. "I didn't have a scale, so I had to guess. If this one is a little more than a half kilo, the other half will be a little less, and vice versa."

"It is okay," Klaus said. He took the bag and put it on the sink counter behind the bar. He removed the half-kilo and put the SAS bag back on the bar. He placed the package of cocaine on an electronic scale he had set up on the counter.

"It is a little more than half," he said.

"That's what I thought," Nethery replied, smiling. He had chosen the one that appeared slightly larger.

Klaus glanced toward the door to make sure no one was coming in, removed some of the tape around the package and opened it. He wet his finger, stuck it into the powder, then put the tip of his finger into his mouth and rubbed it along his gums.

"It is good. Still, I must have it tested," he said. "The first sample you gave me was very high quality. The rest must be of the same standard."

"It is," Nethery said smiling.

"Very well," Klaus said.

"So, the passport deal will take two weeks?"

"Possibly. It may be sooner. But he will not be rushed. He is a serious man. They will be very high quality."

"Okay."

"I may be needing more of this very soon," Klaus said, indicating the coke.

"Great. Just call me."

They both stood and Nethery used the opportunity to look into the eyes of his new business partner, searching for something amiss. It was obvious that Klaus had the same idea and they both recognized this and grinned. They shook hands and Nethery left. As he walked down the side street, Nethery felt a sense of elation mixed with fear. The plan was moving forward, if that's what you could call it. It could just as easily be considered getting in over his head, entering into something in which there would be no way to turn back. He reviewed the meeting in his mind, double-checking in case he missed something. He casually looked around for anyone following him, or any vans that looked out of place. If someone had designs on getting their hands on the rest of the coke without paying for it, they would try to follow him to the stash.

Nethery made his way back down to the Old Port and wandered around looking for a place to eat. Standing at a crosswalk, he noticed a pair of African men looking at him. He had taken note of them earlier, a few blocks away, by their pink polo shirts. He wasn't sure they were following him, and he wasn't even sure they were the same men from earlier, but to be safe he found a restaurant with an outdoor patio, situated so he could see people coming and going in either direction. He ordered one thing and then another and took his time eating, all the time watching discreetly, but the men had disappeared. As he was paying the bill he checked his watch and realized he had forgotten to tell Lily that he would be late returning to the guesthouse. She would be expecting him around five, and that just wasn't going to happen. It was already five and he had no way to contact her.

It was six o'clock. Lily sat on the bench looking out at the sea. The sun was off to her right, sinking over the horizon. Nethery hadn't returned. They hadn't discussed it, but she'd expected him shortly after four. She was trying desperately to remain positive, but after witnessing the cold ugliness of the fashion industry she found very little reason to be. The events of the last couple years had shaped her mind, and it now naturally tended to gravitate to worst-case scenarios. She gazed out at the horizon. It really was breathtaking, and she closed her eyes hoping to imprint, retain the image, but even the panoramic beauty inspired very little hope. It couldn't be something innocuous. Something serious had happened. She imagined Nethery getting arrested, or worse, knifed, or shot, his body lying in an alley or a dumpster. Or maybe they were torturing him in order to find out where the rest of the drugs were? They might be showing up any minute, and then they would kill her too. The images running through her head became like gasoline on a small fire, igniting a visceral type of fear, more intense than any that had come before. She'd felt fear when she'd been black-listed a year ago, but at least then she'd known of a few things she could do to get by, a few places to run to, a couple people to ask for help. Now she was totally alone.

She opened her eyes. The more she thought about it the more certain she was that something had happened to Nethery. She had begun to have confidence that he could actually help her, but now that last tiny glimmer of hope seemed to be gone as well. She scolded herself for getting her hopes up. There's nothing stupider than pretending the world isn't the way it is, she thought. She looked out over the cliff and imagined what it would be like to hurl herself over the edge. She took a deep breath. I'm not going to take this lying down, she told herself, and her pride and anger snuffed out the fear she was feeling until there was nothing left but cold determination. She stood, walked back into the guesthouse and began to get ready.

"Where are you going?" Fanny asked, standing in the doorway of the guesthouse. Lily had put on the same outfit she'd worn the night before. She had added a lot of black eye shadow.

"I am going into town. To club," Lily replied.

"Where is James?" Fanny asked.

"Oh . . . I do not know," Lily said, stuttering slightly.

"What is the matter, *cheri*?" Fanny asked.

"Oh . . . it is nothing," Lily replied.

"*Mon dieu*," Fanny said, "you are very beautiful."

"Will you call taxi for me?" Lily asked.

Lily sat at the bar and sipped a drink, waiting for the night to come. It was still early, and the club was quiet. There were a few girls sitting at a table in the corner. Escorts. The competition. Waiting for men. As the seconds ticked away and became minutes she slipped back into an old way of thinking, comfortable and familiar, like a warm cloak handed down from the beginning of time.

Gradually the club began to fill up. It would soon be time, and yet this knowledge provided no relief or comfort but gave way to a growing agitation. She had always known what she was doing. It had never bothered her much, when she was doing well, or at least when she had the hope that she could make enough money to get out, or become famous enough to parlay that into a future. But now that those carrots were gone, the trade-off seemed repulsive and unacceptable. She desperately wanted to draw a line in the sand and not cross it for once. She tried to disregard this but it was like a flashing red light that stayed in front of her no matter which way she turned. She kept drinking, hoping she could reach the oft-found point of not caring, but it didn't work. She wished she could just get very drunk, wake up, and have it be over. She gulped the vodka. After four drinks, she began to get drunk, and found herself regaining her bearings. This was what she knew. This was all she'd ever known, selling herself, in one form or another. "It's true," she thought, "I am a whore."

"Hello madame," said someone in Russian, but she didn't notice over the music and the chatter of the people at the bar.

"Madame?" She felt a hand on her shoulder, turned and raised her eyes. It was the fat Russian from the other night.

"Oh," Lily replied, "hello."

"It is good to see you again," the man said.

Lily tried to force a smile.

"Where is . . . your friend?" the man asked.

"He is not here," Lily replied.

"I see. Would you like to sit with us?" he asked, indicating a table close to the bar.

She really didn't feel like it, but this was what she'd come down here for after all.

"Very well," she said, and she picked up her drink and followed him to the table. The same two friends were with him. They were younger, and not as physically repulsive. One of them, however, gave her a bad feeling. It was the smile he gave her as she sat down—not creepy exactly, but there was something inauthentic about it, as if his face were made of wet clay, cold and lifeless.

"What is your name? I have forgotten," the old man asked, after she sat down.

"Lily."

"Lily? Of course. Now I remember. What a pretty name. I am Vladimir, and this is Anatoly and Pasha," he said, indicating his friends. Pasha was the one with the weird smile.

"The man from other night? He is not here?" Pasha asked.

"No."

"Is he your . . . manager?"

"No, no, he is just friend."

"Then, this is not a day off for you?" Pasha asked somewhat sarcastically.

"No. Not day off."

Vladimir ordered another round of drinks for everyone, and there was some small talk.

"We having a party later . . . on boat. You would like to come?"

"Boat?" she asked.

"Yes."

"I do not know," Lily replied, acting disinterested, but wondering if they were talking about the huge yacht she'd seen in the harbor.

"It will be a good time . . ." Pasha said, very slowly, "very good time."

"I must wait here," Lily said, playing hard to get, "someone coming for me."

"Ten thousand euro," Vladimir then said, and he looked at her to gauge her response. Lily kept her cool. The men waited for her to respond but she remained ambivalent. She was still good at playing this game.

"I must have half of money, up front," she said. Vladimir nodded and Lily smiled a little, in order to make it seem she as though she wasn't totally disgusted, but she was, more than ever. Anatoly seemed to get very excited. Pasha sat back and smirked. They had another round of drinks. Now that a deal had been struck, the men ignored her and talked amongst themselves. After fifteen minutes Vladimir signaled it was time, and he led the group out to a big black BMW sedan parked behind the club. They drove the short distance to where the boat was moored. It was, as Lily had assumed, the boat she'd noticed when she and Fanny had been shopping. As they pulled up to the dock the two younger men kept glancing at her, seeing if she was impressed. Vladimir got out of the car and opened the door for her.

Nethery leaned on the bench, looking out at the sea. It was 7 p.m. and Lily was gone. He had picked up a handful of stones and was throwing them out into the darkness one after the other. He could see the stones leave his hand and travel a few feet, then reach the edge of the light and vanish into the black night. It had taken him five hours to get back here. He'd sat at a café for over an hour, and then he'd walked or taken a taxi to a few hotels, gone in the front door and out the back, until he was certain he wasn't being followed. He then took a bus back to Cassis in case someone was watching the train station.

The moonlight was bouncing off the sea in flashes of silvery light. The flickering had a sort of hypnotic effect and threatened to distract him. He wished he could have just sat down there and done nothing, but he had taken a peek into the bedroom and found Lily's makeup strewn all over the bed. She had gone out, probably to make some money. Jealousy and concern wrestled around inside him. Nethery grunted and flung the last stone out into space as hard as he could, and then turned and marched up to Fanny's house. He knocked on the door and Jeanette answered.

"Oh! Mr. Nethery!" she said, smiling. She stepped forward and hugged him. "Come in, come in," she said, stepping aside. Nethery was surprised, but then gathered himself, walked in and stood in the living room.

"Do you know where Lily is?" he asked Jeanette. Fanny came out of the kitchen, holding a big bowl. She had a wooden spoon and was stirring something.

"She say she go to club. In Cassis," Fanny said.

"Damnit!" Nethery cursed under his breath.

"What is matter? You have . . . umm . . . problem? Fight?" Jeanette asked.

"No. I was just supposed to be here hours ago."

"She seem very sad," Fanny commented.

"You find her?" Jeanette asked.

"Yeah," Nethery said.

"I call for taxi," Fanny said.

The men led Lily to a lounge in the center of the yacht. Plush leather couches ringed the room, and there was a flat screen television on the wall. An antique bar was situated in the corner. Vladimir made drinks for everyone. He and Anatoly sat on one of the couches, turned on the flat screen and proceeded to become engrossed in a soccer match. Pasha had focused his attention on Lily and was dragging her around the yacht, pointing out this or that. This was a game she'd played before. But

Lily was finding it increasingly hard to play, and somehow she found it very difficult to slip into character, even though she'd done it hundreds of times, even though she knew that not doing so could have consequences.

When she remained indifferent to Pasha's efforts to impress her, a kind of darkness came over him. The smirking face vanished and he stared into space for a few moments. She realized that he had a very bad haircut and she might have laughed, but he had suddenly begun to exude a coldness that she could almost feel. He seemed to become even paler and his face appeared to become damp or greasy. Pasha eventually ushered her back to the lounge. She wanted to move to the couch where Vladimir and Anatoly were sitting, but he steered her to the opposite side of the room. She was beginning to grow concerned, and she wondered if she should have waited longer to see if Nethery would show up. She didn't have the protection of Claude's influence or the leg-breakers at the club, or even her gun. She wondered if she had gone too far.

Pasha got up from the couch, went over to a cabinet and turned on some music, drowning out the soccer game. Vladimir and Anatoly looked up, but didn't say anything. Then Pasha disappeared into one of the bedrooms. Lily was going to engage the others in conversation, possibly even move over to their side of the room, but the way Pasha had looked at her suggested that he wanted her for himself, so she stayed where she was. Pasha reappeared after a few minutes carrying a large clear plastic bag of white powder, another bag full of tablets, and two bottles of expensive champagne.

Pasha threw the drugs down onto the glass coffee table and sat next to Lily. He opened a bottle of champagne and poured a glass for himself and one for her. He then took two of the tablets and washed them down with champagne. He drank more, guzzling straight from the bottle. He took another two tablets out of the bag and set them on the table, then dumped out a large amount of the white powder onto the glass. With a hunting knife he'd gotten from somewhere, he carved out four big lines, probably close to half a gram in each. He rolled-up a euro note and snorted two of the lines. He then sighed, sat back on the couch and closed his eyes. His face and eyes twitched occasionally and he began to visibly sweat. He sat like that for a couple of minutes. Vladimir and Anatoly occasionally looked over, but didn't speak. They exchanged a few words that Lily couldn't hear, as if they were waiting for something to happen.

Pasha eventually moved. He slowly sat upright, his eyes still closed. Then he slowly and mechanically turned to face Lily and opened his eyes. The look he gave her sent chills down her spine. It wasn't blank, without conscience, like Sergei back at the club, born out of stupidity and ignorance; rather this was something else, something more primal and animalistic, a kind of evil that feels itself justified. Without breaking his stare Pasha slowly reached out a white finger and pointed at the two lines and two pills on the table.

Lily felt as if she couldn't move. She glanced down at the drugs and back at Pasha. Beads of sweat were running down his face. The smirk had returned, and Lily now knew why it had bothered her, back at the club. Lily stalled, trying to think of a way to defuse the situation, and out of the corner of her eye she could see Vladimir and Anatoly casting nervous glances her way. Pasha's arm darted out and grabbed a handful of Lily's hair. He yanked hard, and then pulled her closer until her face was two inches from his.

"Do it," he growled, and she felt tiny drops of spit hit her face.

Lily forced herself to start moving, and Pasha relaxed his grip on her hair and let go. She reached for the rolled-up euro note on the table, leaned over and began to snort the coke. There was no way she could do an entire line at once, like Pasha had.

Unlike many models she knew, it had never really been her thing, but Pasha obviously assumed it was, and wouldn't believe her if she said she wasn't. She snorted part of a line, then sat bolt upright, grabbed her nose, and closed her eyes. It took her five snorts to finish the line, and when she had, she sat back on the couch. Pasha grabbed her arm and dragged her back into a sitting position, and indicated she snort the second line. The inside of her nose had gone numb and it made the second one a bit easier to take. It was strong, and clean, not speedy, not the kind of coke that makes you anxious, but the sort that is actually enjoyable. Her entire body was feeling the euphoria of the drug, and would have been pleasant under almost any other circumstances, but then it seemed to move into another gear. Her heart began racing. She felt nauseous and prayed that she wouldn't get sick. Pasha dragged her by the arm into a sitting position again. He handed her a glass of champagne, and then the two pills from the table.

"What is it?" Lily asked, holding the tablets in her palm and looking at them.

"Do it," he said. The tablets were stamped with *OC 80*.

"They will relax you," he said, and then he smiled. The nausea had let up a bit, and there was no other option, so she tossed the pills into her mouth. She took a sip of the champagne and swallowed the pills. There was a pack of cigarettes on the table and she lit one. Pasha allowed her to sit back on the couch.

She smoked the cigarette, and then another. She drank the champagne. Her hands were shaking. Pasha watched her closely and refilled her glass. After about ten minutes she began to feel very warm, a pleasant sort of gentle throbbing of her entire being. It was like opening a door and the energy of her will drained out of her body. Her mind faintly ordered her body to move but nothing happened. She felt like she was becoming gelatin, a soft mass. She attempted to string a few thoughts together, but the drugs had shorted out the connection between her mind and her body. The only thing she could seemingly still do was smoke. She watched her hand approach her face, as though it wasn't hers. She had a hard time finding her lips with the cigarette. Pasha reached over and began to take off her clothes. She resigned to just let them do what they wanted. She had agreed to this, after all, and it was too late to turn back now. She thought about James and a hint of sadness pierced the thick wall of the drugs. She closed her eyes, and prayed that it would be over soon. Pasha was busy trying to remove her dress. She made an effort to sit up but she couldn't. The room was just a blur, fading to black. Someone took her arm and tried to pull her to her feet. A dark shape moved before her, then another, and another, and then she felt something wet on her face, and she made a feeble attempt to lift her arm to wipe it off.

Nethery stood outside the club, trying to figure out the quickest way to get to the waterfront. The bartender had told him she'd been there, had drinks with the Russians, and then left with them. He said they'd probably gone to their yacht. Can't be missed, he said, the biggest boat in the harbor, tied up out near the Hotel le Golfe. He made his way to the waterfront and followed Quai des Baux until it became Quai Jean-Jacques Barthélémy as it turned out away from the town and toward the mouth of the harbor. Within a minute he spotted the sign for Hotel le Golfe on top of a building about a hundred yards ahead and as his eyes moved to the harbor he saw the yacht. It was about four times larger than the any of the others, and looked like it may have had a helipad on the stern. Now that he had a destination fixed in his mind he put his head down and walked quickly in that direction. Nethery came to the cement dock where the yacht was moored and he paused. The yacht was about twenty yards away, shrouded in darkness but for a few lights on below deck. He'd been running on pure adrenaline and now, as he imagined what was happening inside the yacht, a wave of dark and pure anger was added to the mix.

Nethery walked out toward the yacht. His hand curled around the butt of the pistol. He remarked to himself how natural it felt, as if it had been designed specifically for him. When he was about ten yards from the gangway his eyes began to adjust to the darkness and he spotted a dark mass on the dock between him and the yacht. As he got closer he recognized it was Lily, lying in a heap. He jammed the gun into his pants and ran over to her. She was barely conscious, her eyes rolling around in her head. He managed to get her to her feet. She was able to bear some weight but unable to walk. Some part of her was trying, attempting to put one foot in front of the other. She was moaning and trying to form words. He helped her out to the road and sat her down on a bus bench under a streetlight.

"Lily? Lily?" he said, holding her head up and looking into her face. Her makeup was badly smeared, her hair was a mess, and her clothes were wet in places. Her dress was half undone. He smelled something pungent and sour, and then recognized it as piss. Her eyes met his for just a second and then they wandered off, unfocused. Nethery let go of her head and it fell back down to her chest. He laid her sideways on the bench and then ran across the street to the Hotel le Golfe. Inside he found the concierge and had him call a taxi.

Nethery had to carry her down the path to the guesthouse. She had passed out again. Inside he set her gently down on the bed and turned on the lamp on the nightstand. He turned her face so he could see her. His hand touched something cold and slimy in her hair, and he immediately recognized it as semen. She also had the beginnings of a black eye and dried semen on her face. He felt a surge of emotion, more than anger, more than rage—this was a pure and electric fury that burned so bright it threatened to blind him. He looked down at Lily and took deep breaths. It took every ounce of self-control he had to keep from going straight back to town at that moment. He gently let go of her head, went into the bathroom, and filled a washbasin with warm water. He set it down next to the bed and undressed her, carefully removing her cheongsam. It had been hastily put back on her and some of the buttons were gone. Under the dress there were scratches on her skin and semen residue on her breasts and stomach as well.

He became obsessed with getting her clean. He lost track of how many times he rinsed out the rags and refilled the washbasin. When the water was dirty, he dumped it down the toilet instead of in the sink. Every few minutes he checked to make sure she was breathing. She looked oddly at peace. It took over an hour. Eventually he realized it was futile. He would never get her clean, not in the way he wanted. He had at least removed the visible traces of what had happened, minus the black eye, and that was the best he could do. He tucked her under the covers and let her sleep.

He went into the bathroom and scrubbed his hands. Now that he was done caring for her, the fury began to return. It was similar to what he had felt at Claude's and yet different, less focused and deliberate. It was powerful, like a gravitational pull drawing him into Cassis, to the yacht, to those men. He envisioned putting bullets in their skulls and throwing their bodies overboard. He realized he'd been scrubbing his hands for five minutes and they were almost raw. He sighed and turned off the water.

Lily woke the next morning to a throbbing head and a dull pain behind her eyes. She tried to sit up, but collapsed back onto the pillow. As consciousness returned she became aware that her jaw hurt and she had a sore throat. More aches and pains all over her body made themselves known. There were too many to catalog. She tried to remember what had happened. Images of the previous night began to come to her, but they were just fleeting glimpses, incomplete. She was lying on something soft and that made her understand she had no idea where she was. She managed to sit up, propped against the pillow, and she rubbed her eyes and winced. Her face hurt. She tentatively moved her jaw around. Nethery was sitting slouched down in a chair next to the bed, asleep, his head slumped forward onto his chest.

"James?" she asked, not believing her eyes. She looked around quickly, and realized where she was.

"James!" she exclaimed, and lunged in his direction, but her arms and legs didn't work properly and she just fell off the side of the bed. Nethery woke up, slid out of the chair to the floor, and took her in his arms. He lifted her back onto the bed and then sat down on the edge.

"I thought something happen to you," she said.

"No . . . I . . ."

"How I get here?" she asked, on the verge of tears.

"I brought you."

"But . . ."

"Fanny told me. She said you went to the club. I went there, the bartender told me you left with those Russians, and said you probably went to their yacht. He told me where it was moored." Lily took a minute to digest the information, and then a look of concern spread across her face.

"Did you . . . kill them?" Lily asked.

"Nope," Nethery said calmly. "When I got to the yacht, you were passed out on the dock. I just called a taxi and brought you back here."

"Where is my money?" Lily asked.

"I dunno."

"Where is my bag?"

"You didn't have one."

"Fuck! Fuck!" and then she ran off a string of Ukrainian curse words.

"Hey hey hey," Nethery said, stopping her, leaning over and holding her in his arms to try and calm her down, "it's okay."

"I only go for the money," Lily said quietly, her voice cracking.

"I know, I know," Nethery said, trying to soothe her.

"I think you not came back," Lily continued, "I think something bad happen to you."

"No, it just took me a lot longer to get back here," Nethery said.

"I am . . . sorry," Lily said, staring at the floor.

"Hey," Nethery said, placing his finger under her chin to lift her face, "you don't have to be sorry. I know you didn't want to go. You won't have to ever again. I'm doing the deal with the guy in Marseille soon, and we'll have some money after that."

Nethery looked at her face, tears spilling out of her bloodshot eyes, makeup smeared all over her face, snot dripping out of her nose, her hair a tangled mess, and he couldn't believe how beautiful she was, how much more beautiful she was now than when he'd first seen her.

"You were pretty messed up," Nethery said, smiling at her.

"They make me!" Lily said, between sobs. "The drugs . . . they make me."

"It's okay," he said, "you're here now."

From the state of her aches and pains Lily had deduced what had happened. It wasn't too difficult to figure out, in fact, she had expected some version of it when she left the guesthouse for Cassis. She had expected to be used and tossed aside. But she hadn't expected to be beaten up, perhaps naively, and the details were all a fog. She was able to recall tiny fragments, moments, odd details of the yacht, the drugs, and Pasha's smirking face—which loomed large as if projected onto the walls of her mind.

"I want you to stay in bed," Nethery said, "I'm gonna make us some coffee, okay?" She nodded, clutching the sheet to her chest, having ceased sobbing.

Nethery returned carrying a tray with coffee and croissants. Holding the sheet up to her neck, Lily drew her knees up to her chest to make room. Nethery set the tray down on the bed, sat on the edge. They drank coffee and ate in silence. Occasionally, Nethery smiled at her and she valiantly attempted to return the gesture but every single movement brought pain. She chewed the croissant slowly and winced when she swallowed. When they were finished eating she appeared exhausted, and Nethery suggested she sleep a bit more and he retired to the living room. He soon grew restless, and the fury at what had been done to her began to return. It danced around in his mind as if it were taunting him, inspiring visions of bloody vengeance. He tried to distract himself by reading a French newspaper but he couldn't concentrate. It only further frustrated him, attempting to decipher the articles from the few words and phrases he knew. He set the paper aside and turned on the television. The BBC was showing a retrospective of Claude's career, how he had risen from nothing to become a giant in the fashion world, how he'd revolutionized style, given countless models their starts in the business, and there was a parade of models, designers, and celebrities testifying to what a great man he was. The show kept returning to one picture, of him with a bunch of models hanging off him, apparently the encore of a fashion show.

Eventually he switched off the television, walked outside, and lit up a cigarette. His hand was shaking. He should have turned off the television. Nethery had killed Claude, had put a bullet in his head, but it hadn't been enough. A part of him lived on, in the minds and memories of millions of people. His legacy was like a zombie, a lie that refused to die, a lie so great it begged to be burnt to the ground, erased from the annals of history. It was something so wrong Nethery was unable to resist the call to make it right, like the song of a siren. He stood by the bench and looked out at the Mediterranean. It was covered in a thin layer of haze. The blue of the sea appeared almost pastel colored. He was thinking. He took one more drag of the cigarette, flipped it out over the cliff, and rushed back inside. He turned the television back on to the Claude retrospective, found a pen and a piece of paper, watched until the end credits ran, and wrote down a few names.

Lily woke up sometime that afternoon. She piled up the pillows behind her, sat up against the headboard. She felt better, but was cold, and pulled the sheet up to her neck. Nethery brought her soup and she ate slowly, as if she wasn't really enjoying it, but realized the necessity. She then lit a cigarette, and took long drags. Nethery suggested she take a shower. He helped her into the bathroom, turned on the water, made sure it was warm, and then left her to it. The water seemed to rejuvenate her and she became aware of every ache and pain in her body. They must have really had their fun, she thought, the fucking cowards. They couldn't even face her, couldn't do it while she was awake. She still couldn't remember details but acknowledged that it was probably a good thing. A part of her also didn't care. In a way, she was used to this sort of thing. It didn't affect her like it had in the beginning. What angered her most was that they hadn't paid. The fucking bastards could afford it. She washed her hair carefully and then went to work on her body. Her privates were extremely tender and she scrubbed them gently over and over and then directed the showerhead at her privates using the hottest water she could bear. She dried off and wrapped herself in a towel. She brushed her teeth and rinsed her mouth out thoroughly with mouthwash. When she was finished, she swept her hand across the fogged-up mirror and saw her eye for the first time. It wasn't the worst black eye she'd ever seen, but it was obvious she'd been struck. She came out of the shower wrapped in a towel. Nethery was sitting in the chair.

"Feel better?" he asked. Lily stopped, looked at him for a second, and then made her way to the bed.

"What's wrong?" Nethery asked, and Lily pointed to her eye.

"Oh. Yeah. I saw that," he said.

She got into bed, pulled the covers over her, and turned onto her side away from him. Obviously she wanted to be left alone. Nethery went out to the living room, threw himself down on the couch and turned on the television. Some kind of dating show was on, with young men in swim shorts and girls in bikinis. Occasionally they would pair off and go into a box that looked like a telephone booth and make out. Nethery wanted to turn it off, but the utter banality of it was fascinating. It seemed to empty his mind and place him into a kind of trance and when he snapped out of it thirty minutes had passed. He stood, picked up the television and carried it outside to the edge of the cliff. At the last moment, he simply sat down on the bench and set the television down beside him.

Nethery gently shook Lily until she opened her eyes. He knew if she woke up and he was gone she would panic. She saw that he was fully dressed and asked where he was going. When he told her, Lily's eyes widened in fear, until he reassured her that he would return. He stayed for a bit, giving her a stripped-down version of what he had planned. When he felt it safe to leave he took a taxi to the station and caught the train into Marseille. Following a hand-drawn map, he made his way to the computer store he'd looked up on Fanny's computer, found a salesman that could speak English, and bought a laptop computer and a few accessories. He wasn't as elaborate making his way back to the guesthouse and the entire trip took just under three hours. Lily was on the couch watching television. She was visibly distressed.

"What's wrong?" Nethery asked, sitting down next to her on the couch.

"They have something on TV. Something about Claude . . ."

"Oh yeah. I've seen that. It's been on almost every day."

"It is . . . wrong."

"I know it is. Do you want to do something about it?"

Lily looked at him, not understanding.

"We can give them the tape."

"What? No! I do not want them to see!"

"They won't see you. That's why I bought this," he said, removing the computer from the bag. "We can erase your face from the video."

"E . . . erase?" she asked.

"Yes. Remove," Nethery said, swiping his hand across his face to illustrate.

"Oh James . . . I do not know . . ."

"Well, let me see what I can do. Then I'll show you what it looks like. If you still don't want to, then we'll just throw the tape, and the computer, and the camera, everything, out into the sea."

"Ohhh . . . very well," she said.

"How are you feeling today?" Nethery asked.

"Better, a little. I am still . . ." she said, searching for a word, and unable to find it she brought her hands up to the sides of her head and shook it, to indicate she was still disoriented.

"You take it easy," he said. "Let me work on this and you take a nap."

He hooked up the video camera to the computer and started the tape so it would download to the computer as it played. He would have to watch the entire thing to see what needed to be edited out. As it played he became more and more distressed and enraged, but only about the rape. When it came to the murders he merely felt a strange kind of detachment, watching as he casually walked right up to the first man and shot him in the head, and then the other man. It seemed as if it were someone else, he moved so calmly and surely, so precise and mechanical. It all seemed very cold-blooded. Claude's face appeared clearly for a second, as he pulled his mask off backing away from the table. Then he stumbled backwards and disappeared off-screen. Nethery moved off-screen as well, as he moved to block his exit. In the background, the broken window where Lily had thrown the vase could be seen. Then you could hear Claude pleading, then the pause, then pleading again. Nethery could understand some of what he was saying now.

"I am Claude Dutronc, please, please, I am Claude Dutronc," he kept repeating, as if that meant something. And then there was the final gunshot and only the music playing in the background. Nethery then came briefly onscreen as he tended to Lily. Her face was down when he brought her to her feet. Nethery's face appeared for a split-second, in profile near the edge of the frame but not long enough to be recognizable. The only part of the video that required editing was when Claude yanked Lily's head up by her hair and stuck the camera in her face to show how terrified she was.

He disconnected the camera and went to work on the digital version. He used the editing program to place a black spot over Lily's face that moved wherever her face moved. When that was done Nethery copied the edited video onto the computer's hard drive and simultaneously burned it to a DVD. When he was finally finished he stood up, sighed, stretched his arms and rolled his head around, trying to work out the tightness in his neck.

He found his jacket, removed the gun, stuck it into his pants and went outside. The sun was beginning to set, but in the half-darkness he managed to climb down the cliff to the first beach. He took the gun out and walked close to the water where the sand was wet and dense. He fired the gun into the sand, knelt down, and dug down until he recovered the bullet. He placed it and the shell casing in his pocket. Later that evening, Lily came out of the bedroom. Her condition seemed to be improving. They had dinner at the little table and she talked a bit and even smiled. Nethery thought she could handle it and after dinner he showed her the video. She watched, and while she sat there expressionless he could sense that she had reservations, and was hesitant about going ahead with this.

"They cannot . . . remove that . . . and see my face?" she asked, when the edited video had finished playing.

"No," Nethery replied, "your face is visible only on the original tape."

Lily was quiet for a minute, and slowly the look on her face began to change from one of concern and worry to something harder, more solid, revenge and determination.

"Very well," she said, standing up from the table, "we do it."

PART III
THE STORM

Clive Wallace was hungover. His head throbbed and he squinted down at the glass of water before him, watching two Alka-Seltzer tablets dissolve. He drank the medicine in one gulp. He went to grab his coffee to wash the taste out of his mouth and knocked the cup over. Coffee spilled all over the papers on the desk, notes on a piece he was working on. He grabbed a handful of napkins to try and mop it up, but there was too much and it had run off the edge of the desk and gotten on his pants. He gave up and in a moment of fury hurled the soaked napkin into the trash bin, flinging coffee everywhere. He slumped down in his office chair and closed his eyes. His head was still pounding and the office seemed to be painfully noisy. He rubbed his temples. He looked up and spotted his boss Bertrand Dupuis, making a beeline across the room toward him. Here we go again, Wallace thought, rolling his eyes, another lecture from the moral compass of Western journalism. Wallace prepared himself for the assault. Bertrand arrived at his desk, and stood there for a moment doing nothing but glaring down at him, arms folded across his chest, an unpleasant look on his face. Of course it was about the Claude Dutronc piece. What else? Wallace, as usual, hadn't been able to resist asking some of Dutronc's associates questions that weren't on the script, namely about the rape allegations from a few years back. He remembered it well. A model had come forward and said Dutronc had kept her passport hostage, made her do things. It had seemed so credible at first. She'd said she had proof. And then the model suddenly changed her story, and it faded from the spotlight. Wallace had been working on something else at the time, but he'd smelled something fishy, a payoff, a cover-up. Bertrand was still talking and Wallace sat there, not really listening, but looking off into space. He noticed a spot of wine on Dupuis's otherwise clean white shirt. He smiled.

"Clive? Clive! Are you listening?" It snapped him out of his trance, and he stopped smiling.

"Um, right."

"You have to stop going off-script."

"I know, Bertrand . . . but . . . what difference does it make? You guys edited it out of the program anyway."

"This piece was not meant to be an investigation, goddamnit! The man is dead, and you're asking these sordid questions. You just can't do that."

Bertrand continued for another minute, very loudly so the entire office could hear. He covered all the usual issues, his going off-script, his shabby appearance, his boozing, his blog, missing days, his coming in late. Finally, it ended and Wallace began going through the papers on his desk, background information on his new assignment, a piece about the wine crisis in France. Competition from other countries was causing a huge glut in the French wine industry. The Bordeaux region especially was having problems. He'd been told to portray the situation as a tragedy without cause, and not mention regulations and rule changes enacted by the government that were the obvious cause. Wallace was flipping through a stack of papers when he realized he wasn't even looking at them. He sighed, set them down on the desk, and headed for the coffee machine. When he returned his phone was ringing. He set his coffee down and answered it.

"Clive Wallace, BBC Paris Bureau."

"Mr. Wallace?"

"Yes."

"You are going to be receiving a package."

"Eh?"

"Tomorrow, or the next day at the latest, a package will arrive at your office there."

"Look mate, I don't know what the hell you're on about . . ."

"I killed Claude Dutronc," Nethery said, and there was a pause.

"Piss off," Wallace replied. He was about to hang up, but there was something in the caller's voice that stopped him.

"The package contains a video of the murder," the voice said.

"Sure it does. Of course it does. And I'm Father Christmas."

"Mr. Wallace," Nethery said, speaking very calmly, "bear with me. Take five minutes. Call your police contacts. I'm sure you have some. Ask them about the tripod they found in Dutronc's apartment. Or the masks they discovered at the scene. Two of the victims were wearing masks. There hasn't been mention of any of that in the media."

"Look here," Wallace said, "what . . ."

"I have the video camera that was on that tripod. And the video. It shows everything that happened that day. In the package you will also find a bullet, and a shell casing. Have them tested. They will match the bullets and casings found at the scene."

There was a moment of silence.

"What's on this video, then?" Wallace asked.

"You will have to see for yourself."

"Okay, look here, mate. If this is true, you know I will have to turn this over to the French police."

"Yes. I know."

"Why? Why send this to me? Assuming, of course . . ."

"The truth, Mr. Wallace."

"The truth?"

"The media are portraying Dutronc like he was some kind of great man," Nethery said. "It's bullshit."

"Look, I don't know what you're talking about. The Dutronc thing is over. He may have been a creep . . ."

"A creep? Have a look at the video, Mr. Wallace. You will see Dutronc was much more than just a creep. I am placing my faith in you, Wallace, as a journalist. There is a story here. A big one. Run with it. If you don't, I will simply approach someone else. Someone with some balls."

"Balls? Listen, mate . . ."

Wallace could hear the caller chuckling, slightly. But it didn't alter the serious tone of the conversation, the thing that had prevented Wallace from hanging up in the first place.

"Well, this is your chance to prove it," Nethery said. "You won't hear from me again." There was a click.

Nethery flipped the cell phone shut. He stared out at the sea. Every last bit of haze had vanished and the ocean shimmered like a thousand flashbulbs. He knew this was a risk. But it was such an affront to the truth he simply could not let it stand. But rather than the fear he expected it brought about enlightenment; for the first time in his life, he understood the meaning of sacrifice. What kind of world is this, he asked himself, where a man could go thirty-five years without knowing what that means? It boggled the mind. And it wasn't the only thing. A sense of pride, a sense of honor, of duty, had also been utterly lacking in him and probably, he realized, his entire generation. He, and everyone like him, thought there was some profound value in merely being, rather than doing. They had been taught that everything in the world could be theirs, should be theirs, and they would have to give up very little. He stood at the edge of the cliff and became acutely aware of the taste of the salt air in his mouth. He continued waiting for the fear to come, to grip him as it had so often in the past, and to begin thinking of ways to undo what he'd done, but all he felt was an even stronger commitment to see this out to the end. It was invigorating. He sat down on the bench and looked down the shoreline toward Cassis. Soon the sun would go down, and there would be nothing but the glow of the town, rising over the headlands.

Wallace sat at the bar, nursing a drink. He'd received prank calls before, misinformation, leads that went nowhere, but something told him this was not one of them. There was something in the caller's voice. But still, a video of the Dutronc murder? It was highly improbable. Nevertheless, he'd left a message for one of his police contacts involved with the case. He and Wallace had traded information in the past, and the two had established a certain degree of trust. They'd even gone out occasionally to booze it up. He had just finished the drink and ordered another when his cell phone rang. He saw Lieutenant Pascal's name on the screen, got up, and walked back near the toilets where it wasn't so noisy. He answered and asked how Pascal was doing, and if he would like to come out for a drink. Pascal said he was too busy working on the Dutronc murder. Wallace then casually mentioned he'd heard something about that, and he mentioned the masks, the tripod, and the missing camera.

There was a long pause, and then Pascal demanded to know what Wallace knew. Wallace felt a surge of adrenaline, and told Pascal he didn't know anything, yet, but that he might be on to something. Pascal agreed to let it go, for the moment, as long as Wallace promised to keep him up to speed on whatever he dug up. This was a serious case, Pascal said, and if Wallace withheld information he would be in serious trouble. Wallace asked again about the masks and the tripod but Pascal reiterated that he couldn't say anything at the moment. Pascal said he needed to get back to work and hung up.

Wallace walked back to the bar, his mind sorting through what this meant and how he should handle it. Pascal's reaction told him everything he needed to know; there was something to this masks and tripod business. Screw the Bordeaux assignment, he said to himself. There was no way he was letting this story fall to anyone else. He ordered vodka on ice.

ethery was on the TGV to Paris. Lily had woken before him, made coffee and brought him a breakfast tray, even smiled a bit. But her mood darkened when Nethery told her he was traveling to Paris. He sat next to her and calmly explained that he had no choice, that if he sent the package from Marseille or Cassis, the cops would be able to trace it and have a general idea of their location. And they still needed more time to get the passports. Eventually he was able to reassure her. The conductor's voice over the PA woke him as the TGV pulled into the Gare de Lyon. He'd napped most of the way, the package in the SAS bag on his lap. It was just after three in the afternoon. He disembarked and found his way to a post office. There was a long line and it took half an hour, plus some verbal wrangling with the clerk. The return address he'd placed on the package was that of the Picasso Museum. He stopped for a coffee on the way back to the station, and by five, he was on his way back.

Lily had accepted Fanny's offer to join her and Jeanette shopping in Cassis. She had done her best to enjoy the outing, but as the day wore on she began to grow more and more concerned. She was standing before a fountain in Place Baragnon, the village square. But she was looking at nothing.

"Lily?" It was Jeanette.

"Oh . . . um . . ." Lily replied, finding her way back to the present.

"What is the matter, *cheri*?"

"Oh, nothing."

"Come, come," Jeanette said, and she led Lily over to the outdoor market.

"Look at the fish," Jeanette declared. Lily dragged her mind the rest of the way out of her worries and looked at the incredible array of seafood on display. Mussels, clams, mackerel, cod, squid, shrimp, and countless others that Lily did not recognize. Some of it didn't look so appealing, eels and strange ugly fish. Fanny was a couple of tables down, talking and gesticulating wildly with one of the seafood dealers.

"You must make something, for James," Jeanette said, looking up at her.

"Oh, no," Lily answered, "I do not know . . ."

"I will help you," Jeanette answered. The idea must have appealed to her, as she suddenly got very excited, turned her attention to the man behind the table, and began barking out orders. She turned back to face Lily.

"I know what we will do. I have best recipe. He will love you forever," she said smiling. "You will see." When Jeanette had finished buying a few varieties of seafood, she said they needed to get home as soon as possible as what she was going to make required a good deal of time. But then she took a detour to a linen store, as she had determined that a new tablecloth and napkins were also needed. Lily tried to give her some money but she wasn't having it. There was nothing for Lily to do but just follow her around. She was impressed with how much energy and drive Jeanette had. It reminded her of her mother and other old women she remembered from her childhood. They never seemed to get beaten down by life, seemed to manage the hardships and heartbreaks and tragedies and not become cynical. But then again, they most likely had never experienced what she had.

When they arrived back to the guesthouse Jeanette went to work on her special cioppino. It required as much time as possible to simmer, she said. Lily helped her, preparing the tomatoes, chopping vegetables and herbs, cutting fish, peeling shrimp. Jeanette put the soup on to simmer and told Lily that when Nethery got home she should add the seafood, turn up the heat, and it would be ready in twenty minutes. She then showed her how to make her special garlic bread. After Jeanette had gone Lily spread the new tablecloth over the kitchen table, fixed the place settings, and installed brand-new slim white candles in the holders.

Nethery walked in shortly after eight. He was greeted with a wonderful smell. He took off his jacket and threw it over the back of the couch. Lily came out of the bedroom. She was wearing a tight pencil dress and her Gucci high-heeled sandals. She had tidied up her bob so it almost looked like a molded helmet, her dark hair curving forward along her jawline, framing her face. She had put on dark eye shadow and mascara that gave her an alluring and sexy look. Nethery stood there and stared for a minute. A wry smile eventually played across her mouth, when she recognized that he was pleased.

"Are you hungry?" she asked.

"Oh, hell yeah," he said and smiled. She hurried over to the stove, turned up the heat, and began adding the seafood to the cioppino. She turned on the oven to get it ready for the garlic bread. Nethery sat down on the couch and when she had set everything to cook she joined him. He lit a cigarette and noticed that Lily seemed happy and untroubled, and there was no trace of the recent ugliness on her face or in her mood.

"God," he said, "you are really something," he said. She leaned over against him and put her head on his shoulder. She was relaxed for a few moments, and then Nethery felt tension creep into her body.

"When you leave," she said quietly, "every time. I am worry."

He put his arm around her.

"Don't worry. If something happens to me, Fanny and Jeanette will help you. There'll soon be enough money for you to stay here for quite a while if you need to."

A buzzer went off in the kitchen.

"Sit down," she said, looking back and nodding at the kitchen table, in a tone that suggested he should have known to do that already.

Nethery had been preoccupied all day and the pangs of hunger hadn't gotten their foot in the door, but now they kicked it down. He devoured two bowls of the cioppino, mopping up every drop with the garlic bread. After, he plopped down on the couch and put his feet up on the coffee table. Lily took the dishes to the sink, then came and sat next to him. He lit a cigarette and passed it to her, and then lit one for himself. He turned on the television, absentmindedly flipped through the channels, and stopped at the BBC. They were reporting on something that had happened the night before when a pair of hedge fund managers had been found impaled on the horns of the Wall Street Bull, in Bowling Green Park. The bull had been painted with the words *This is what we do,* in blood. They were blaming it on the People's Mafia. There was more confusion as to how the perpetrators had gotten past the private security forces, and there was talk about the government sending in the National Guard. Nethery grinned. He changed the channel again but there were only French shows, and eventually he returned to the BBC. They were interviewing a renowned social scientist in Chicago.

". . . we could very well be witnessing a new kind of revolution, something totally organic. Picture Al-Qaeda without a Bin Laden, a revolution without any sort of figurehead, without a manifesto, an ideology or religious dogma, without a chain of command or any stated goals. No organization, no nothing, just the law of physics applied to a population of people, just the action of the wealthy and politically connected pushing the American people down toward or into poverty, and the reaction of them pushing back. How would you stop it? That's a huge problem for the government and the power structure. Even if they enacted martial law, it probably wouldn't do much good."

"You're making these terrorists sound like rational people."

"Well . . . they are, in my opinion."

"Oh come on . . ."

"Look. These people aren't starving for food, which is how most revolutions begin, but they're starving for something else, for meaning in their lives. Human beings can only placate their inherent and primal drive for meaning with shallow and banal pursuits for so long before critical mass is reached. That point has come and it has sent them over the edge. It's made them mentally, emotionally, and physically unstable. The chemical fixes and entertainment distractions have reached the limit of what they can do. They just don't work anymore, and besides, at best they just cover up the fundamental problem, that human beings are simply not designed to live like this. The chemical solution was bound to fail at some point."

Nethery chuckled and changed the channel to a nature show.

"What funny?" Lily asked.

"Oh," Nethery said, "they're havin' a real party back home," he said and chuckled again. On the television a pair of cheetahs flew across a grassy plain, chasing down an impala.

"Party?" she asked, confused. One of the cheetahs went for the impala's hind legs. It tripped and fell. The other cheetah lunged at its throat.

"Yeah. They should have never fucked with the Indians."

"What? I do not understand."

"It's not important," Nethery said. He kicked off his shoes and lay down lengthwise on the couch. Nethery wrapped his arms around her and they dozed off.

Wallace weaved his way down the Rue Jules Simon. He'd had to put his sunglasses on even though it was overcast. Those fucking clouds, he thought. The whiteness seemed to pierce right into his brain. All of a sudden he felt dizzy and nauseous and had to stop and lean against a wall. He had stayed at the bar for hours the night before thinking about how to proceed. He was still skeptical, but just in case the package turned out to be something, he wanted to be at the office when it arrived. He had seen key pieces of evidence disappear before, get lost, vanish, then turn up missing elements or having been altered in some way. That was their first method of getting you to write the story they wanted, controlling the materials and the facts. When he'd been in Iraq it meant not letting you go certain places, see certain things. Denying you access to people and places. Here if it was a controversial topic they gave you an implied script, a position to take before you'd even asked any questions, and casually hinted that you could be in a tight spot if you deviated from it.

He entered the building and went straight for the mailroom. The clerk, André, was sitting at his desk eating a croissant.

"*Bonjour,*" Wallace said. André looked up for a second, grunted, and then turned his attention back to chewing and ogling a men's magazine laid open on his desk.

"André?" Wallace asked, trying to get attention.

"Mmm-hmmm," Andre said, nodding, without looking up, his mouth full of food.

"André!" Wallace shouted.

André slowly stopped chewing and looked up, like he was being put out. Wallace was holding up a twenty-euro note, slowly waving it back and forth. "When the packages arrive today I want you to call me," he said. "I will be upstairs at my desk." André looked confused, but he reached out for the note. Wallace pulled it back.

"Before you take another bite of food, before you take a piss, before you draw another breath. Call me. Got it?" André had gotten his fingers clamped onto the free end of the bill, but Wallace held on to the other. André looked at him and nodded and Wallace finally released the bill.

Wallace was asleep, his head on his desk when the phone rang.

"Yes," he said, yawning and wiping his eyes, ". . . uh . . . Clive Wallace. BBC Paris."

"It is André. There is a package . . ." and Wallace hung up the phone while he was still talking. He stood up too quickly, became dizzy, and almost fell over. He pulled himself together and ran down to the mailroom, got the package, and took it to the media center where video and audio used to be edited before the internet made it possible for all those things to be done in London. It was still used for a few things, but at the moment it was empty and the technician was not around. Wallace closed the door behind him, sat down at the station. It was a fairly small box, and he cut open the tape sealing the top using one of his keys and folded back the flaps.

· · ·

Lily woke up early on the couch. The front door was open and she could see Nethery outside talking to Fanny. She was still tired and stumbled into the bedroom and went back to sleep. When she woke up again it was two in the afternoon. Sunlight peeked in from around the blinds on the window, forming thin sheets of light that sliced across the room. She piled the pillows up behind her and lit up a cigarette from a pack on the night table. The drugs had finally left her body and she was almost back to normal. She suddenly felt restless and got up, went outside and found Nethery, sitting on the bench at the edge of the cliff. He was looking at a French newspaper. She stood before him and stretched her arms, reaching for the sky. The sun was directly overhead, and it would have been uncomfortably hot but for the slight breeze blowing in from the sea. Lily had finished her cigarette and flipped it out over the edge of the cliff.

"What you do?" she asked. Nethery smiled a bit at her broken English.

"I'm trying to read this newspaper," he replied.

"It is bad news?" she asked.

"Nope."

"What you do today?"

"Nothing."

Lily turned and looked out at the Mediterranean, as if she had heard something, and then she sat down next to him on the bench. He folded up the newspaper, set it down beside him, and looked at her. She had closed her eyes. The sun was behind her and it made her look as if there were a halo around her face, the edges of her profile glowing, stray brown hairs appearing translucent and red. He felt the powerful desire for her again and this time was unable to stop. He leaned over, wrapped his arms around her and kissed her. She drew back.

"What you doing?"

"Uh . . . kissing you?" He said, and Lily wrenched herself free. She stood up and glared down at him for a moment, and then walked back into the guesthouse.

Lily sat on the edge of the bed and began to put on her sneakers. She finished tying the laces, sat up straight, and then sighed and collapsed onto her back and stared at the ceiling. Why had she reacted that way? There had been dozens of moments when he could have made a move. She had actually been waiting for it, possibly even hoping for it, so why had she freaked out? She told herself it was because he'd surprised her. She wasn't certain it was true, but she didn't want to consider it might be something else—an inability to allow someone to truly care for her. She took a deep breath and exhaled, puffing out her cheeks, and then she stood up. She turned her frustration into anger, and then left the guesthouse and walked right past him without saying a word.

She began to make her way down the cliff, and when she got to the larger of the two beaches she looked back. He was following her and catching up. She kicked off her sneakers, ran into the sea, dove through a wave and began to swim straight out. After a few minutes she stopped and turned back to the beach, treading water. She was about fifty yards out. Nethery was heading straight for her, about thirty yards away. She repeated what she'd done before, and swam parallel to the shore for a bit and then without looking turned back and swam straight toward the beach.

Lily collided with something and pulled back. She knew that she hadn't reached the beach yet and treading water, she shook the hair out of her face. It was Nethery, and somehow he had timed it perfectly and cut her off and gotten between her and the shore. They were about ten yards from the beach, in about seven feet of water.

"Damnit!" she exclaimed.

"I didn't mean to scare you."

"Well you do," she spat, and tried to swim around him to the beach. He tackled her around the waist.

"Let me go!" She tried to keep swimming, but Nethery had a good hold on her and all she succeeded in doing was towing him a few feet until he could touch the sand on the bottom with his feet. He braced himself so she couldn't go farther. She stopped trying to escape and faced him.

"What you doing?"

"I want you."

"Do not . . . oh! Do not tell me these things," she said. She struggled to get free, but he had both his arms around her now and their bodies were pressed together. His cock had become hard and it was rubbing against her. She looked into his eyes and her resistance began to fade, gradually drowned out by desire. They had drifted out again to where Nethery could barely touch the bottom.

"Do not *say*," she said quietly, "*do*."

Lily began to pull down her shorts with her one free hand. Nethery did the same. She wrapped her legs around his waist and rubbed herself against him. She pulled up, and floated down onto him. She threw her arms around his neck. Nethery held her close, and they floated there, buoyed by the salt water, not moving, not feeling gravity, temperature, wind, nothing but the place where they were connected. Occasionally they would sink, slowly, until Nethery's foot touched the sand of the bottom and then he would propel them gently upwards again. They kissed that way for about a minute. Eventually Lily couldn't stand it anymore, and she began writhing against him.

When it was over Nethery carried her toward the beach until she could touch the sandy bottom. She unwrapped herself from his body and they walked out of the water. Lily collapsed on the sand next to her sneakers. Nethery fell to his knees in front of her. She reached for one of her sneakers but Nethery grabbed it before she could put it on.

"What you do?" she asked, puzzled.

"Shhhh . . ." he said, tossing her sneaker aside. He reached down and took hold of her foot. He raised it up and began to brush the sand from it with his hand. She leaned back onto her elbows and watched him. He was very focused on the task, and occasionally he would glance up from what he was doing and smile at her. Each time he did she felt an ache, almost like a twitch in her heart. First he brushed the sand from the top of her foot, then the underside. It took a few minutes, but it seemed like longer, and when he had the majority of the sand brushed off he raised it close to his mouth and blew off the last remaining bits of sand until it was completely clean. Then he kissed the top of her foot, picked up her sneaker and slipped it on. He began doing the same to her other foot, and she felt incredibly hot and as if her face was swelling up. It was such a gentle gesture, so natural and spontaneous. A barrier somewhere within her broke and tears began to leak out of her eyes from an enormous reservoir. He finished cleaning her other foot, and kissed it. He slipped her shoe on, looked at her and smiled. Lily stared at him with a kind of tortured disbelief. He stood, held out his hand, pulled her up and took her in his arms. She began to sob, her body gently convulsing.

She stopped sobbing on the way up the cliff. He led her into the bedroom, and was going to leave but as he went to go she grabbed his arm. She said nothing, and she pulled him down. He undressed, and they made love again. Later, after they'd woken from a nap they enjoyed a dinner of fried fish and bread. There was nothing fancy about the meal, but as they sat there eating on the bench overlooking the cliff Nethery thought he'd never tasted anything so good. After dinner, they watched some television curled up on the couch, and Nethery caught something about a United States senator being killed during the opening of a new exhibit at the Guggenheim. An employee had removed an ancient spear from one of the displays and run it through him, screaming *This is what we do!*

Of course the media were blaming it on the People's Mafia. That was followed by a report from China where workers at an Apple plant had taken over the factory and thrown a few bosses from the roof of the building and then set the factory on fire. That was followed by a report from Japan, where some girls dressed up as characters from the manga *Elfen Lied* flipped out and killed four women getting their hair done at a beauty parlor, hacking them to death with sword-like weapons that were strapped to their arms. Nethery kept staring at the television after the report was over, unable to process what he was hearing and seeing. Eventually he changed the channel to a soccer match, but he quickly grew bored.

He began watching Lily, who'd fallen asleep with her head in his lap. He watched her chest slowly rise and fall with a sense of wonder and amazement. They hadn't said much to each other since returning to the guesthouse, but rather communicated with looks and smiles. He reached down and stroked her hair. She was so lovely like this, so peaceful, and he wished that he could freeze this moment in time. His cell phone rang, and he tried to answer it quickly but she began to stir. Nethery had been so caught up in what was happening between them that he had forgotten about the cocaine, Klaus, the passports, and even the danger they were in. It was all part of a world completely separate from the one they had been living in. Lily sat up and rubbed her eyes. She watched Nethery while he spoke with Klaus and a look of concern spread across her face. Nethery saw this and winked at her. When he was finished she tried to question him about the call but he just smiled, got up from the couch, and pulled her into the bedroom.

Lily had immediately drifted off to sleep, but Nethery lay awake and stared at the ceiling. The phone call had popped the bubble they'd been living in. And what was worse, he had to go back out there. There was no way around it. Klaus wanted two more kilos, and they needed the money. He forced his mind back into the old way of thinking, trying to picture all the angles, all the different possible scenarios, points where something could go wrong. And then he stopped himself. It would either go, or it wouldn't. Things had been set in motion, acquired a life of their own, and if something were to go wrong he felt certain it would be unforeseeable, and inevitable. It was almost like his relationship with Lily, something delicate, organic, and rare, and his meddling would only foul things up. This was something that he could not alter for better or worse. He had to show up of course, go through the motions, but after that it was out of his hands. It was unusual, and his head told him he should be worried, and plotting some desperate action in case it all went sideways, but there was a sense of destiny to what had been set in motion. He curled up next to Lily and immediately fell asleep.

The train pulled into the St. Charles station. Nethery disembarked and began to make his way down toward the Old Port. He had an hour before the meet so he took an indirect route. Out of habit he kept his eye out for pink polo shirts, although he knew it was absurd, and that surely the men had changed shirts. Nevertheless he stayed alert and kept looking at men, imagining they were cops, or members of the group that owned the drugs, and that they knew who he was, but none of them were paying him the slightest bit of attention. He arrived at the bar ten minutes early.

Klaus was standing behind the bar washing glasses. He noticed Nethery and then directed his attention back to what he was doing. An older couple was sitting at a table along the wall. They had a couple of beers on their table and looked like tourists. Nethery gave them the once over as he walked past and made his way to the bar. He sat down and set the SAS bag on the counter.

"Hello," Klaus said.

"How's it goin'?" Nethery asked.

"It is going well, thank you."

"Are we going to do this here?" Nethery asked quietly, tipping his head toward the tourists.

"Sure, why not?" Klaus said, smiling.

"Okay," Nethery said.

Klaus pulled a manila envelope from under the bar and slid it over to Nethery. He reached into the envelope and pulled the money out to the edge of the envelope and casually flipped through the bills very quickly, just to make sure it wasn't a bunch of ones. While Nethery was checking out his end Klaus had pulled the SAS bag down behind the counter and removed the packages, squeezing each one gently. He then placed the bag back on the bar.

"Aren't you gonna test it?" Nethery asked.

"No, I do not think it is necessary. The last was the same as the sample. At some point one must have faith, no?"

"Yeah," Nethery said, grinning.

"Would you like something to drink?"

"Sure, how 'bout some seltzer water this time? On ice. With lemon."

"Coming right up," Klaus said. "Isn't that what they say where you come from?"

"Yes, it is," Nethery said, smiling.

Klaus brought the seltzer and set it down on a coaster. Nethery took a long drink.

"Thank you for doing this," Nethery said, looking up, and patting the manila envelope.

"Yes, well, I'm not doing it for free, am I?"

"No, I know that. But the passports especially, are really gonna help someone."

"Someone?" Klaus asked. "Not you?"

"No . . . I kind of . . . in a way, I think my fate has been decided already."

"Really?"

"Yeah, sort of."

"I knew some in the Legion who were like that." Klaus remembered some of his more fatalistic former colleagues. Most of them walked straight into firefights, and most of them had also survived.

The two tourists came to the bar, paid their bill, and left.

Klaus climbed onto a stool behind the bar and began to talk. He went on about his time in the Legion, and Nethery could tell he missed it, and listened with interest, occasionally laughing when Klaus told a joke.

"And then after . . . ?" Nethery asked, looking up from his drink, implying that if Klaus wanted to continue he could.

"After the Legion, I worked for the old-time Mafia bosses."

"Is that how you went to jail?" Nethery asked, feeling it was safe enough to ask now.

"Yes, yes. There was an assassination attempt. Someone drove up on a motorcycle and tried to kill . . ." Klaus said, hesitating when he came to the name, "the one I was working for."

"And you took care of it?"

"Yes. I took care of it."

"You shot him?"

"Yes."

"Wow."

"The whole thing was quite unnecessary, you see," Klaus said, looking down and shaking his head.

"What?"

"Every day, same time, same place, the boss, walking his dog. That damned dog. I tried to tell him . . . but it was like a show. To show that he could go where he wanted. That he did not have to hide."

"Oh, right."

"But I was the bodyguard. This is what we do."

"Of course. Still, that's kind of a drag it turned out like that."

"Yes. But I should not complain."

"I dunno, man," Nethery said, shaking his head, "I think I'd be pretty pissed off." Klaus laughed, and then the smile vanished from his face.

"James?"

"Yeah?"

"I have told you many things about myself . . ." he said, leaving the sentence unfinished and after a moment he continued, and Nethery knew where this was going.

". . . and I know . . . almost nothing about you."

Klaus looked at him, waiting. This is what relationships were built on, some degree of trust, Nethery thought. It seemed only fair. If Nethery refused to reveal anything now it would ruin what they had going on.

"You know Claude Dutronc? The fashion big shot?"

"Of course, I read the papers. I watch the TV."

"Well . . . I killed him," Nethery said casually, then took a drink of the seltzer. He set the glass down on the bar and stared at the drink. "And," he continued, "I killed his two asshole friends too."

Nethery looked up, saw the look on Klaus's face and laughed, but just for a moment.

"Look, they deserved it. My friend, the girl? In the photo? You wouldn't believe what they . . . were doing . . . the most terrible things you can imagine . . . to her."

Klaus sat there silent, listening intently.

"It wouldn't have done any good to call the cops," Nethery continued, "you know that."

"Yes," Klaus replied.

"A guy like that . . . would have gotten away with it. So I stopped him."

"All of France is looking for you."

"They're looking for *someone*. Not me."

Klaus had overcome his shock, but wasn't quite sure what to say. Despite the fact that Nethery didn't look like a killer, he knew what he was hearing was true, and because of it, an even deeper level of trust had been established.

"*Merde*," Klaus said. "The television said they were still looking around Paris."

"Hmmm. Good thing I'm in Marseille then, right?"

"You would not like something stronger to drink?" Klaus asked, grabbing a bottle of whiskey.

"No," Nethery said, chuckling, "that's okay."

Klaus poured himself a shot. He held it out to Nethery, and he toasted with his glass of seltzer. Klaus drank the shot and looked at Nethery, not doubting, but he was obviously curious about the details and Nethery recognized this. He shrugged.

"It was just one of those things. It had to be done. You know what I mean."

"Yes," Klaus replied, seriously, "I do know."

"Some people get away with anything," Nethery continued, "like your old boss. Not because they're good, or because they deserve it. They just have money."

Klaus nodded, and there were another few moments of silence.

"What are you going to do?" Klaus asked

"I promised the girl I would help her get home. After that, I dunno."

"Can we make another deal?" Klaus asked.

"When?" Nethery replied.

"I am not sure. In a few days?"

"No problem." Nethery finished his glass of seltzer water.

"I would like to do it sooner, but that kind of money is hard to arrange."

"Sure, I know."

"What if you do not answer the phone?" Klaus asked.

"It could mean I have been caught, I suppose. Or that I'm dead," Nethery said chuckling, "but let's hope those things don't happen."

Klaus laughed.

"Yes. Let us hope," Klaus said, chuckling at Nethery's nonchalance. "Is there anything I can help you with?"

Nethery paused.

"No. I don't think so. But thanks."

Nethery sat on the bench at the edge of the cliff, watching the blanket of morning haze slowly burn away. The sea was gradually becoming visible, and the blue became deeper and more vivid. He took a long drag of a cigarette. A broad smile spread across his face. What had happened to his inherent cynicism, pessimism, negativity? Somehow over the last three days with Lily it had all vanished. He hadn't thought about it until now, swept along on waves of joy, as if the fundamental nature of the universe had shifted and it was finally on their side.

The day before Nethery had chartered a boat to take them on a tour of the *calanques*. They'd been following the coastline, on their way to one of the designated attractions when Nethery spotted a tiny beach, barely visible through a narrow channel. It wasn't on the listed destinations. Nethery glanced at Lily and she was looking at it too. She smiled, and he knew what she was thinking. The skipper objected, said the channel was narrow, but Nethery gave him some extra money. It took some doing, the boat scraping on the limestone walls of the channel, and he and Lily had to stand on each side of the boat and push off, but eventually they made it through and into an idyllic little harbor lined with rocky outcrops and cliffs, inaccessible by land. They spent the entire day there. And there were other instances as well, where it seemed they were reading each other's minds. Over the last three days one of them would get an idea—to go into Cassis for dinner, to go dancing, to do something for Jeanette and Fanny—and they would look at each other and smile.

Lily came out of the guesthouse. She walked around in front of Nethery and plopped herself down on his lap and rested her head sideways on his chest. Her hair was a tangled mess, stiff from too much hairspray the night before and sticking out every which way.

"What are you doing?" Nethery asked, feigning irritation, "can't you see I'm busy?"

"Mmmm, you are not busy."

"Yes, I am," Nethery said, and made a slight move to dump her off his lap.

"Nooooo," she cried softly as she flung her arms around his neck and drew her knees up so she was curled in his lap.

"Hey you," Nethery said.

"Yes," she replied, looking up at him.

"Kiss me."

"I have sleepy mouth," she said, making a funny face.

"I don't give a flying fuck," Nethery said, smiling. She smiled too and then they kissed, and she laid her head on his chest again. Nethery's cell phone rang, and he felt Lily grow tense. He took the phone out of his pocket.

"Hello?" Nethery said.

"Hello. It is Klaus."

"Yeah. Hi Klaus. What's up?"

"I was just . . . I have not spoken to you in some days, and I . . . wanted to make sure . . . everything was okay."

Nethery laughed.

"Yeah, I'm okay. It's all good. Thanks for asking."

"Because there is something I must tell you."

"Oh yeah?"

"I have heard, through my contacts, that some very bad people are looking for an American with cocaine."

"Oh really?"

"Yes. I do not know them. It is only what I have heard."

"Shit."

"They are, I have heard, part of this People's Mafia from the United States. You know of this . . . this Mafia?"

"Yeah, I've heard of it."

"I also wanted to tell you that I am wishing to see you again."

"Oh yeah?"

"Yes. I can accommodate another two . . ."

"Yeah, okay. We can do that. Is it safe for me to come into Marseille?" Nethery asked.

"I believe so. As I said, I do not know these people. I have only heard in the . . . grapevine. But if it is you they are looking for, they will not find out from me. I would like to continue doing business."

"What about the people you're giving the dope to?"

"They are not really part to the underworld. They are more . . . with the Monaco crowd. High rollers."

"All right. When do you wanna meet?"

"How about tomorrow?"

"That will be fine."

"Three?"

"Yes."

"Okay, see you then," Nethery said, and he flipped the phone shut.

"What is happen?" Lily asked.

"I'm gonna sell another two kilos tomorrow."

"Oh," Lily said, and then she paused as if she were searching for words. Nethery could tell she was worried.

"It's okay. This guy is cool. He's an old Foreign Legion hand."

Lily didn't understand, and Nethery continued.

"He used to be a soldier. Their motto is honor and fidelity. As long as we don't fuck with him, he won't fuck with us."

Despite Nethery's attempts to reassure her, the phone call had shattered the mood. She slid off Nethery's lap and looked around at the sea and the guesthouse as if she had never seen them before. Fight-or-flight response, or something, Nethery guessed. He suggested they take a picnic down to the beach to get her mind off it. She agreed, but didn't seem too enthused about the idea and while she was getting dressed Nethery fixed up some ham and cheese baguettes, a couple cans of soda, and placed them in a picnic basket.

It was afternoon when they finally set out down the cliff. They made their way to the second beach, and Nethery spread out the old tattered tablecloth. They undressed and waded out into the sea. Nethery swam close to the shore, keeping an eye on Lily. The water seemed to work wonders and very quickly she was in a good mood again. Nethery was floating on his back, about twenty yards from the shore. The sky was clear, the most incredible blue. He looked to his left and right, couldn't see Lily and assumed she was behind him somewhere, and then she popped up between his legs, having swam up from underneath. She giggled, looked at his crotch and made biting gestures with her mouth. Nethery reached for her and tried to close his legs, but she was too quick and was gone. She popped up about five yards away, slowly swimming for the beach.

Nethery caught up to her in about five feet of water. She was just getting ready to stand and walk out of the sea when he tackled her from behind. She squealed. They had a mock wrestling match, Nethery allowing her to throw him about like a rag doll. After, they sat on the tablecloth and caught their breath. Lily lay back on the tablecloth and closed her eyes. Nethery took a bite of his baguette and was immediately overwhelmed with the taste. There was nothing special about the sandwich. It was just a baguette, with butter and ham and provolone, but it was simply exploding with flavor.

He savored the overwhelming taste of the sandwich and then from somewhere a dark cloud crept over him. It happened very quickly, as if it were an automatic reaction to the euphoria he'd been drunk on, a security protocol. He felt the energy drain from his body, and a fatigue washed over him that morphed from concern into fear and then paranoia. His chewing slowed and stopped. He knew they were alone on the beach but he looked to the right and the left, almost expecting to see someone in a uniform. He looked at the outcroppings of rock that bordered the beach and imagined teams of police behind them, gearing up for an assault. He forced his eyes away from the rocks and the beach and aimed them straight ahead at the small waves, lapping at the sand. But his mind had switched back to a familiar and well-worn track. The French cops were out there. The owners of the drugs were out there. The world was out there. They had all pushed him and Lily out of Paris and down here to the coast. And they would not rest until he and Lily were pushed out to the center of the sea and then left there, to exhaust themselves trying to stay afloat, and then eventually drown.

That evening Nethery and Lily were curled up on the couch, after a meal up at the main house with Fanny and Jeanette. Lily had dozed off and Nethery was watching television. He had been occasionally checking the news to see if anything had come of the package he sent, but there hadn't been anything on the television, in the papers, or online. He assumed that the whole thing had been covered up. Maybe Wallace had tried to run the story and been stopped. Maybe he had just thrown it in the trash, or given it to the cops. It was impossible to know.

Suddenly a banner announcing a BBC Special Report scrolled across the screen. The banner dissolved and a man appeared. Nethery recognized him as Wallace, and he was standing outside Claude Dutronc's apartment. He announced there would be a special report about the Dutronc murder after a commercial break. Nethery sat up straight and the movement stirred Lily out of her nap. She sat up and rubbed her eyes.

"What happen?" she asked, drowsily.

"Look," Nethery said, pointing at the television.

"What?" Lily asked. It was still a commercial.

"Keep looking," Nethery said.

"This is Clive Wallace of the BBC. I'm live outside fashion icon Claude Dutronc's apartment in Paris near the Place de la Bastille in the 11th arrondissement. As reported just over a week ago, Dutronc was murdered upstairs in the apartment building behind me. Three days ago a package arrived at our offices here in Paris. It contained a DVD that allegedly shows the murder of Mr. Dutronc and his two associates. It is far too disturbing and graphic to air, but the DVD appears to show Mr. Dutronc and two other men torturing and raping an unidentified young woman. It shows one man holding her down on a table while another rapes her and the third stands off to the side whipping her. All the men are wearing black masks. Then they are interrupted. A man walks into the frame with a pistol and kills the rapist and the

man holding her down. The man whipping her then removes his mask and looks toward the camera. He appears to be Claude Dutronc."

Across the screen flashed a series of still images from the video, played in sequence as a kind of stop-motion movie: a masked Dutronc whipping Lily, his arm in the air; the lash striking her back; the welts on her back; Nethery's back as he walked toward the man raping Lily, the gun in his hand at his side; Nethery standing behind the rapist, the gun to the back of his head; Nethery's arm raised, the second man falling back through a cloud of smoke; a masked Dutronc looking toward the camera; and then, a second later, obviously the same man; Dutronc's surprised face and the mask in his hand. Then the slideshow ended and they cut back to Wallace, still standing outside the apartment.

"We have no way of knowing the veracity of the DVD, but the background appears to be that of Dutronc's apartment, including the broken window. The time and date stamp that appear on the DVD, edited from the original video, match the time and date the crime was committed. The two other men were killed in the same manner as Dutronc's two associates, one with a gunshot to the back of the head, the other by a bullet to the chest. Toward the end of the DVD a man can be clearly heard off-screen pleading, 'I am Claude Dutronc, please, please, I am Claude Dutronc.' Then there is a single gunshot and the killer comes back into the frame with his back to the camera to help the girl. Both of them disappear off-screen and the DVD ends.

"*The identity of the girl is still unknown, and the killer, or someone, has gone to great lengths to prevent her from being identified. The DVD has been censored but only to hide the girl's face. We are waiting for the French police to verify some other items that we received with the DVD, apparently included to prove it is authentic. We will have more on this breaking story soon. This is Clive Wallace, BBC, live from Paris.*"

After shooting the report, Wallace drove back to the newsroom. Some of his colleagues stopped by his desk to congratulate him. Most of them valued their jobs too much to try anything like he had and without being too overt they came and paid their respects. He reached into the drawer on his desk and took a drink from the flask he kept there. He'd been prepared to go all the way this time. After formulating a plan he'd walked into Dupuis's office, shown him the DVD and the evidence and told him that if the BBC didn't run this story he would quit and go somewhere else, maybe sell it to AP, or Agence France-Presse, *Paris Match*, or to one of his colleagues at another newspaper. He said they could fire him, sue him, throw him in jail, and given his recent appearance and behavior, Dupuis knew he was serious, or at the very least unbalanced enough to go through with it.

After yelling incoherently at Wallace for ten minutes, Dupuis made some phone calls to the higher-ups, and a few hours later the piece was given the green light. Wallace was warned about making any assumptions about Dutronc. The cops came to the office not long after the program aired. They hadn't wanted to release the information about the tripod and the masks and were furious. They interrogated him in the media room, demanding the original materials he had received and that they get advance notice of any other information that he received and any further programs on Dutronc. After grilling him for almost two hours they left, stressing that he would be in a tight spot if he went ahead with more stories without alerting them first.

After they'd gone, Wallace took another sip from his flask and returned to his desk. He reveled in an immense satisfaction. These were the kind of moments he'd gotten into journalism for. The big stories, the ones certain people don't want to hear, the ones that made you enemies. They'd been increasingly difficult to find, especially at big corporate media conglomerates like the BBC. He leaned back in his chair, put his feet up on the desk, and smiled.

Klaus was sitting at the bar, a drink before him, staring up at a small television mounted high on the wall. Since the report the night before, the news had been nonstop about the Dutronc murder and the video. Nethery was late, and every few minutes Klaus would tear his eyes from the television and glance at the door. He was watching some new personalities discuss the Dutronc case when he heard someone walk in.

"*Merde!*" he exclaimed.

Nethery smiled and hopped onto the stool next to him.

"How's it goin'?" he asked, setting the SAS bag down on the bar.

"I thought something happened to you. You have seen the television!?" Klaus asked.

"Yeah, I saw it," Nethery replied, casually.

"Who send them the movie?"

"I did," Nethery said, grinning.

Klaus opened his mouth but said nothing, and shaking his head, he looked down for a moment and touched his finger to his head, like he was trying to figure something out. He then groaned and then quickly looked up.

"Wha . . . what?" he asked, a pained expression on his face. "*You* send movie?"

"Yeah," Nethery replied, chuckling now, amused at Klaus's reaction. "Those fuckers were videotaping it. I took the tape after I killed them."

"I see . . . but . . . why would you send the tape?"

"You saw how they were talking about that guy. He was a piece of shit."

"But . . . he is dead."

"Yeah, I know, but . . . not his image. Not his ghost. I wanted to kill them too. I wanted to kill that asshole all the way."

"All the way?" Klaus asked, not understanding.

"Yeah. All the way."

"I see . . . remind me not to make you angry," Klaus said, and Nethery laughed. "Will they not find you now?"

"I don't think so," Nethery replied.

"Are you certain?"

"I think I covered my tracks pretty well."

"*Merde*. I hope so."

"Yeah, me too," Nethery said, chuckling.

"You are . . ." Klaus said, pausing, looking at him with his head cocked to the side, "I don't know . . ."

Nethery burst out laughing.

"Go ahead, you can say it," Nethery said.

"Say what?"

"What you were gonna say, that I'm crazy."

"Very well. You are crazy," Klaus said.

"Fuckin' A," Nethery said, and he smiled. "Have you heard any more about the people looking for me?"

"No," Klaus replied, "I have heard that they are not Americans, but Africans. I do not know much about them, if that is what they are. I worked for the Corsicans. The two groups do not mix very much."

Klaus handed Nethery the envelope with the money, then walked around behind the bar to make drinks for both of them. Nethery had seltzer water again, and this time he asked for two slices of lemon, which he carefully squeezed into the water. They sat for a while, drinking and talking. Eventually they came around to the subject of Lily, and Klaus asked how she was doing. Nethery told him that she was well, and went on to tell Klaus a little about her, that she used to be a model, how it had all gone wrong, the incident with the Japanese businessmen, how she'd been screwed over by Claude, and how she just wanted to go home. He talked about her at length, saying she was strong and proud and honorable, that she was smart and funny.

"You are in love with her," Klaus said, smiling.

Nethery looked at him, stunned. "What?"

Klaus raised his eyebrows and nodded, a grin on his face. "You should hear yourself," he said, laughing.

Nethery stared at the condensation on the side of his glass. It was true. He had even told her as much, or that he'd thought he was falling in love with her, but he'd seemingly forgotten as if it were such an alien concept that it hadn't seemed real until Klaus said it.

"Yeah. I guess you're right," Nethery said.

"It is very unusual," Klaus continued, "that she is okay with this idea of sending the tape."

"What?"

"Most women I think would rather forget."

"Yeah well, she's tougher than she looks. She was all for it."

"What's the word on the passports?" Nethery asked.

"I have spoken with the man. It is on schedule. About a week."

Nethery looked down, and Klaus took note of this.

"This is a problem?" he asked.

"Well, now that you know what's going on, what I need them for, exactly, you know. Eventually they're gonna catch me," Nethery said and shrugged.

"What?" Klaus exclaimed.

"People only get away in the movies."

"I don't understand."

"I'm not sure I do either . . . it's just . . . I have a feeling . . . that . . . once I finish this . . . once she's gone, it'll be over."

"You can get away," Klaus said.

"Oh come on. Where am I gonna go? Back to America? I don't think so . . . the damned place is falling apart."

"But . . . stay here! I can get you new papers."

"France? Oh, I dunno."

"Then go with her."

"No, what would I do in . . ." Nethery asked realizing he was about to divulge Lily's home country, "no, no . . . I can't do that. I have a feeling I'm gonna be in a tight spot soon. I don't wanna take anyone down with me."

Klaus continued trying to persuade him, but Nethery made it apparent he didn't want to discuss the subject. They sat for a bit in silence, sipping their drinks. Nethery drifted off into a daydream, and he began to imagine what it would be like. But the rest of the world wasn't like their little beach in Cassis. The people who were after him were not going to forget, and he had a strange aversion to the idea of running, being on the lam, wondering when they were going to kick down the door. It sure as hell wasn't freedom. And if there was one thing he wanted to give her, one gift that was within his power to grant, it was a new start. It would take a long time for what she'd been through to fade into the mists of time, years probably. She would have to totally rebuild herself. And having him around would remind her of everything. He would be like a stone in her shoe.

He knew now how he felt about her, but the feelings were not like any he'd experienced, totally unlike the obsessions and desires of the sort he was used to that always ended badly. Something had changed inside him, tectonic plates had shifted. He'd been invigorated, but was it because he'd discovered purpose, meaning, and honor, or was it because he'd developed a taste for killing? These questions had been hovering in the back of his mind as well every time he pondered a possible future with her. The pull was still there, the drive for vengeance, a primal force. He would catch himself fantasizing about it. He wasn't sure how to stop, or even if he could, and until he did he felt it was best to operate under the assumption that when the passports came he would simply send her on her way, however difficult that might prove to be.

Klaus watched Nethery leave the bar, staring after him as he walked out. He could not understand his unwillingness to at least attempt to escape and start a new life. Klaus had done it, after the Legion, and again after prison, but he didn't know what was going on in Nethery's head. Klaus took the shot glass over to the sink and rinsed it out. There's nothing I can do about it, he thought. Nethery would have to decide for himself. He picked up the packages of cocaine, carried them to his office in the back, and locked them in his safe. He sat down at his desk and picked up the phone.

Klaus had known the counterfeiter for almost twenty years. He often did work for the gangs—passports, new identity cards, work visas, phony business contracts—you name it he could do it. He was legendary among the Marseille underworld. His exploits were almost unbelievable. In one, he'd forged papers to get a guy out of jail. Associates of the prisoner had dressed up as guards and a court officer, gone to the jail, presented the papers to the jailers, and they looked so authentic and contained the correct signatures that they were accepted and the man walked out. He was old now, in his seventies, but he still did work for a select few people. Klaus was one of them, due to not talking when he'd gone to prison.

"Hello?"

"Mr. St. Seurin?"

"*Oui?*"

"It is Klaus. From the bar."

"Yes, Klaus. How are you?"

"Fine, thank you."

"What can I do for you?"

"It's about the . . . passengers."

"Ah, yes."

"Do you know when they will arrive?"

"I believe it will be in five days or so."

"I see. Is there any way to speed that up?"

"Well . . . I do not think so. It is a delicate process. One must have the right materials, and . . ."

"I can get my hands on another two . . ." Klaus interrupted, "for your friend, same deal as the last," he said, referring to St. Seurin's nephew who'd been buying the coke. Klaus had been charging twelve thousand euros each, which made a tidy profit of seven thousand per kilo. And even at that price it was still a good deal. The stuff was so pure it could be cut three times and you would still have the best in town.

"Ummm, well . . ." St. Seurin said.

"There is a situation that is urgent," Klaus said.

There was silence on the other end.

"It would be extremely helpful to begin this vacation at the earliest possible date," Klaus continued, "Do you understand?"

"I think so, yes. I will see what I can do."

"Thank you."

"But I cannot perform miracles, Klaus."

"I have heard that you can," Klaus said, joking.

"Yes, well . . . not in this particular instance."

"So I will hear from you then?"

"Yes, I will call you in a day or two. I do not think they will be ready, but I will let you know how it is going."

Wallace was sitting at his desk going through some background info on his next assignment when the phone rang.

"Clive Wallace, BBC Paris."

"Hello, Mr. Wallace," Nethery said. He was sitting on a bench at St. Charles station, waiting for the train to Cassis.

Wallace recognized the voice immediately.

"If you're thinking of tracing this call, it won't do you any good."

"No, I . . . oh, I don't know . . ." Wallace finally said, "I suppose they could be doing it without my knowledge, but . . ."

"It doesn't matter, Mr. Wallace. This won't take long. Give me your cell phone number. Then go outside, walk around, and I will call you in five minutes. I'll be watching, so don't alert anyone. You can tell the cops I called later."

"Uh . . . okay."

"I did something for you, Wallace . . ."

"Yeah, okay sure," and then Wallace gave the number. Nethery wrote down the number on his hand and immediately hung up. He sat on the steps, watching people. He could see the Mediterranean in the distance, glowing in the afternoon sun. There were dozens of people coming and going from the station and they were very loud, so he moved off to the side of the plaza away from the entrance where it was quieter. He smoked a cigarette and when he was done he dialed the number.

"Hello?"

"Hello, Mr. Wallace."

"I ran the piece today."

"I know. I saw it."

"They wouldn't let me run the DVD . . ."

"I knew they wouldn't."

"Here, are you American . . . ? Because . . . I may . . ."

"Mr. Wallace? I do not have much time. I only wanted to thank you."

"Oh . . . okay . . . here, why don't you turn yourself in? Now that, you know, the video is out . . ."

"That is not possible."

"Then meet me," Wallace said.

"Yeah, right," Nethery said, chuckling.

"I'm serious."

"I don't think so, Mr. Wallace."

"Look, the police called me. They tested the bullet and it does match."

"I told you it would."

"Yes, but they said it also matches the bullets from a killing of a couple the day after the Dutronc thing."

"So?"

"So . . . people might forgive you the Dutronc thing. But this other thing . . . come on, it was like an execution. Meet me and give me your side of the story."

"No."

"But . . ." and then the connection went dead.

Nethery got back to the guesthouse around six. Lily was doing the dishes. She was wearing rubber gloves that were way too big for her tiny hands. She didn't bother taking them off, and gave him a hug and a kiss and then went back to work. Nethery took off his jacket, sat on the couch, and watched her. He remembered when he'd first met her. He hadn't been able to imagine her doing some basic chore like dishes without it being ridiculous, but now it seemed natural and normal. It seemed right. He lit a cigarette and put his feet up on the coffee table. He felt so at home here now. This little place, that wasn't even theirs, felt so lived in, so safe, it felt like more of a real home than his apartment back in the States ever had—and he'd lived there for eight years. In fact, the little bit of time they'd spent in the guesthouse meant more to him than all the years of his life that had come before.

"Let's go into town tonight," Nethery said when she was finished. "Somewhere nice. This dough is burning a hole in my pocket."

Lily understood the first part of his statement and smiled, but frowned at not understanding the second. Nethery responded by pulling the ten grand out of his pocket and waving it, then doing a hot potato act, tossing it from one hand to the other and hopping around the room. Lily looked at him as if he were an idiot. Nethery laughed and she ran over and kissed him.

It was a warm night and they walked into town. Fanny had recommended La Villa Madie on the Avenue du Revestel, above the beach on the east side of town, a short walk from the village center. It was an upscale place for the trendy and rich crowd. They were ushered outdoors to a patio that overlooked the long stretch of white sand beach that Nethery had seen from the cliff at Fanny's. Halfway through the meal Nethery noticed that Lily's mood had darkened. She seemed to be thinking about something, drifting off to some other place. Nethery assumed she was simply in a bad mood, maybe overwhelmed, both of which were totally understandable.

. . .

As they were leaving the restaurant Nethery asked her if something was wrong and she just shrugged her shoulders. She didn't know how to explain it, but she was aware of the pull to treat Nethery just like any other man now. That was how she had always kept control of situations, and the more aware she became of this the more difficult it was becoming to accept what was going on. Neither of them spoke in the taxi back to the guesthouse. When they got there Nethery had to use the bathroom, and when he came out Lily was not there. He found her outside, standing out at the edge of the cliff, leaning on the back of the bench, staring out into the night. He came up behind her and put his arms around her and her entire body stiffened. He tried to kiss her neck and she pulled away.

"All right," Nethery said, turning her to face him, "What the hell is going on?"

"Nothing."

"Bullshit. Tell me."

"I . . . I think maybe . . . we should not be doing this."

"Doing what?"

"Oh! You know."

"No, I don't. Why don't you tell me?"

"This thing . . . it is going to end."

"Yeah? So what?"

"Oh, you . . ."

"The whole world might end tomorrow."

"You just want to fuck me!" she shouted.

Nethery turned away from her and took a few steps away, sighed, looked down at the ground for a moment and then turned to face her again.

"Lily? Don't pull this shit."

"It is not shit!" she exclaimed. He made a move toward her

and she turned and walked back into the guesthouse. Nethery sat down on the bench and put his head in his hands.

"Goddamnit," he muttered, rubbing his temples, feeling the rejection solidify into anger, at himself, and at the world, and yet he wondered why it was bothering him so much. What difference did it make if they stopped now, or two days from now? It was going to end, and that was all there was to it. He suddenly found himself very weary, and he stood, walked into the guesthouse and threw himself down on the couch. He turned on the television, kicked off his shoes, and eventually went to sleep.

The next morning he woke up early. Lily was still asleep and he carefully got out of bed and went outside. He sat on the bench and thought about the events of the previous night, the anger a flickering flame that quickly became a blazing inferno. A new kind of hatred burned inside him, sharp and in focus, a hatred directed at this world, this culture, at every single thing that had contributed to making Lily into the damaged girl she was. At least that was what he told himself. He lit a cigarette and noticed his hand was shaking. He went inside and got dressed quickly, walked up to Fanny's, and knocked on the door. Jeanette answered, and invited him in for coffee. He sat for a minute and had Fanny call a taxi for him, saying he had some things to do, that Lily was still sleeping and he didn't want to wake her. He asked Fanny if she would go down to the guesthouse in a half-hour and tell Lily he would be back later.

Nethery was impatient that morning and decided to skip the Cassis station and take the taxi all the way to Marseille. He napped on the train to Paris and when he got there, he made his way to the Champs-Elysées neighborhood where the BBC offices were located. He checked out the area, devised a plan and sat down in a café. He ordered lunch and pretended to read a newspaper. On the front page of the paper was a huge picture, a still from the videotape, Nethery with his gun to the back of the rapist's head. The headline read *Héro ou Bandit?*

Wallace was on the phone with a London correspondent. Since the live report outside Dutronc's apartment all hell had broken loose. He was trying to track down a model in London who claimed that Dutronc's friends had raped her as well. His contact there had spoken to her, but she had disappeared. He was supposed to be assembling a follow-up piece but it wasn't going well. The video had proved exceptionally divisive. Some of the previous models and fashion industry people who had spouted off about what a great man Dutronc was had changed their tune after the DVD came out, but now that Wallace wanted to talk to them they suddenly didn't want to go on record. He assumed they'd been paid off. Dutronc's business associates had no such crisis of conscience. They were standing by him and refused to acknowledge the possibility that he might have been a scumbag. Wallace had expected that as well. There was a lot of money involved and he was very accustomed to people selling out their principles for money. He'd seen it a million times. The problem he faced wasn't to assemble a preponderance of witnesses for one side or the other but to provide an objective perspective on this follow-up. At first it had appeared to be fairly straightforward, the piece evenly balanced between those condemning Dutronc and those who refused to accept it was him on the DVD, but now that he was asking people to go on record they were bailing out. If he couldn't find anyone to come forward, and the report was too one-sided in favor of Dutronc, all his work would have been for nothing.

Wallace had already done the hard part, gotten the story out there, and it was so big that it couldn't be swept under the rug.

But it could still be forgotten very quickly unless he got more people to talk. Line three of his desk phone lit up. He put the London guy on hold and switched over.

"Hello?"

"It's me."

Wallace recognized the tone and tenor of the voice.

"Do you still want to talk to me?" Nethery asked.

"Uh . . . yeah."

"Okay. Can you broadcast this phone call live right now?"

"No, they would never allow it. I might be able to get it on the air tonight. Or a transcript of it."

"Okay. That'll do I guess. Get it ready. You have five minutes until I call back," and there was a click.

Wallace immediately got up and headed for Dupuis's office. An assistant cut him off, waving some papers.

"Clive? What do you want me to do about . . . ?"

"Not now, Tom," Wallace said, walking past. Dupuis was sitting at his desk, going over some reports. He looked a bit haggard.

"I need to talk to you," Wallace said.

"Oh shit. Very well. What is it now?"

"The Dutronc killer just called. He's calling back in five minutes. He wants us to record the conversation and broadcast it tonight."

"What? Oh fuck. Hey, wait a minute? How do you know it's him?"

"It's him. Believe me. He knew that the return address on the package was the Picasso Museum. That information was never released."

"Oh fuck. Fuck. *Merde, merde!*"

Dupuis bent over the desk and put his head in his hands, and then he looked up. He was almost shaking.

"If we don't do it, he'll just go somewhere else," Wallace said, bluffing.

"Well, go record the damned thing then," Dupuis said, sighing. "I don't think they will let us broadcast it, but . . ."

Wallace reached across the desk, grabbed the phone and immediately called down to the video room. He got the technician on the line and asked him to come up to record a phone call. Word quickly spread around the office about what was going to happen and within a few minutes a crowd had gathered around Wallace's desk. After exactly five minutes the phone rang, the technician gave the thumbs up, and Wallace answered and switched on the speakerphone.

"This is Clive Wallace of the BBC and I'm on the phone with . . . a man who claims to be the killer of Claude Dutronc. What shall I call you?"

"Call me . . . Travis."

On the train back to Marseille Nethery was exhausted. He sat there and stared out the window, analyzing the events of the day, trying to sort out his conflicting emotions. On the one hand he felt that what he'd done was quite stupid. If he'd been thinking rationally he wouldn't have gone back to Paris, wouldn't have called Wallace again, or stayed on the phone so long. He wouldn't have told him about the couple, and he wouldn't have gone to that neighborhood. He would have simply stayed at the guesthouse. But Lily's rejection had triggered something, and in a way he felt a strange kind of satisfaction. He hadn't noticed it until he'd gotten on the phone with Wallace but something had come over him and the words had just flowed out as naturally as water flowing down a stream. When he thought about some of the things he'd said, he marveled at how composed he'd been, talking about things that he really hadn't thought of much before, that had been lying dormant on the edge of his consciousness. The whole thing had been a revelation of a great many things that up until that point he had not wanted to see, that he had rationalized and disregarded as nonsense, that until now he had just been too distracted and self-absorbed to take seriously. The countryside flashed past outside the window. A slight smile spread across his face. His cell phone rang. It was Klaus.

"Yes?"

"James?"

"Yeah, it's me."

"The passengers will be ready the day after tomorrow."

"Great," Nethery said, automatically.

"I would like to see you again. Can we do that?"

"Yeah, sure. I only have one left, you know. And the other half of the deposit."

"Yes."

"You wanna do it when I pick up the other thing?"

"Yes. Where are you? There is a lot of noise . . ."

"I'm on a train."

"I see."

"The usual time?" Nethery asked.

"Yes, I believe so. Three o'clock. I will call you tomorrow to confirm."

"Okay, good. Hey Klaus . . . ?"

"Yes?"

"Thanks."

"Of course."

Nethery closed the cell phone. He sat there with the phone in his hand, suddenly unable to move. Lily's face rose in his mind, and a feeling of intense sadness swept over him, a kind of warmth with a honey-sweet sickness to it. But this was what he'd been waiting for, the moment he'd known was coming. He thought he had prepared for it. His chest became very heavy. His heart felt as if it were pumping air, and in the strange workings of his mind the lounge car appeared like a shining beacon and became his destination, all in a matter of seconds.

Lily woke up and seeing she was alone she looked at her watch. It was 10 a.m. She stumbled out of the bedroom and into the kitchen. There was no coffee and Nethery was nowhere to be found. She ran outside, frantically looking around. She ran up to the house and knocked on the door. Fanny answered and she recognized that Lily was distressed and invited her in for breakfast. Lily had coffee and croissants with the sisters, but after she had been informed of what was happening, she had a difficult time following the conversation. She kept drifting off and after a while she excused herself and went back to the guesthouse.

Lying down on the couch, she tried to watch some television. She could smell Nethery on the cushions, and it had a strange effect on her, sparking her desire, which quickly became tenderness and then morphed into anger. What was she so mad about? She didn't think she was in love with him. She had always fallen for a certain type. "As if a woman ever loved a man for his virtue," she remembered reading somewhere. For her, it had always proved true. She had always chosen the wrong men, and as her modeling career progressed they seemed to get even more wrong. She hadn't had a relationship that had lasted more than a few months. At the time it hadn't bothered her.

She went to the kitchen sink and began to fill a glass of water. When it was full she looked at it for a moment and then poured it out. She went outside the guesthouse and looked out at the sea. Her mind understood that what she was seeing was incredibly big, yet somehow it felt very small. She decided to climb down to the beach to clear her mind. As she was descending the cliff she slipped and dislodged some rocks. She watched them fall, bouncing off the cliff a couple of times and then vanishing. When she reached the bottom she walked along the base of the cliff until she found a tiny alcove protected from the sun by an overhang of rock. She sat down in the shade and tried to figure out what she was feeling. Maybe she did love him? She certainly did miss him, and was completely on edge when he was gone. When he was not around she felt a new and different kind of emptiness that had nothing to do with fear. It was totally unlike anything she'd felt with her previous lovers, and it confused her.

Lily curled her toes in the cool sand and she stared off at the horizon, but what she was seeing was clearer picture of herself than ever before. She was beginning to understand just how damaged she was, and how it had come about. As it sunk in she felt an intense feeling of regret, for what she'd lost, and all the time she'd wasted. In the beginning she'd been very happy to be a model. She'd been good at it. She enjoyed the money, attention, and prestige. When it began to go south she ignored it with the booze and drugs, still dreaming to reach a point high enough to where she couldn't see the ground, and what she'd done to get there. But this newfound clarity also showed her that she was lucky to have gotten out. If she'd stayed where she was it eventually would have destroyed her.

And yet, even after everything she had been through, and everything she now knew, she was still filled with rage at how it all had turned out. She still dreamed of being a model, and her mind automatically looked for ways she could get back there and make it work.

Far out by the horizon she could make out a boat. It seemed to shift and change shape in the heat and haze rising off the sea. She looked down between her legs, and picked up a handful of sand. She made a fist and slowly let it trickle down in a stream to her other palm, where she toyed with it for a minute and then let it slip through her fingers and back from where it came.

• • •

Nethery got back to the guesthouse around 8 p.m. He was a little drunk. Lily was at the kitchen counter, putting dishes away. When she heard him she gave a start, and dropped a plate to the floor. It didn't break and she bent down, picked it up, and placed it in the cupboard. Nethery stood there for a minute, waiting for her to acknowledge that he was there, but she ignored him. He had to stop himself from saying something. He sat down on the couch, turned on the television, and began fuming. These games where people pretended to ignore one another were stupid, he thought. Mindlessly he flipped through the channels, landing on BBC World News for no other reason than an almost subconscious recognition of the language. Lily was still putting dishes away, and making more noise than she needed to. This was one of those stand-offs he'd been in before. Who would break first? Who would swallow their pride? He'd be damned if it was going to be him, the booze and the anger combining to make him more obstinate than usual. He tried to forget it and watch the television, but Lily was making much more noise than she needed to. He couldn't even concentrate enough to take in what was happening on the television. Fuck this, he thought, and got up and went outside. It was a cool night and he sat on the bench and lit up a cigarette. He looked up and saw the stars. After a few minutes he heard Lily behind him.

"James?" Nethery turned and saw her standing about ten feet behind the bench. She had a dishrag, and was drying her hands off with it.

"What?" he said, perturbed.

"There is something on the television," she said.

"So what?"

"James, please," Lily said, imploringly.

Nethery sighed and got up, went inside and sat on the couch.

Lily joined him, but she slid over against the armrest, as far away from him as she could. Nethery almost said something, but forced his anger back down and turned his attention to the television. The BBC Special Report banner scrolled across the screen. Wallace came on the screen announcing that the Dutronc killer had phoned the BBC that afternoon and they would be playing the recording of the interview next. Nethery glanced over at Lily and she was leaning forward, staring at the television. On the screen were stills of Wallace and Dutronc, and the recording was accompanied by French subtitles at the bottom of the screen.

"This is Clive Wallace of the BBC and I'm on the phone with . . . a man who claims to be the killer of Claude Dutronc. What shall I call you?"

"Call me . . . Travis."

"Very well, Travis. How do we know that you're actually the Dutronc killer?"

"The package I sent you? The return address was the Picasso Museum."

"That's true. That information hasn't been released to the public. Are you American?" Wallace asked.

"Yes."

"What are you doing in France?"

"Killing."

There was a long pause.

"Well, yes, we know that, but why? Why Dutronc?"

"He had it coming."

"He did?"

"You bet your ass he did. He was a corrupt piece of shit who couldn't get it up anymore so he took it out on young women he had power over. Under all the flash and glitz, he was an intensely ugly man. That's why he surrounded himself with pretty young women. Just like all those guys."

"Surely they all aren't like that."

"I wish I could kill every single one of them."

"Now wait a minute . . ."

"These fuckers, they ruin people's lives, they steal their youth, they steal their beauty, they steal their innocence, they steal their futures, their dreams, they encourage them down these paths in life that lead . . . nowhere, that lead only to degradation and self-hatred. And they don't even do it for the money. They simply do it to ruin young people, out of envy. They do it because they can get away with it. They do it because no one stops them. That kind of ugliness needs to be . . . utterly destroyed."

"Oh, come now. Who are *these people?*"

"People like Dutronc. People with money and power. When did we forget that power corrupts people? We've known about that since the Greeks for Christ's sake."

"But surely . . ."

"I learned something when I killed that piece of shit."

"And what was that?"

"These people, they do not grasp the damage they cause. They really don't. The system allows them to disconnect from it somehow. It allows them to rape and pillage the rest of us, and tells them it's okay."

"You seem to have a problem with the rich."

"No, not really. It's a systemic problem. The system has become corrupt. It's working backwards. It's not advancing the most worthy among us, the most virtuous, the hardest working, the most humble, the smartest, even the strongest, but the most devious, the best liars, the sociopaths and narcissists, the weak and the soft, the shit like Dutronc. These people need to be stopped."

"Um, but there are ways . . ."

"Don't make me laugh. Look, this isn't a left or right thing. It's not even a rich people thing. It's a corruption thing. Corruption is the enemy."

"So, what? Are you going to stop it?" Wallace asked.

"I have a message," Nethery said quietly.

"A message? For whom?"

"For all the fuckers like Dutronc."

"And what is that?"

"We know who you are. There will be no more bailouts, no more revolving doors, no more golden parachutes. It's time to suffer the consequences. It's time to pay. We're coming after your ass."

"We? Who is we? Are you a part of that terrorist group? The People's Mafia?"

"I thought they didn't exist."

"No one knows. But they're committing terrorist acts, so . . ."

"So they must be terrorists?"

"Yes. Terrorists."

"You call them terrorists. Maybe they're something else."

"Like what? Revolutionaries?"

"You said it, not me."

"Is that what you are? A revolutionary?"

"No," Nethery said.

"Are you an anarchist? A fascist?"

"I'm not any of those things."

"Well, what are you then?"

"I'm just a man. I'm just one man."

"Are there more of you here in France?"

"Yes."

"There are?"

"Yes, I do believe there are men in France," Nethery said, and he could be heard chuckling.

There was another pause.

"You think I'm the only one?" Nethery said. "Have you seen the papers lately?"

"And so . . . your solution is violence?"

"I didn't start this," Nethery said, "I didn't denigrate all meaningful action until all that remained was violence."

There was a pause.

"Where is the girl from the video?" Wallace asked.

"She's gone. She went . . . away."

"Why doesn't she come forward?"

"She doesn't want to."

"Where is she from?"

"You know I'm not gonna answer that."

"Was she one of Dutronc's models?"

"Next question."

"Have you killed anyone else?"

"Yeah."

"You have?"

"Yeah, I killed this couple in St. Germain."

"The couple?"

"Yes."

"Why?"

"They were making a lot of noise."

"Making noise? Is that any reason to kill someone?"

"It is if nothing can make them stop except a bullet."

"I see."

"Look . . . they were making people suffer. That was their grand accomplishment in life. They thought it was funny. I thought it was sick. I took action."

"Are you planning on killing more people?"

"If I need to, yeah."

There was another pause.

"Look. I didn't set out to kill anyone in the first place," Nethery continued, "I just found myself in a situation that called for it."

"Are you trying to justify your actions?"

"No," Nethery said.

"No? Well then, why don't you turn yourself in?"

"I'm not finished."

"Finished with what?"

"What I'm doing."

"And what is that?"

"Living."

There was a click as Nethery hung up. The stills on the screen vanished and a live shot of Wallace came on, saying the police and the government would be making a statement next.

Nethery looked over at Lily. She was staring at the screen with her mouth open. It had been strange, hearing his voice on the television. It had seemed so much like him and yet also unlike him. As if he'd been possessed by some vengeful spirit. Those thoughts lingered for only a moment, drowned out by his anger at Lily for sitting at the other end of the couch.

"It was you?" Lily asked, knowing that it was.

"Yeah."

"The English too? You kill them?"

"Yeah."

"Why?"

"'Cause I wanted to."

"What is happening?"

"It's none of your goddamned business!" Nethery shouted, losing his temper. Lily stared at him for a second and then began to cry. Nethery sighed, got up from the couch, and walked outside. He lit up a cigarette and cursed, but what he was most angry about was the rejection. What the hell was her problem? Couldn't she see that they had found something incredibly rare? And she was ignoring it. Her behavior reminded him of someone seeing a hundred-dollar bill on the ground and just walking past and not picking it up. It made no sense. This thing they had found was going to end, but that didn't mean they should stop now. They should stop when the goddamned world made them stop and not one second before. For a day, a week, a month, for five fucking minutes, they had to make the most of it, and there was so little time left.

But maybe she *was* trying, and simply couldn't manage it? Nethery paused and thought for a moment and then walked back into the guesthouse and sat down on the couch next to her. She was curled up like a cat and was still sobbing.

"Look, Lily? I'm sorry," he said, slurring his words a little bit. He thought about telling her that she would be going home the day after next, but somehow he couldn't. She looked at him, tears streaking her face, and then she wailed and threw herself on him and held on tight. On the television a man appeared standing behind a podium, set up atop the steps of an ancient building. It was the French Minister of the Interior and he was preparing to make a statement. Nethery spotted the remote on the couch behind Lily. He pushed her back slightly until he could reach it, and changed the channel to some cartoons.

Eventually Lily calmed down, and they went outside and sat on the bench. She ran back into the guesthouse, grabbed a bottle of wine, returned to the bench, and began to drink from the bottle. Nethery reached for the wine, and Lily gave it without hesitating. Neither of them said anything. Lily stared out at the sea, as if she could see something. They drank until the wine was gone. Nethery walked out to the edge of the cliff and flung the empty bottle out into the blackness. Lily said she was tired, and got to her feet, but she was very unsteady. Nethery helped her into the bedroom where she sat down on the edge of the bed and kicked off her shoes. She bent down to arrange them side-by-side right next to the bed. Nethery turned and began to leave.

"James?"

Nethery turned to look back at her. Her eyes were wet and her mouth moved as if to speak but nothing came out. Nethery turned again and walked toward the door and he heard her voice.

"Stay," she said. "Please."

Nethery got into bed with her. She laid her head on his chest and immediately fell asleep. His head was swimming with alcohol and he could feel sleep trying to claim him as well, but became aware of the limited time they still had together. One day was all they had, one more day. Twenty-four hours. He realized he would be unable to sleep and that it would be a long night but not nearly long enough. He looked at Lily and had an impulse to wake her, but she was sleeping so peacefully he just lay there staring at the ceiling. Eventually he went out to the living room, flopped down on the couch, turned on the television, and eventually dozed off.

Nethery woke up to the noise of Lily in the kitchen. He tried to sit up but became aware of an incredible throbbing in his head. He groaned and fell back onto the couch. He looked up at the ceiling but the light was hurting his eyes. He rolled onto his side and groped on the floor for his cigarettes. There was some sort of game show on the television and he watched it because everything else hurt to look at. After a few minutes Lily came over with two cups of coffee.

"Good morning," she said cheerfully. Nethery moved his legs out of the way and groaned as he sat up. She sat down and slid over until she was up against him. She smiled and handed him the coffee.

"I'm not so sure about that," he replied.

"What?"

"It's morning, yes. It's the good I'm not so sure about."

"What is matter?"

"I had a lot to drink last night."

"So?"

"I'm just not used to it," Nethery said, chuckling.

"Ohhh."

"Look at this," Nethery said, pointing at the television. The game show had ended and on the screen were multiple scenes of rioting, from different cities all over Europe. In London and Manchester masked gangs were setting fire to shops and looting. In Paris overturned cars were ablaze, and crowds of young people were battling the police, throwing rocks and Molotov cocktails. Hordes of people were marching and chanting *"Vive Travis! Vive Travis!"* They were pronouncing it Trav-ees! Some were carrying signs that said *Vive Travis!* Others had signs that read *C'est ce qu'on fait!* A building was on fire and on it were painted the words *Travis était ici.* The television cut to the president of France, standing at a podium crammed with microphones. He was preparing to speak. The cameraman slowly moved around to the side and then aimed the camera at his feet. He was wearing platform shoes and standing on a box about eight inches tall.

Nethery changed the channel to France TV5. It was a report from Rio de Janeiro, where an armed group had taken over the airport and blown up some jets. The next channel was covering something similar unfolding in Africa. The next channel was CNN. A reporter was describing how a man had crashed a light plane into the mansion of a Wall Street tycoon somewhere in the Virginia countryside. There were images of the smoldering ruins of the house. The pilot had used a cell phone to alert the media prior to the crash, and an amateur video had caught the approach of the plane towing a banner that read, *This is what we do.*

Nethery turned off the television. He looked at Lily, at her face. She was transfixed by what was happening on the television. You would never know it from looking at her how much ugliness that face had seen, taken in, absorbed. Lily looked over at him again and smiled. Strands of hair had curved down to her mouth and were stuck to her lips. She made no effort to brush them away. She reached her arms around Nethery's neck and lay down beside him. He suddenly felt very emotional, knowing that he had to tell her soon.

"What we do today?" she asked, as if she didn't have a care in the world.

"Let's go down to the beach," he said, getting a grip on himself. "We'll have a picnic."

They were out of food, and took a taxi into Cassis. They bought some things at a Monoprix and walked down to the waterfront to catch a taxi back. As they waited on the Quai des Baux Nethery's eyes were drawn to the Russian yacht, still moored out by the mouth of the harbor. He felt a powerful urge to go out there, find them, and kill them. He imagined tying them up, and lowering them over the stern by their ankles to be chopped to pieces by the propellers of their own damned boat. Instead he went to a small store and bought a can of black spray paint. When Lily returned they walked out to the yacht and Lily giggled as Nethery painted *This is what we do* in huge letters across the side of the yacht. A few people around the Hotel le Golfe saw them but Nethery could have cared less. Laughing like kids they ran off and grabbed a taxi back to the house.

Lily made some sandwiches and they climbed down to the beach. Nethery spread out the tablecloth and watched as Lily stripped down to her underwear and ran into the water without a word. Nethery began to undress but then he stopped. Lily was swimming out, her arms and legs flashing. He could not move. He stood there, watching her. She swam out fifty yards as she had done before. She then turned and looked back toward the beach, expecting Nethery to be right behind her, but he had stayed ashore and was standing there, head bowed, looking at the sand. She waved. He stared at the ground, his legs buckled, and he collapsed to the tablecloth. He could feel it now, the pain that was coming, that would get worse, an absolute certainty, but what it made him want to do was not tell her, nor alleviate the pain, even try to enjoy the time they had left, but leave the beach at that very moment, go into town and kill those Russians. Stand before them, tell them what he was going to do, and then do it, the strongest one last. Make sure they know fear. It's sick. I'm sick, he thought. The recent events that had set him free had also unleashed some of the most primitive human urges, the sort that made people capable of the most barbaric atrocities. He buried his head in his hands. They combined inside him, a whirlwind of rage and pain, and he felt like lashing out. He felt Lily sit down on the tablecloth next to him.

"What is matter?" she said.

"You're going home tomorrow," Nethery said, staring straight ahead, choking back his emotions.

"What?"

"Yeah. The passports will be ready tomorrow, and then I'm taking you to the airport."

Lily sat there, trying to take it all in, staring out at the sea. Nethery had not looked up.

"James?"

"Yes," he replied, still looking down. Lily reached over, placed two fingers under his chin and raised his head. His face was twisted into a mask of pain and his eyes were wet. She knew, at this moment, everything he had done for her, everything he was trying to do, and why.

"I love you," she said. She reached for him and he groaned and tipped over and his head fell into her lap. She stroked his hair. She felt very sad, but also responsible for his sadness and she mustered the courage to be supportive. Nethery lay there, overwhelmed by emotion but the tears would not come. Lily bent down and kissed his head, and stroked his hair for a few more minutes. Then she stood and took his hand. He managed to get to his feet, but he was unsteady, and he looked around as if he didn't know where he was. Lily helped him back up the cliff to the guesthouse. They spent the rest of the day making love, but it was different, a desperate and frantic lovemaking. They stayed in bed the rest of the day, taking breaks for food and cigarettes outside on the bench. Each time they went out Nethery noticed the position of the sun. It moved across the sky, far too quickly.

Nethery woke up first. He went out to the kitchen to put on some coffee. What had to be done that day immediately drifted into his mind, like a curtain of dark clouds blotting out the sun. It caused his stomach to tense up and his hands to sweat. Searching for something to do, he began going through the cupboards for no real reason, but he gave up. He couldn't even stand there and wait for the water to boil so he went outside and smoked. A layer of haze hovered over the sea, waiting for the day to come and burn it away. He walked back inside, fixed two cups of coffee, and took them into the bedroom. Lily was just waking up. She pushed herself up into a sitting position, took the coffee from him, had a drink, and then set the cup on the night table. She blinked her eyes, smiled, and reached out her arms at Nethery who was standing next to the bed and clenched and unclenched her hands. He set down his coffee and got into bed. They made love and fell asleep.

Nethery woke around noon. He found Lily sitting on the couch. She was staring so intently at the television she didn't even notice him. Nethery grabbed a croissant from the basket on the kitchen table and sat down next to her. She raised her arm and pointed a finger at the television. A building was on fire in Marseille. Flames poured from the windows of the lower floors and from the edge of the roof hung a huge banner made of white cloth and red letters that read *C'est ce qu'on fait!* It changed to a scene of riot police marching in formation down a wide street covered in broken glass, past burned-out hulks of cars. Molotov cocktails exploded around them, apparently hurled from nearby rooftops, breaking their formation for a few moments.

"Lily?" She turned to face him.

"Yes?"

"We have to get ready to go."

Her lips were trembling and she looked like she was going to burst into tears.

"Yes," she said, her voice creaking under the strain.

Nethery found the remote control and turned off the television. Lily reached over, took his hand, brought it to her mouth and kissed the back of it, and then she held it against her cheek for what seemed a very long time. She stood, and slowly headed for the bedroom, not letting go of his hand until the very last second.

Nethery watched her until she was through the doorway. He stood up from the couch and busied himself getting dressed and then gathering the kilo to sell and the other half he owed for the passports. He realized then that the last kilo was the one he'd taken the samples from and made a mental note to tell Klaus. He placed the packages in the SAS bag, put on his jacket and stuck the gun in the waistband of his pants.

On the train to Marseille they could see dark clouds of smoke rising from the city. At St. Charles the entire station was strangely quiet except for the footsteps of rushing people, contrasted by teams of black-clad policemen who stood around. They were all carrying automatic weapons and watching everyone very closely. The Boulevard d'Athènes was very quiet and there were not many cars about. When they came to Boulevard Dugommier people became even scarcer and the occasional car was smashed up. The Canebière looked like a war zone, and there were burned-out cars and garbage scattered all over the street. There was no activity but for the occasional cop car, cruising slowly. Storefronts had been destroyed and windows broken, but the damage was mostly to the bigger stores. The smaller shops had been left alone. Lily clutched Nethery's hand tightly and occasionally glanced at him with an apprehensive look on her face. He smiled to reassure her. They came to a section of the street that looked especially bad. Some cars were still on fire and shouting could be heard overhead, coming from the rooftops. They detoured off onto the Rue Thubaneau, which was relatively untouched.

It took them about ten minutes to get to Klaus's bar, and they found the door locked and the lights turned off. Nethery cupped his hands around his face and looked in through the glass and then knocked on the door. They were an hour early, as they had planned on having lunch at La Samaritaine. Nethery got out his cell phone, but there was no signal. He knocked again, very loudly, and finally he saw Klaus peek his head out the doorway of the office. Klaus sprang from the office, ran to the door, and unlocked it. As soon as Nethery and Lily were inside he locked the door again and ushered them into the office. Klaus took a seat at his desk. There was one more place to sit, an old wooden chair, and Nethery pulled it out and offered it to Lily. She sat down and placed her hands in her lap.

"What have you done?" Klaus asked, looking up at Nethery.

"Uh, what're you talking about?"

"All of this madness, the riots . . . it's all because of what you said on the television."

"What?"

"Yes," Klaus said, nodding his head, "they think you are some kind of Che Guevara."

Nethery looked surprised for a moment, and then he laughed.

"They do not think it is funny," Klaus continued. "They are waiting for you."

"Waiting for me? To do what?"

"To lead them."

"What? That's crazy. The French would never let an American lead them anywhere."

"That may have been true in the past, yes. But something has changed. They do not care that you are American. You could be an Arab and they still would not care."

"Wow. Well shit. I'm sorry, but I have no intention of leading them anywhere. I have things to do."

"It does not matter to me, my friend. I was only worried that you would not come."

"Well, I'm here."

"Yes, you are," Klaus replied, smiling. "Is this . . . ?" he asked, nodding at Lily, who was sitting there quietly, her hands still folded in her lap.

"Yes, this is my . . . friend."

"I see. *Bonjour*, madame. I am Klaus," he said, holding out his hand. Lily removed one of her hands from her lap and held it out. Klaus took it and kissed the back of her hand. She blushed slightly.

"Do you have the passports?" Nethery asked.

"Yes."

"Oh good."

"It was hell to get them, I must tell you."

"Oh yeah?"

"Yes. The man refused to drive because of the madness."

"Oh?"

"Yes. I had to go to the seventh arrondissement to get them.

Down by the Vieux Port it was very bad. I was on the Rue de Breteuil and suddenly the road was blocked by police. Behind me there were explosions and people on the rooftops throwing Molotov cocktails. I was trapped. I managed to turn my car onto a side street and leave it. I walked the rest of the way and then I found a taxi to drive me back but we had to avoid the city center and go around."

Nethery stared at the wall, deep in thought.

"Is something wrong?" Klaus asked.

"Oh. I just was hoping you might be able to drive us to the airport."

"I would, yes, absolutely, but now . . . I have no car."

"It's okay. We'll make it. The trains are still running, from the looks of it. There are cops all over the stations."

"Yes," Klaus said, "they have sent the police and the army to try and keep things running."

Klaus grinned. "You have started a revolution."

"Yeah, well, it's about time I guess. Somebody had to do it."

"Why did you do it?"

"Oh, shit, I dunno. We had a fight," Nethery said, nodding at Lily, "and I guess I went a little crazy."

Klaus burst out laughing. Lily frowned.

"Of course, of course," Klaus said, "I should have known it was something like that."

"Here's the stuff," Nethery said, placing the SAS bag on the desk. Klaus pulled out the two packages of cocaine, set them on the desk, and handed the bag back to Nethery. He then opened a drawer, removed a stack of bills and the passports, and handed them to Nethery.

"Klaus, I forgot something," Nethery said.

"Yes?"

"That last kilo is a little short. It's the one I took the samples from. I would guess it's about three ounces light."

Nethery counted out ten hundred-euro notes and handed them to Klaus, who looked a bit perplexed.

"Oh . . . thank you for your honesty," he said. "What are you going to do now?"

"I'm taking her to the airport, and then . . . I'm not really sure what I'm doing," Nethery replied.

Klaus got up from his chair and stood before Nethery.

"Well, at any rate, it has been a pleasure doing business with you," he said, extending his hand. It wasn't a dismissal, or a sign that Klaus wanted Nethery to leave, just a soldierly show of respect. Nethery took his hand and shook it, and then Klaus sat back down at his desk. Nethery looked at the passports, opened one and examined it, and then the other. His was a U.S. passport and hers from Ukraine, like they'd requested. The issue date on both was a few years before and they looked used and each had stamps from various countries.

"These look really good," Nethery said.

"Yes. You will have no problems. Even the magnetic stripe corresponds to someone in the system. Why don't you come back here tonight?" Klaus asked.

"Oh, I don't know. Maybe . . ."

"Well if you'd like, here is my mobile number," Klaus said, writing the number down on the back of a card.

"The bar number is on the card," he said.

Nethery took the card and placed it in his pocket.

"Thank you," Nethery said. "Did you know there is no cell phone signal?"

"Oh yes, I had forgotten. They have done something to the towers in some parts of the city. It was working when I was down by the Vieux Port, but here . . . nothing."

"Well, I will try to call you later," Nethery said. "I suppose we'd better get going."

"Very well. I will show you out."

Klaus led the way to the door and unlocked it. He shook hands with Nethery once again. Nethery ushered Lily outside, and they were gone.

They stayed on the back streets. They were mostly deserted except for the occasional person hurrying like a rat caught out in the open. Every so often they heard shouting from the rooftops and sirens in the distance. Clouds of smoke drifted past and pieces of ash floated through the air. Nethery led the way, trying to stay on the side streets and come out near the steps leading up to St. Charles station. Lily clutched his hand tightly. The closer they got to the station the calmer the city became, and finally they emerged onto the Boulevard d'Athènes a few blocks from the station. There were even a few cars around and Nethery was able to flag down a passing taxi. Nethery asked for a ride to the airport, and the driver demanded one hundred euros. Something about the man's arrogance set him off and he reached around behind his back for the gun. Lily grabbed his arm, stopping him. He looked over at her and his anger dissipated in an instant. He paid and oddly, despite everything going on around them, they dozed off in the back seat.

Nethery awoke to the driver saying something in French. He looked around and saw they had arrived at the airport. He removed his arm from around Lily and gently shook her awake. He climbed out and helped her out of the taxi. He became acutely aware of how difficult this was going to be, and he seemed to lose focus in what he was doing. This was going to hurt, he said to himself, and the closer it got, the more painful he knew it was going to be. Lily stood on the curb holding the handle of her wheeled suitcase. She looked around as if she were bewildered. Nethery eventually snapped out of it, took her hand and began towing her toward the terminal. Lily followed for a minute and then began to lag behind, occasionally tugging at his arm as if she wanted to stop. Nethery kept on walking, staring straight ahead. They entered the terminal and he led her to the departure screen. She tried to talk to him and he put up his hand up to silence her. He examined the flights, but there were no direct routes to Kiev. He towed her over to the Lufthansa counter and spoke to a woman. They had a flight, in a little over two hours to Munich where she could transfer to a flight to Kiev. He bought a first-class seat in Lily's new name. It was expensive, almost two thousand euros. When he had the ticket and boarding pass he towed Lily to a café close by and they sat down at a booth that afforded a measure of privacy.

"Here is your passport," Nethery said, looking at it. "Your name is now Vera Voronina. You got that? Say it."

"James . . ."

"Say it!"

"Do not be mad at me . . ."

"I'm not mad, Lily. Or Vera. But we can't screw this up now, after making it this far. So say it. My name is Vera Voronina."

"My name is Vera Voronina," Lily said quietly, rolling her eyes. "James . . ."

"Say it again."

Lily glared at him, beginning to lose her temper. "My name is Vera Voronina," she said, rocking her head from side to side, "my name is Vera Voronina, Vera Voronina. Okay? Is good?"

The mocking went right over Nethery's head. He was singularly focused on eliminating anything that could go wrong.

"You don't have anything else with your old name on it, do you?" he asked. "Old identification cards, letters, bills, anything?"

"James . . ."

"Lemme see that purse," Nethery said, grabbing it from her lap. He poured the contents out onto the table and began to look through them.

"Stop!" Lily shouted. Nethery kept on and finally she tried to grasp his hand and stop him but he pulled his hand free and continued fumbling through the lipstick, makeup, and cigarettes.

It was clear that there was nothing in the purse that would give away her identity, but Nethery kept on.

"This is where most of these plans go wrong," he said, "when you're so close to home. I won't have it. Not for you."

"James, please," she said.

His hands stopped moving as he finally gave up, but he continued to stare at the table. And then he closed his eyes. Lily took one of his hands and brought it to her mouth and kissed it. Nethery felt this and opened his eyes. He turned and looked at her.

"We go outside and smoke," Lily said, her voice cracking. Lily placed her things back into her purse, including the passport and ticket. They walked out of the terminal and found a bench, sat down, and both lit up cigarettes. The sky was clear and blue. Travelers walked past, as well as the occasional heavily armed soldier. When the coast was clear Nethery handed Lily the five thousand euros he'd gotten from the deal that day, and another five from his pocket. He would have given her all of it, but he guessed there would be trouble if she had more and it was discovered.

Nethery was unsure what to do next. He sensed Lily's eyes on him, but he was afraid to look at her. He stared at the sidewalk in front of him. The silence grew awkward. Finally Nethery asked Lily for the address of her mother's café in Kiev.

"What you want that for?" she asked, writing it down on a slip of paper.

"So I can send you more money," Nethery replied.

"I do not want money," Lily said quietly. "I want you."

"What?"

"Come with me," she said.

"Huh?"

"Kiev is beautiful city. You will like it. There are many many parks, and the Dnieper, and . . ."

"That's not a good idea right now," Nethery interrupted, trying to remain composed.

"But . . . why?" Lily asked.

"Lily, these people? The cops, the government? They're gonna be looking for me. They're not gonna stop. With all that's happened . . . it's just not safe for you."

"They cannot find you in Kiev," she said.

"We don't know that."

"I want phone number then," Lily said in a demanding tone.

"Oh, um . . . no," Nethery replied.

Lily glared at him.

"Why? Damn you . . ."

Lily turned away from him and stared straight ahead, crossing her arms in front of her. Nethery touched her shoulder and she pulled away.

"You don't want them to find you, do you?" Nethery said. "You don't want them tracking you down, asking all kinds of questions, right?"

She turned to look at him.

"What if I get caught? Then you call and they will know where you are."

Lily understood. She moved closer to him on the bench, but then she stopped and looked at the ground, thinking.

"But . . ." she said, "you have address of café . . ."

"Yeah, well, I'm gonna get rid of it right away."

"Pfft," Lily spat, and then she looked at the ground between her feet again. "I do not want you to be caught," she said, softly.

Nethery didn't know what to say.

"I do not want to go," Lily said in a voice barely more than a whisper.

"You have to," Nethery said firmly, and he raised his head and looked at her.

"What will happen to you? I am wanting to see you again," she said.

"I just have to sort out a few things here. I'm not gonna get caught," Nethery said, trying to sound as confident as he could. "You just need to get away from me for a little while," he continued. "When it's safe I will call you. We will see each other again," he said.

"I'll give you the number to Klaus's bar," Nethery said, trying to move forward, "he can be our intermediary."

Lily didn't understand and looked puzzled.

"I will call him, you will call him. We can stay in contact through him. But when you call him, make sure you use a pay phone, okay? Just in case."

"Very well," Lily sighed.

Nethery looked for the numbers to the bar and wrote them down for her on the back of a matchbook, tore it off and gave it to her. She scooted back over next to him, put her arm through his and laid her head on his shoulder. Nethery lit two cigarettes and passed one to her. They sat there in the sun for about twenty minutes without saying anything, both of them trying to enjoy their last moments together.

Nethery glanced at his watch, stood up, and held out his hand. She looked up at him and her eyes looked very big, as if they were waiting to be filled with tears. She stood and Nethery took her into his arms. He was reminded of the first time they danced, in that little room at the brothel. She clung to him and he had a feeling that she was not going to let go. He gently broke the embrace, put his arm around her, and began to walk toward the terminal. Because of the gun he was unable to go with her to the gate and he waited as she passed through the security checkpoint. When she was finished being processed, she stood there on the other side of the barrier and blew him a kiss. He smiled and waved, and she seemed to be unable to move, or unwilling. Nethery blew her a last kiss, and then forced himself to turn and walk away.

PART IV
SOMEWHERE OVER
THE WAVES

Outside the airport Nethery found a taxi. He bargained a ride all the way to Cassis for two hundred euros. He felt drained, as if he'd been running for weeks and could finally stop. His mind was filled with half-formed thoughts. He stared blankly out the window, watching the sun as it crept over the horizon. When he reached Cassis it was almost dark. Nethery told the driver to take him to the waterfront. He couldn't bear to face the emptiness of the guesthouse, and had an urge to get drunk. The town seemed unaffected by the madness going on elsewhere in France, as if it were protected somehow. People were out walking their dogs and couples strolled along the waterfront. Nethery got out of the taxi on the Quai des Baux, but as he looked around he felt out of his element amongst all these seemingly normal people and without thinking he began wandering in the direction of Club Santos in a kind of shock, guided by a vague memory of how he'd gotten there before.

He wasn't sure how long he'd been there when someone clapped Nethery on the shoulder. It was one of the Russians, the one called Pasha, sliding onto the barstool next to him. Nethery sighed, pretended to ignore him and stared at his drink.

"Where is friend?" Pasha asked, slurring his words. "Where is girl?"

Spit was flying out of his mouth when he spoke. Nethery saw his two friends standing at the bar a short way down.

"Where is girl?" he said again.

Nethery remembered his visions of murdering these men, but he was tired, and even more than vengeance he simply wanted to be left alone. He finished his drink in one gulp, climbed down from the barstool and walked away.

"Hey Yankee!" he heard Pasha shout.

He glanced over his shoulder and saw the three of them coming after him. What would they want with him? Lily was not there. She was gone. But it was men like them that had made her leave, and when he thought of this, he slowed. He almost turned to confront them but he forced himself to keep walking, driven by a vague sense that the best thing for him would be to get as far from them as possible. He was outside and halfway down the block when he heard Pasha shouting behind him again.

"Hey Yankee!!"

Nethery found himself at the entrance to a back street. He ducked into it and kept walking. The street was long and dark and narrow, one side packed with parked cars, the rest barely wide enough for a car and a narrow sidewalk. He was halfway down the street when headlights hit him from a car pulling into the other end. The car approached slowly and Nethery stepped onto the sidewalk so it could pass, but the car slowed and kept coming until it was about ten yards away and stopped. Pasha got out of the passenger side, then the other young one, Anatoly, and then the old fat man Vladimir, who'd been driving. Something was going to happen. In the past, situations like this would have frightened him. The three Russians moved in front of the car and stood there, side by side, silhouetted in the electric blue headlights of the big Mercedes. They had left the car doors open and music could be heard, the slowly building bass beat that signaled the beginning of Massive Attack's "Angel."

Nethery stepped into the center of the street and faced them. Pasha took a step forward.

"Where is girl?" he asked.

"She's not here," Nethery said.

Pasha snorted.

"I see she is not here," he said. "But where is she?"

"She's gone."

"We want her."

"Well you can't have her. Not now. Not ever."

"Listen, Yankee. You will tell us where girl is. We want her."

Nethery chuckled and said nothing.

"You know what we do to her?" Pasha asked, taking a drink from a flask. "We do everything," he said, grinning.

"We do *everything*," he said, dragging out the last word. Anatoly laughed, and the two of them stepped in front of the fat man and began a pantomime of fucking, standing a few feet apart and thrusting their hips at each other to show they had screwed Lily from both ends while she was passed out.

"We do *everything*," he said again. "She was good girl. We like her. We want her. You will tell us."

They began really getting into the pantomime, grunting and thrusting and Anatoly laughing his head off. Nethery remained calm and stood there, watching. They kept up their game for about thirty seconds. Pasha stopped and took another drink from his flask. He was a little unsteady on his feet and almost lost his balance.

"Now! Yankee. You will tell us where girl is."

"Why don't you go back to the club?" Nethery said. "Pick out one of the skanks there? That's more your speed anyway. Fuckin' losers."

"You will tell us where girl is, you damn Yankee," Pasha said, threateningly.

Nethery paused for a moment, and then he spoke.

"Are you sure you wanna do this?" he said, shaking his head and sighing.

"Do what? You stupid! We want girl!" Pasha yelled and then he and Anatoly began their pantomime again.

Nethery could have walked away. It wouldn't have been so hard. Now that Lily was gone the last shred of justification had gone with her. If he did something now it would be purely retribution, nothing but vengeance, and he knew it.

"All right," Nethery said, shrugging his shoulders, "have it your way."

He took two steps forward and pulled the pistol out from behind his back. He leveled the gun, shot Anatoly right in the chest, moved it and shot Vladimir, but missed slightly and hit him in the shoulder. He spun and fell to the ground. Pasha stopped moving and stood there, holding his flask, looking down at his friends. Anatoly was dead and Vladimir was writhing on the ground and moaning. Slowly Pasha turned and looked at Nethery.

"You . . . what you doing? You crazy!"

Nethery laughed.

"Yeah, I keep hearing that," he said, "but you know, I'm not so sure."

"You . . . you . . ." Pasha said, still staring at his friends.

"Look," Nethery said, his ears ringing from the gunshots, "this is it for you. It's not gonna be like the movies. I'm not gonna go on some religious rant about *furious anger* or the price of butter. I'm just gonna end you. Right now."

Pasha screamed and charged. Nethery put two bullets into his chest and he fell on his face, dead, his flask skittering across the cobblestones.

Nethery walked slowly among the bodies. Anatoly had fallen back onto the car, slid to the ground, and was sitting against the bumper of the Mercedes. His head was on his chest, the side of his face lit up cinematically in the headlights. Pasha was spread-eagled and facedown on the cobblestones. There was something terribly beautiful and peaceful about them. Nethery stopped next to Vladimir, who was facedown writhing on the ground in front of the car, and Nethery thought his desperate moaning was horrible and ugly. He pointed the gun down at his head, but only stepped on his shoulder. Through the ringing in his ears he heard him scream, but it was so faint it seemed to come from another time and place. Nethery stepped back, and after curiously surveying the scene for a few moments he began to hear the song coming from the car again. "*Youuuuu . . . are my angel . . .*"

He squeezed past the car and continued down the street. He kept the gun in his hand and his arm dangling at his side. A few onlookers had gathered at the end of the street. As he approached they scattered. Occasionally he looked down at the gun as if it was some strange thing he had never seen before. He emerged onto a wide, well-lit street and began walking toward the waterfront. He could see it a few blocks ahead. A well-dressed older woman approached him on the sidewalk, walking a white poodle on a leash. It began barking when he was about ten feet away. The sound was dull, his ears still affected by the gunshots, but the noise brought him out of his trance. He stopped and watched. As the dog passed it lunged and tried to bite his ankles. Only the woman jerking hard on its leash kept it from getting at him. He turned as they passed, following the dog with his eyes. He looked up at the woman. She had seen the gun now and was standing there wide-eyed. Nethery looked down at the gun in his hand again, raised it and aimed at the dog, but then he just smiled and lowering his arm, turned and kept walking.

At the waterfront he crossed the street and sat on a bench. He set the gun on the bench beside him and looked out at the harbor. The ringing in his ears had gone and he was able to hear again, the small waves lapping against the sides of boats, the creak of ropes, cars on the street behind him, and the voices of

people out walking along the promenade. Without really thinking he took the piece of paper from his pocket. He held the tiny
slip of paper up to the light, stared at it for a few moments. The
name of the café was in Ukrainian but he was able to decipher
the word café and Frunze Street, number 110. He said this aloud
a few times, hoping he would remember, and then he put the
piece of paper in his mouth and began chewing. He swallowed.
He gazed out over the water of the harbor. The beam from the
lighthouse swept over the Russians' yacht at regular intervals.
After a few minutes he noticed it was quieter. He heard fewer
and fewer people behind him, and then none, and he heard cars
pull up, their tires screeching as they stopped. And then he was
illuminated in a spotlight and a voice came over a megaphone.

Nethery was handcuffed, placed in the back of a Renault police car, and driven to the Cassis police station. He put up no
resistance, and was barely aware of what was happening. As
he was being led into the station he noticed a Buddhist prayer
wheel bolted to the wall right next to the front door, and it was
so out of place that he became slightly more conscious of what
was going on. Inside there were polished hardwood floors and
an ornate wooden staircase on one side of the room. An officer
led him across the lobby, through a steel door and down a darkened hallway to a cell, where he removed Nethery's handcuffs
and locked him in.

There was a cement platform built out from the wall, a thin
but clean looking mattress on it, a blanket and a couple of pillows. There was a steel toilet in the corner and a tiny sink. Nethery sat down on the bed, and leaned back against the pillows.
After ten minutes an official-looking man came and spoke to
him through the bars. He spoke French, and Nethery said he
could not understand a word he was saying. The man looked

confused for a moment and then left. He appeared again half an hour later and in broken English explained that they did not have a lawyer in town that spoke English, but would have to request one from Marseille. Nethery gathered that because of the chaos the lawyer might not get there until the next day. Nethery asked the man if there was something to read in English. The man understood apparently, and said he would see what he could do. A few hours later a very young police officer arrived and handed him a copy of *The London Times* through the bars. The officer then sat on a chair outside the cell. He seemed very curious about him and kept looking in his direction. Finally he spoke.

"You are . . . American?" he asked.

Nethery looked over at him, and then began laughing.

"Why you laugh?" the officer asked.

"People keep asking me that . . . and I don't really know what to say."

"Ahhhh," the officer said, clearly not understanding.

"Hey," Nethery said, "can I ask you a question?"

"Of course."

"What's with the prayer wheel outside?"

"Oh yes. That."

"Yeah, *that*."

"This place was Buddhist temple."

"Where'd they go?"

"The . . . police bosses, they go to landlord, they make landlord raise rent so they have to leave. We move in. It is nice place, yes?" he said cheerfully, nodding his head.

"Yeah."

"*Merde*," he said, "I must thank you. I have been ordered to take care of wheel and I forget," he said and then got up and walked down the hallway. He soon returned, walking past the cell, grinning and carrying a sledgehammer. A few minutes later

Nethery heard the faint banging of the young officer hammering away at the prayer wheel. It went on for a half an hour.

The young officer never returned, and Nethery sat up against the wall and opened the newspaper. The rioting in France and America had spread to England. Someone had attacked Big Ben with an RPG. The clock had been destroyed. *This is what we do* had been painted on the pillars at Stonehenge. Back in the States, a corporate jet carrying the CEO's of two major banks had apparently been hijacked and crashed into the Hudson. A few seconds before impact air traffic controllers received one message: *This is what we do.*

Nethery folded up the paper and set it aside. He didn't care what was happening elsewhere in the world. He had never been socially or politically engaged, and now that he'd woken up and was aware of a few more things, he was even less so. He found it all interminably boring. He did not understand activism, or meddling in affairs outside one's immediate circle of influence, that of family, friends, and maybe community. Everything beyond that was out of one's control, dictated by madmen who sought power. There was something he despised about people who thought they knew what was best for anyone but themselves. His former coworkers had thought him extremely odd. They had accused him of being uncaring but he didn't see it that way. He'd been cold and aloof simply because there had been nothing worth caring about. He closed his eyes and thought of Lily. He cared about her, he truly did. He had expected to feel pain when she left, but the emptiness was so deep it had shocked him. He'd never had much of an inner life, but there had been something growing there, especially after Lily, a small plot of dry grass, a dandelion here and there kept alive by the faintest of hope, surrounded by a lush and rampant jungle, and now the entire area had been razed to the ground. Scorched earth as far as the eye could see, a flat and monochrome desert.

He gazed up at the ceiling and tried to picture Lily, what she was doing, where she was. There was nothing. He looked around the cell. It wasn't so bad. Not nearly what he'd imagined a French prison to be. There were only a few pieces of graffiti scrawled on the walls and the smell wasn't particularly offensive. It wasn't much worse than some hostels he'd stayed in years before. He felt it curious that he was responding to everything so calmly. He had imagined situations like this, and at the time it had nearly paralyzed him with fear. It simply wasn't happening now. Some internal shift had occurred, some transformation, a paradigm shift in his emotional state. The result was a strange and unexpected kind of peace or resignation, he wasn't sure which. Events had unfolded as if guided by a dark and divine force, his own personal manifest destiny. Irreversible and inevitable, a dark gravity. He had thought briefly about intervening somehow, trying to change the course of events but it seemed wrong, immoral even. Getting Lily home was the first truly good, useful, and selfless thing he'd ever done in his life. That was all that mattered. He thought about trying to escape and quickly rejected the idea. He was tired. Contemplating escape, all the planning and plotting, talking to other prisoners, just seemed pointless. Fate was in control now. He had done what there was to do. It was over. He would accept what was coming. He had made others pay for their actions. Now it was time for him to pay for his. He folded his hands behind his head and stared at the fluorescent light on the ceiling. He found it fairly easy to fall asleep.

The next morning Nethery woke to an officer entering his cell. He was handcuffed again and brought to a room, given a croissant and a cup of coffee, and told to sit at a table. The handcuffs were locked through a steel ring in the table. After fifteen minutes a woman was let into the room. She sat across from him and they were left alone. She looked to be about forty, fairly good-looking, and reminded him of the French actress Nathalie Baye, pale with reddish-brown hair that tumbled over her shoulders. She put on a pair of fashionable rectangular eyeglasses, pulled a few papers out of a briefcase, and set them on the table.

"I will be your counsel," she said, looking up, in English with a French accent. "My name is Betty."

"I would shake your hand, but . . ." Nethery said, shrugging his shoulders and holding up his hands as far as he could.

"It is fine," she replied, looking at the papers again. "Your name is . . . Jeremy Blackstone, is that correct?"

"No."

"It says here," she said, pointing to the paper, "that you were carrying a United States passport in your possession, and the name on it is Jeremy Blackstone."

"It's a fake. A . . . forgery."

"That is not your name?"

"Nope," Nethery replied, grinning.

"Are you American?"

Nethery grinned. It was that question again.

"Yeah . . . I suppose," he said.

"You suppose?"

"Yeah. I suppose."

"Do you want me to notify the American authorities?"

Nethery sat back and said nothing.

"What is your name?" she asked.

"That doesn't matter."

"It doesn't matter? Of course it does."

"This is a dumb game. When they examine the gun I was carrying they will know who I am."

"And who is that?" she asked, peering over the top of her glasses. Nethery grinned. She looked back at him, confused and waiting for him to elaborate.

"I'm the guy who killed those Russians in the alley. I'm the guy who killed that couple in Paris, in St. Germain. And I'm the guy who killed Claude Dutronc and his two friends."

It took a few moments for the words to sink in, and then Betty's mouth opened slowly, and stayed that way. Nethery chuckled.

"You are . . ." she said, not daring to say the name.

"That's right," Nethery said, with a smirk.

". . . Travis," she gasped. "Oh, *mon dieu*," Betty said. She sighed and lowered her head. She seemed to be thinking and then after about thirty seconds she looked up.

"Okay. You must listen to me now," she said. "You must not tell them who you are."

"Uh, why? They're gonna figure it out soon enough."

"Yes, of course. But it will take some days."

"What's the difference?"

"You do not understand, Mr. . . . the entire country has gone mad and they blame you. The president of France himself has put out a reward for you. Once they know who you are . . . they will take you away . . . you will disappear. I will not be able to help you. No one will."

Nethery shrugged and Betty looked at him strangely.

"You do not care?" she asked.

"Not really," Nethery said.

"*Merde*. Very well, will you do this for me? Do not tell them who you are, at least until tomorrow, okay?"

"Sure. No problem," he said.

L ily made it through customs without incident and out into the main concourse of Boryspil Airport. It was extremely busy, and she found a place to sit. She felt odd. She was back on her native soil, back home, but there was no warm feeling of familiarity. Something had changed. Whether it was her or something else she could not tell. She found a kiosk and bought a pack of cigarettes, walked outside, and had a smoke. It was partly sunny, pleasant and warm. Clouds drifted incrementally across the sky. She flagged down a taxi for the half-hour ride to Kiev. She asked the driver for a piece of paper, and he gave her one from a pad on the dashboard. She dug out the matchbook cover with Klaus's phone number scrawled on it out of her pocket, and wrote down the number again in large numbers and wrote it on her hand as well. To be safe, she told herself. She then placed the piece of matchbook back in her pocket and the other piece of paper in her bag. She closed her eyes, and drifted off into a half-sleep, occasionally rousing herself as the taxi neared Kiev. She began to recognize parts of the city. As they crossed Patona Bridge she was able to see up the Dnieper to Podil, where she'd grown up.

She told the taxi to stop down the street from the café. She sat in the back and did not move. Now that she was close she didn't want to get out. She should have been happy. But all she felt was a kind of dread. Her mother had advised her not to leave, to stay close to home, to family. The taxi driver snapped his fingers and asked for his payment, saying he had to respond to another call. She paid the driver, got out, and made her way up to the corner. She ducked into a darkened doorway across the street, smoked a cigarette, and watched. It was a slow afternoon and there were only a couple of customers, probably having her mother's crepes. She could see a pretty young girl bringing food to the tables. Her cousin, probably. Her mother walked amongst the tables, chatting with customers and making sure the food was to their liking. Her mother had always done that. She liked people, or at least believed the best of them. Lily used to have that kind of faith. She reached into her pocket and pulled out the piece of matchbook with Klaus's phone number scrawled on it, just to make sure she hadn't lost it. She closed her hand around it, reminding herself to call that man Klaus at the bar when she got a chance.

After standing there for twenty minutes, Lily still hadn't found the will or the courage to cross the street to face her mother. She finished a cigarette, dropped the butt down to the ground with the others, and stepped on it. She sighed, raised her head and rather than crossing the street she walked in the opposite direction. She wound her way through the neighborhood for a few blocks guided by memories until she found the winding road that climbed up the hill to St. Andrew's Catholic Church. She took her time, stopping to browse the tables of the merchants that lined the lower end of the road. She knew she was wasting time, avoiding the inevitable. At the top of the hill she crossed the parking lot and paused outside the heavy wooden doors of the church. It felt almost as if there was a barrier of sorts preventing her from entering. She ignored this, pushed the doors open, and walked through the lobby. The church was empty but for an old woman wearing black sitting in the second row near the front. Her eyes were drawn to the stoup. She walked over, dipped her fingers in the holy water, and stared at her hand for a minute, half expecting the water to start boiling. She removed her fingers from the water, crossed herself and said a prayer, then sat down in the back of the church on one of the old wooden pews. The smell was the same as always—old wood, oil, and furniture polish, and it ushered in a flood of memories. Lily and her mother had come here often when she was young. Back then she had been able to find comfort in this place. She sat there quietly and closed her eyes, trying to find what she once had, but there was nothing but an uncomfortable stillness as if she were in a cavern deep underground. She didn't want to move. She felt if she made the slightest sound, it would come back a hundredfold and crush her.

Lily left the church and walked back down the hill to the neighborhood where she stopped at Kontraktova Square. It was June, almost the hot season, and there were many children playing in the park, watched closely by their mothers. She sat on a bench for a half-hour and then she made her way back down to the Dnieper. She gazed at the dark water. She smoked a cigarette and started back to the café. On the way, she passed a print shop. She stopped, stood there for a moment, and she turned back and went inside. She spoke to the attendant, and then left and went into a cheap goods shop a short way down the street. She bought some black yarn and a telephone calling card for Europe, then she returned to the print shop. The attendant had finished laminating the piece of matchbook and then punched a hole in the plastic. Lily threaded the yarn through the hole, tied a knot, and placed the necklace around her neck.

She walked back up to the corner across from the café. Her mother would be happy, but there would be the inevitable questions. Her mother had been right about Claude, but she hadn't done much to stop her from leaving. Finally, Lily crossed the street.

She grasped the door handle and opened it, ringing the bells. She closed the door behind her and stood there, fidgeting, more nervous than she'd ever been on the runway under the lights. Her mother appeared from the kitchen. She was looking down, wiping her hands on an apron, and then she raised her head. She saw Lily standing there, and a smile spread across her face.

Wallace made his way unsteadily down the steps in front of the police station, holding on to the handrail. He'd been without booze for two days and was in a cold sweat, his body tormented by the conflict of nausea and hunger. They'd only given him a piece of stale bread once in a while to eat and hadn't let him sleep the entire time, interrogating him in teams. Where is Travis? How do you know him? Why did he choose you to approach? Is he a part of the People's Mafia? It went on and on. The entire thing had also been so they could search his apartment, tap his phones, and he knew this. It also meant that soon they would look through his phone records and find Travis's number from the second phone call, the interview, and see that they had spoken before that. That's when the real trouble would start. Wallace took his cell phone from his pocket and called Dupuis. His hands were shaking and his muscles didn't seem to be working properly.

"Hello?" Dupuis answered.

"Bertrand?"

"Wallace! Are you okay?"

"Yeah, fine. I just need a drink."

"Oh *merde*, you do not need a drink! Tell me what happened."

"Not much. They put me in a room and asked me questions about the Dutronc killer."

"And?"

"I told them what I knew. Nothing."

"Well I am going to speak to the lawyers. They can't just pick up our journalists and interrogate them for two days."

"Hmph. They can do whatever they want, Bertrand."

"Well, it's not right, goddamnit!"

"Whatever. I'm gonna go home. I haven't slept for two days. I'll be at the office tomorrow, but probably not until the afternoon."

"Very well."

Wallace took a taxi to his apartment, stopping on the way to pick up a bottle. About a third of it was gone when he reached his apartment. He was punching the code into the door when he heard a woman's voice behind him.

"Mr. Wallace?"

He turned and almost dropped the bottle.

"Goddamnit," he said. He steadied himself and looked her over.

"Who the hell are you?" he said.

"My name is Betty Marais."

"Well, Betty Marais? I've just spent two nights in a cell being grilled by the cops. I'm tired as hell and I don't want to talk to you."

"I think you do," she said.

He rolled his eyes, shook his head in disbelief, turned, and began punching the code into the door again, but had lost the sequence.

"Bloody hell!" Wallace shouted and he began punching the code again. Finally the door buzzed and he pushed it open.

"I know where Travis is," she said, before the door could close. Wallace caught the door, pulled it back open, and turned and looked at her. Something told him she was dead serious.

"Goddamnit," he sighed, shaking his head and looking at the ground, "come in."

. . .

Nethery was awakened by a police officer and taken to the meeting room again where he was chained to the table. He asked what was going on but the officer ignored him, left, and then came back with a croissant and a cup of coffee. He sat there, gnawing on the croissant and washing it down with coffee. The chains only allowed him to raise his hands from the table to his mouth, and he became irritated and lifted and tried to pull the table but it was bolted to the floor. After fifteen minutes Betty appeared at the cell door with a police officer and another man, who looked familiar. Betty explained to the officer that the man was her assistant and they were there to take a deposition for the U.S. consulate. Nethery looked the man over. He was carrying a video camera and a tripod. The officer examined the equipment and then told Betty they had ten minutes. He opened the cell door and allowed them in. Betty checked her watch, then dragged a chair over and sat across the table from Nethery. The man set up the tripod next to the table, pulled a chair over, sat down, and began fiddling with the video camera. He looked a bit ragged, like he'd woken up hungover in an alley after a bender.

"Hello, Travis," Betty said. The man stopped what he was doing and looked over at her, and then turned and looked at Nethery closely. He set the video camera on the table.

"Do you know who this is?" she continued, nodding at the man.

"Nope."

"Clive Wallace," the man said, holding out his hand.

Nethery recognized him, and noted that he wasn't so disheveled on television.

"What's he doing here?" Nethery asked, looking at Betty. Then before she could answer, he looked at Wallace. "What are you doing here?"

"We're here to document your presence," Wallace said. "If we have proof that you're here, they won't be able to just spirit you away somewhere."

Nethery shrugged.

"You weren't kidding," he said to Betty, "he doesn't care."

"I told you," she said, shaking her head.

"I don't think you understand the seriousness of your position . . ." Wallace said. Nethery sighed.

"Let's just get this over with. Okay?"

"Okay," Wallace said and shrugged. He stood and mounted the camera on the tripod, adjusted the picture so that all three of them could fit in the frame and turned it on. He then sat back down and turned to face the camera.

"This is Clive Wallace of the BBC. I'm in the Cassis jail with the man who calls himself Travis, and his attorney Betty Marais."

"Let's start. You are the Dutronc killer?"

"Yes."

"How do we know this is true?"

"The police have the gun I used."

"How did you end up here?" Wallace asked.

"I shot three Russians here in Cassis."

"Why?"

"I wanted to."

"You wanted to?"

"Yeah. Well . . . they had it coming."

"You said that about Claude Dutronc too."

"Yeah . . . *c'est la vie*, right?"

"What did these Russians do to deserve it?"

"They came after me."

"They came after you? Why?"

"They wanted to know where the girl was."

"Why did they want the girl?"

"So they could do what they do."

"And what was that?"

"The same thing that Dutronc did. Look, I tried to walk away. But they wouldn't leave it alone. They asked for it. They were begging for it."

"They were asking to get shot?"

"It's not my fault they didn't understand the consequences," Nethery said.

"How did you get caught?"

"I walked down to the harbor and sat down."

"You sat down?"

"Yeah."

"Why?"

"It was a lovely night."

"You didn't try to run away? Flee?"

"Nope."

"Why not?"

"Remember our last conversation?"

"Yes."

"When I said I wasn't done living?"

"Yes?"

"I'm done now."

"You are?"

"Yes."

"What has changed?"

"The girl is gone."

"She is?"

"Yeah. She was still here when we last spoke on the phone."

"And now she's gone?"

"Yeah."

"Who is this girl? Where is she?"

"She's everywhere," Nethery said and then he laughed.

Wallace sat there, baffled, trying to figure out what to ask next when Betty got his attention and pointed at her watch.

"Very well," Wallace said. "We have to stop now. The officer will be back soon. This is Clive Wallace of the BBC from the jail in Cassis, France."

Wallace stood and turned off the camera. He'd wanted to ask Nethery if he was part of the People's Mafia, and a number of other things, but he'd run out of time. He removed the camera from the tripod and sat down again. He explained that he was going back to Paris and would try to get the video on the news that evening. Betty said she would stay in Cassis, keep an eye on things and that she would call Wallace if they tried to move Nethery.

ily saw her mother smile, and she ran across the floor of the café, arms out. She collided with Lily and embraced her.

"Ohhh, Agnieszka," she said, holding her tight.

It sounded strange. She would have to get used to her name again. Her mother would never accept Lily calling herself anything but the name her family had given her.

"Oh mama," she said, holding back tears, dreading the questions, wondering when they would come. She wanted to delay it as long as possible. Lily's mother sensed it already and pushed Lily away so she could look into her eyes.

"You do not have to worry, my daughter. I am not going to ask you why you came home to me."

It was too much, and Lily stumbled over and sat down on the nearest chair she could find. She buried her head in her hands. Tears were forcing themselves out of her eyes. She took a deep breath, and then a switch seemed to flip and she got a grip on herself. She wiped her eyes. The young girl she'd seen waiting tables was standing next to her mother, and she smiled. Lily recognized her.

"You remember Natalia, your cousin?"

"Of course."

Lily hadn't seen Natalia since she was eight years old. She had grown almost as tall as Lily, thin, with small breasts and long limbs, square shoulders, and a unique face—perfectly symmetrical. She had big greenish-hazel eyes, wide apart. Lily stood and took the girl's face in her hands and kissed both her cheeks. The girl beamed.

"I'm going to be a model. Like you!" she exclaimed.

Lily's heart skipped a beat, but she forced a smile and then looked over at her mother, who was looking down at the ground, her hands on her hips.

"Oh really," Lily said, trying to seem excited, "that's great."

"I want you to tell me all about it!" Natalia said.

"Of course."

There was a small window of thick glass high on the wall of Nethery's cell, so chipped and cloudy it was impossible to tell whether it was day or night. But what did it matter? Time had no meaning anymore. At first he had continued to glance at his wrist out of habit, but now every time he thought of it a split second later he remembered that a watch was useless in here. Nethery piled up the two pillows against the wall, leaned back, and dozed off. He awoke a short while later to footsteps approaching out in the hall. He raised his head and there were three men at the cell door, all wearing suits. They made no move to open the cell door so Nethery closed his eyes again.

"So you are the great Travis," a voice said, in English with a French accent. Nethery pushed himself up into a sitting position. He grinned. The man in the center, the one who'd spoken, had stepped forward from the other two and was gripping the bars of the cell door. He was glaring at Nethery.

"You think it is funny?" he said bitterly. "Do you know how many people you have killed?" the man asked.

Nethery figured he must know how many he'd killed with his own hands, and that he must be referring to the riots. So, now they want to talk about collateral damage, he thought, but he merely said, "More than you," and kept grinning.

Nethery could see the man grit his teeth. His knuckles had turned white where he was gripping the bars of the cell. He barked out some orders to one of the other men in French. He left and returned a minute later with two of the local officers who opened the cell door. One of them drew his pistol and stood off to the side while the other handcuffed Nethery. The two cronies of the man in the suit then entered the cell, took Nethery by the arms, and began to lead him out. In the lobby there were dozens of police officers, guards, and men in suits. They all stopped what they were doing and stared at Nethery. He spotted Betty, sitting in a chair along the wall. When she saw him she jumped up and tried to approach but was restrained by a couple local officers.

"They are taking you to Baumettes Prison in Marseille!" she shouted. "I will follow. I will see you there as soon as I can! Do not go outside of your cell! Stay inside your cell!"

Nethery nodded. The two men led him outside to a waiting van and pushed him into the back. They sat him down on a steel bench and one of them attached his handcuffs to a ring on the bench between his legs. The guards and the man in charge sat on the bench opposite. One of the men gave a signal to the driver, banging on the wall of the van three times.

"This will be a short trip," the one in charge said, "make your-self comfortable," he said sarcastically, and then he smirked. The others seemed quite nervous and apprehensive. They avoided making eye contact with him.

Lily had gone back to work immediately in an attempt to quiet her mind. It had worked for the most part. The day passed fairly quickly—taking orders, carrying plates of food, chatting with customers, most of them residents of the neighborhood. A few of them she even recognized from her childhood. Her mother had hired a cook named Victor who sang and whistled tunes all day in the kitchen. She had enjoyed the work. It had turned off certain circuits and allowed her to relegate some things to the back of her mind. They never stayed there for long however, and were awakened often, triggered by ads in magazines, television, billboards. The only time she wasn't able to box them up and put them away was when her cousin wanted to talk about modeling. She was relentless. It was all she wanted to talk about, seduced by false idols and the phony glamour of the fashion industry, just as Lily had been. Apparently there were some modeling scouts in town, two men that had been hanging around the café, and Lily's cousin wanted her to meet them.

The dinner rush had died down, and Lily needed to clear her head. She grabbed a pack of cigarettes and left the café, walking in the direction of the Dnieper. The sun was about to set, and the buildings cast long shadows across her path. At the river's edge she found the old concrete abutment she'd played on as a child. She lit another cigarette and gazed out across the river. It looked like a dark ribbon. She leaned on the railing and hung her head. She was having a hard time adjusting. Her life in Paris seemed bizarre to her now, like a bad dream, and in a way, she couldn't believe some of the things she'd done while she'd been there. She raised her head and gazed at the Dnieper. She felt as though she had returned from another world, a world with an entirely different set of rules and values.

She finished her cigarette, and flipped the butt into the river. She walked to the pay phone on the corner, pulled the laminated piece of paper out from under her sweater, and dialed the phone number to Klaus's bar.

"*Oui?*" Klaus answered.

"Hello . . . umm . . . it is Lily? James's friend . . . ?"

"Oh yes. Hello, Lily."

There was a pause, and Lily didn't know what to say.

"Is there something I can do for you?" Klaus asked.

"Have you . . . have you spoken with James?"

"You do not know what has happened?" Klaus asked.

Lily took in these words and her heart began pounding in her chest.

"No . . ."

"James has been arrested."

"What?"

"He is in jail. Later that night . . . after . . . I suppose it was after you had left . . . he killed two Russians in Cassis."

Lily knew immediately what had happened.

"He didn't even try to escape," Klaus continued, "he just walked down to the harbor, sat on a bench, and waited for them to arrest him."

Klaus heard Lily sobbing on the other end of the line.

"I'm trying to get in contact with his counsel," Klaus said.

Lily couldn't speak and clutched the phone tight to her ear.

"Is there something I can do?" Klaus asked. "Would you like me to give him a message?"

"Yes . . ." Lily said, choking back sobs. "Tell him that . . . I love him."

"Very well," Klaus said. "I will do my best. It may be impossible. But I will try."

"Thank you."

"Why don't you call me tomorrow night?" Klaus asked, feeling bad for her.

"Yes."

Lily hung up the phone. She forced herself to stop sobbing and tucked the phone number back inside her sweater. She walked back to the café, weaving a little. Her mind was elsewhere and she barely looked where she was going. She crossed a street against the light and a car screeched to a stop. The driver blared his horn and Lily just stood there, a few inches from his bumper, and glared at him. Slowly she made her way around toward the driver's side door. The man sped off. When she got back to the café it was empty. Lily sat down at a table, and stared blankly out the window. Her mother came out of the kitchen and sat down next to her, and she immediately sensed that something was wrong.

"What is the matter, my daughter?"

"Oh, nothing," Lily said, trying to avoid eye contact. Just then Lily's cousin came out of the kitchen and approached the table.

"Natalia?" Lily's mother asked. "Can you be a dear and go down to the little store down the street and buy a few bananas for tomorrow's breakfast? I'm afraid we don't have enough for crepes in the morning."

"But . . . oh, very well," she said. Lily's mother gave her some money and she left.

"Now you can tell me what is wrong," Lily's mother said.

"Nothing."

"So you say."

"We need to talk about Natalia," Lily said, looking at the table.

"What about her?"

Lily paused for a moment and took a deep breath. She exhaled slowly, and realized there was no way to go about this without raising more questions.

"Where are her parents?" Lily asked, looking up.

"Oh . . ."

"Oh, what?"

"My sister, Alla? She has run off. To Odessa, with a man. Grigori, her father, he has . . . fallen apart. Natalia said he disappears for days, weeks. Her grandmother called me. I took her in."

"I see. That was good of you, mama. But . . ."

"But what? What else can I do?"

"These men that have been coming around to see her? These *model scouts*?"

"Yes?"

"We need to get rid of them."

Lily's mother shrugged her shoulders. Besides feeling that teenagers should be free to make mistakes, she had always been very meek and deferential in the presence of men.

"Why haven't you told them to get lost?" Lily asked. "Leave Natalia alone?"

"She is sixteen. I cannot stop her. I could not stop you."

Lily looked at her mother for a moment. What she said was true, and Lily knew it. Finally, she spoke.

"Yes, I know mama, but . . . I wish you would have tried."

Nethery stepped out of the back of the van. The sun was terribly bright, and after a moment his eyes began to adjust. About fifty yards away was the entrance to Baumettes Prison, carved into a hillside like the entrance to a bunker. The two guards grabbed Nethery by the arms and walked him toward the door, the arrogant cop leading the way. Nethery could feel the guards looking at him, but when he tried to look at them they turned away.

Inside they entered a series of dark hallways. It was quiet and they passed only an occasional corrections officer. They came to a processing station and the arrogant cop filled out some forms. Nethery was placed in a cell and left alone. After about fifteen minutes two guards came and escorted him down more hallways and into a large room filled with dozens of people working at desks. When Nethery's presence became known everyone stopped what they were doing and stared. The officers led him through that room and into another where the same thing happened. Nethery had begun daydreaming. He saw himself being led deeper underground, and he felt a profound sense that he was coming to the end of something.

They moved him to another holding cell for almost an hour and then he was led into the prison proper. It was even noisier in there, people shouting and yelling, and it made the quiet that followed him everywhere even more pronounced. This prison was in much worse shape than the one in Cassis. There was chipped paint and grime on everything, and a dark and violent energy floated around the place. Eventually he was placed in a cell that smelled of stale sweat and human waste. There was another man in the cell, youngish and blond. He sat on his bunk watching. The guards unlocked Nethery's handcuffs very carefully and then quickly left as if he were some kind of extreme threat, sliding the cell door shut behind them.

There was a cement cot on each side of the cell, and Nethery sat down on the one opposite his cellmate and looked over at him. He had a magazine on his lap and was looking at Nethery curiously.

"They're terrified of you, mate," he said in an Australian accent.

Nethery smiled, thinking it was a joke.

"They are?"

"Aye."

Nethery recognized that he was serious.

"Why?"

"Because you're Travis."

"So?"

"Don't you know what's going on, mate?"

Nethery shrugged.

"Well, I don't either, really, anymore. They stopped letting us see the newspapers three days ago."

"Why'd they do that?"

"Because people in here were reading about you and starting shit."

Nethery shrugged again.

"There was a mass prison break at Le Santé in Paris."

"And?" Nethery asked.

"Look, mate. You've really started something. All the riots, the people . . . they're all waiting for you."

Nethery made a funny face and his cellmate laughed.

"The name's Simon," he said, reaching out his hand. Nethery reached across and shook it.

"But let's get something straight. I don't care who you are," Simon said, reaching under his mattress and removing a home-made knife, "you try anything with me and I'll stick you. Got that, mate?"

"Yeah," Nethery said, chuckling, "I got it."

It was a busy night at the café. Lily and Natalia had been work-ing nonstop for almost three hours. Every time they'd had a break her cousin tried to grill her about modeling, coming at her with dozens of questions. Lily had put her off, but she knew that her cousin would keep at it, probably until she heard what she wanted to hear. Someone had filled her pretty little head with nonsense. Every magazine cover, every advertisement on the television, every billboard across town, told a story. And they were all lies. As the day wore on Lily began going over ways to convince her cousin that this was not a road she wanted to go down. How could she, without coming right out and telling her all the grisly details? And then even if she did, her cousin prob-ably still wouldn't listen. She imagined her cousin responding by saying that Lily must have done something wrong, must have invited it, caused it somehow.

There were only two tables of patrons left. They had finished their meals and were having coffee. The bells that hung from the door jingled, two men entered, and as soon as she laid eyes on them Lily knew who they were. They were well-groomed, wore expensive suits, and carried themselves with a certain kind of chic arrogance. Seeing them made her stomach tighten up and she suddenly felt cold and clammy, as if the blood had stopped flowing to her extremities. Her cousin was back in the kitchen helping her mother, so she approached them, thinking maybe she could get rid of them before her cousin came out.

"Good evening," she said.

"Hello," the taller one said, "I haven't seen you here before . . ."

"We're getting ready to close," Lily interrupted, bluffing. It was only 7 p.m., still two hours before closing.

"Close? Nonsense," the shorter one said, pushing past her and making his way to a table. The taller one followed him. Lily stood there for a minute, following them with her eyes, contemplating what to do next. After they sat down they whispered to each other, casting occasional glances back at her. Lily approached the table.

"We would like some coffee, my dear," the shorter one said, smiling. He was trying very hard to be charming. Lily had seen it before.

"You are," the taller one said, sighing, ". . . very lovely."

"Have you ever done any modeling?" the shorter one said.

"You could, you know," the taller one said, "you have the look . . . one in a million . . ." and then he flashed a smile and Lily noticed he had a gold tooth.

"Coffee? That's all?" Lily interrupted, sharply. It surprised them and they simply nodded. Lily walked away and headed for the kitchen. These two were even more subtle and charming than Claude had been, better looking too, younger. She quickly got their coffees and when she emerged from the kitchen she saw Natalia standing at their table. Lily walked over and set their coffees down.

"This is my cousin Agnieszka," Natalia said, excitedly. "She is a model. She has been on many magazines."

"It's not hard to see why," the taller one said.

"I thought I had seen you somewhere . . ." the shorter one said.

"This is Fabio," Natalia said excitedly, indicating the short one, "and this is Marcello. They are from Italy! They want to take me to Milan."

"That's great," Lily said, trying to hide her disgust. Her cousin was clearly under their sway, just like she had been with Claude. Lily walked away from the table without a word. Her cousin stared after her for a moment, confused, but she only shrugged and turned her attention back to the two men.

Lily went about preparing the café to close for the night, occasionally glancing out to see what was going on. Her cousin was sitting with them now, and she was very excited, smiling and hanging on their every word. Exactly like she had been when Claude had begun coming around after she'd met him at the Arena Club. No one had been able to talk sense into her, and she knew in her heart that it would be the same with her cousin.

That evening two prison guards showed up at the door of Nethery's cell. One of them kept a watchful eye as the other handcuffed Nethery, and they led him down a series of long corridors and to a small room where he was seated at a table that was bolted to the floor. They handcuffed him to the table and left. He sat there for ten minutes. He took note of the two-way mirror on the wall. A guard appeared and let Betty into the cell. He told them she had fifteen minutes.

"Hello," Betty said, sitting down in a chair across the table.

"Hey," Nethery said, smiling.

"Hold on for a moment," she said, pulling her cell phone out of her briefcase. She dialed a number and set the phone between them on the table.

"What's that for?"

"They are most likely listening. I want a record of our conversation."

"Hmm. Okay. What's up?"

"Wallace is being held by the police."

"What?"

"Yes, the BBC showed the jail interview on television. It caused more riots and the French police shut down their office. They are questioning him. They were quite unhappy that the public knows you are here. It has made things worse out there. But now they can't simply take you away. You will have to go through the normal legal proceedings."

"Hmmm."

"I think they are going to charge you with murder, and inciting terrorism."

"Whatever."

"I have spoken with your friend, at the bar."

"Oh?"

"Yes, he called me. He wanted me to tell you that the girl is okay."

"Really?" Nethery said, excited.

"Yes. She made it home."

"Thank God."

"He told me she has a message for you."

"Oh?"

"She said she loves you."

Nethery felt a hot flash, and it caused a fissure in the glacier inside him. The emotional response struck him as unusual, as if it had been lying dormant for a time. He looked down to hide his face. Betty smiled, but said nothing.

"How are the conditions here?" she asked, changing the subject.

"Not bad," Nethery said, raising his head, "I'm in a cell with an Australian drug smuggler."

"You must stay in your cell. Do not go out into the yard," Betty urged. "It would be very easy for someone to kill you there."

• • •

Lily saw the two men leave the café. She ripped off her apron, ran out of the café, and caught up with them halfway down the block.

"Well, hello, Agnieszka," Marcello, the taller one said. The shorter one, Fabio, grinned and took out a cigarette.

"That is not my name," Lily said, catching her breath.

"What is your name then?" Marcello asked.

"That is not important."

"Oh?"

"Yes. Oh."

"You know that you look very silly working at that café," Fabio said. "A girl as beautiful as you should not have to work in such places."

Lily flashed him a dirty look, and opened her mouth to say something but no words came out.

"What is it you want, my dear?" Marcello asked. The way he said "my dear" made her cringe. Marcello was very tall, over six feet, and he looked down at her with a supreme smugness. Fabio stood off to the side, smoking and leering at her.

"I want you to leave my cousin alone," Lily said.

"What?" Fabio said.

"I want you to stop coming around the café, filling her head with ideas."

"But she is beautiful," Fabio said. "One in a million. She could be a top model."

"I don't care. I want you to forget about her."

"Surely that is not your decision to make."

"Why don't you come down to our hotel?" Marcello said, a gruesome grin on his face.

"What?"

"Yes, come down and we can discuss it," he continued. "Maybe you would like to work with us."

"No."

"No?"

"No. And I want you to leave my cousin alone."

"I'm sorry, my dear," Marcello said, "but frankly that is none of your business."

"But there might be some way," Fabio interrupted, ". . . you know . . . something you could do . . . to convince us."

"But . . ." Lily said, surprised.

"My dear, you must understand," Marcello said. "We are model scouts. Finding girls like your cousin is what we do."

"Well," Lily said pausing, both repelled and confused.

"Come down," Fabio urged, "we are at the Premier Palace. Room 412."

"When?" Lily asked, staring at the sidewalk.

"Tomorrow night," Marcello said.

"Yes," she said, in a strange way, as if she had just gotten the first faint flickerings of an idea. She stood there and waited for them to begin walking away, then looked up and stared after them. They were laughing. It would be useless to try to talk them out of it. It would be useless to call the cops. It would even be useless to fuck them. She knew that now. There was only one thing they would understand.

Nethery was sitting at a steel table that was bolted to the floor. This was a larger room than the one he'd been in the day before. It was a little bit cleaner and just like the other it had a large two-way mirror on one wall. An officer opened the door and three men in suits filed in. They took up chairs across from him.

"My name is Pierre," said the one in the center. "I am from the Ministry of the Interior. This is my assistant," he said indicating the man to his left, "and this is Mr. Rogerson of the U.S. Consulate."

"What's he doing here?" Nethery asked, indicating the American.

"I'm here to observe. You will probably be deported back to the States after France is done with you."

"Damn."

"What's the matter?" the American asked.

"I really don't want to go back there."

The man from the Ministry of the Interior grinned, and the American noticed.

"What's so funny?" the American said.

"Nothing, nothing," Pierre said. "Let's get underway."

He removed some papers from his briefcase. Nethery heard

some faint sounds coming from outside the room, possibly gun-shots and explosions. The men in suits looked slightly alarmed but they continued the questioning.

"We know who you are now, Mr. Nethery," Pierre said.

"Well whoop-dee-doo."

"Mr. Nethery . . . ?"

"Big fucking deal."

"You don't care that we know who you are?"

"Not really."

"Why?"

"It doesn't matter who I am."

The three of them exchanged confused glances, looking to each other for the explanation of what he meant. They all shrugged.

"What do you know about the People's Mafia?" the American asked.

"Nothing."

"Nothing? Oh come now, Mr. Nethery, are you trying to tell us you didn't send these people out to riot and destroy?"

"Nope."

"We don't believe you, Mr. Nethery. We think you are in-volved with the People's Mafia. Did they send you to France?"

"I thought they didn't exist."

"That is still unknown."

Nethery chuckled.

"It doesn't look unknown to me," he said.

"Why did you kill the Russians?"

"I had to," Nethery said, and he grinned.

"What's so funny?"

"Hey look, if I had a jail I might have just locked them up. But I don't have a jail. All I have is a gun."

"Do you know how many innocent people are being killed?"

"That's your problem, buddy. I didn't start this."

"What?"

"You guys wanna make me out to be the bad guy? Go ahead. Call me a terrorist. But be careful. Because I'll be the best god-damned terrorist the world has ever seen."

"You must really hate yourself," the American said angrily, trying to get a rise out of Nethery, who grinned.

"Hate? You betcha. Genuine American, USDA Prime, Grade A hatred."

"Wha . . . ? You are insane."

Nethery laughed.

"You think you can change anything? We will crush you," the American said, trying desperately to control his rage.

"Listen," Nethery said, putting his hand up to his ear, "you hear that sound?"

Even through the heavy door of the room it was apparent that something was happening outside. The noise had gotten slightly louder—yelling and the faint sound of gunfire. The walls shook slightly twice from what could only have been explosions.

"That's the sound of the future," Nethery continued, assuming for a moment the role. "You guys had a chance, you had dozens of chances to be reasonable. Well now it's over. You guys wouldn't stop it, so we will."

"I knew it! You're part of the People's Mafia!" the American said.

"I'm gonna clue you in on something. It's not gonna be like it used to be, somebody flies off the handle and blows something up, then five years pass and it happens again, and then ten years. It's gonna be happening every five minutes."

The Petrovka black market was just as Lily remembered, rows of tables and tents lined up on either side of the street. Merchants sat on folding chairs, hawking counterfeit DVD's, watches, purses, and sports gear. Off the main street ran covered alleys filled with black market and counterfeit goods. It hadn't changed at all. And it was still the place to go to get things you couldn't get anywhere else. It hadn't taken her long to find the salesman. The deal had gone smoothly, but she had been nervous, the way the man blatantly ogled her, his eyes roaming over her body, the way he licked his lips and smiled. But Lily had maintained a serious tone until the deal was done. She paid with some of the money Nethery had given her. She made her way out of the abandoned building and down the alley until she came to the street. She stood there for a moment and looked up and down at the rows of tables. She looked in the direction of Petrovka station and her brain told her to start walking but something held her back and she couldn't move. She raised her bag and clutched it to her chest. She took a deep breath and set off in the direction of the Metro station.

She got off at Kreschatik station. She found the Tolstoy Square entrance and rode the escalator down into Metrograd, a large underground shopping center. She reached the main floor and headed for the boutique quarter of the mall opposite the Independence Square entrance. As she walked she realized that the place she'd met Claude, the VIP club on the top floor of the Arena entertainment complex, was probably right above her somewhere, at street level.

Lily turned and posed, looking at herself in the dressing room mirror from different angles. This was the third outfit she'd tried on, and she liked it. It was sexy. She had already been to the lingerie boutique. Now that she'd decided on her outfit she placed her normal clothes in her bag, and carefully applied her makeup, heavy dark eye shadow, blood red lipstick, mascara. She teased her hair up. When she was finished she left the dressing room, paid at the front counter. She found the nearest exit and hailed a taxi. The Premier Palace would have security cameras, so in the taxi she put on the extra-large sunglasses she'd bought and wrapped a dark green silk scarf around her head.

The taxi dropped her off a block from the hotel. She stood on the sidewalk for a moment. She felt the presence of the gun in her bag, a dark gravity that filled her with a kind of joy. It forced a deeper realization of what she was about to do. But there was no fear. No hesitation. It made her feel lighter. She became aware of every single thing going on around her. An Asian woman with a black mole on her cheek walked past wearing a worn leather overcoat. A woman crossed the street holding the hand of a child. Time seemed to slow down as she noticed tiny details of every car and bike and person that passed her. Eventually she made her way to the crosswalk and waited for the signal. She felt a very clear sense that she was about to cross a line and she briefly wondered how different it was from the dozens of lines she crossed modeling. She thought of Nethery. His face appeared in her mind and through the sadness she wondered if he had felt the same thing she was feeling that day at Claude's apartment.

The light changed and as she crossed the street a question came to her: why was she doing this? The way her modeling career turned out wasn't a given. Natalia could make a go of it. She was without a doubt pretty enough to make it to the top. Just because Lily's career had turned out badly didn't mean hers would as well. Was it really her business to meddle in this? If anyone had been watching, they would have seen the corner of her mouth turn up in what may have been a very brief smile.

Two guards led Nethery back to his cell. They were obviously nervous. Other guards were running down the halls and shouting, and many of them had armed themselves with machine guns. Simon was reclining back on the bunk, oblivious to it all, reading a teen magazine.

"What the hell's going on?" Nethery asked, after the guards had locked him in.

"It's the Corsicans, mate," Simon said, sitting up on the bunk. "They're trying to break out one of their guys. I heard a helicopter right before all hell broke loose."

"A helicopter?"

"Aye. They've used them to break out before. It's why they put those wires up over the yard."

A half-hour passed, and the noise out in the yard had died down. Guards were no longer running back and forth past their cell. Three officers suddenly appeared at the cell door. One unlocked the door and the other two stepped inside.

"Let's go," one of them said, looking down at Nethery.

"Go where?"

"Out into the yard."

"Now wait a damned minute, mate," Simon said, sitting bolt upright.

"You stay out of this!" the guard shouted, glaring at Simon and pulling out a nightstick. The other guard stood there, clutching the pistol on his hip.

"It's okay," Nethery said. He stood up and he and Simon walked out of the cell. The guards accompanied them down a few hallways and to a steel door. They opened it and ushered them down a concrete staircase. At the bottom was a door, and outside a cage made of chain link fencing with razor wire on top. The guards unlocked the door of the cage and waited. Simon hesitated, but Nethery stepped through the door and out into the yard, and then Simon followed. The guards stayed inside and Nethery heard the door lock behind him.

"Stay close to me," Simon said, and they walked out into the sun.

"Those are the Corsicans over there," Simon said, nodding to one side of the yard at a group of men gathered around an old silver-haired man sitting on a concrete bench. "See the old man there?" Simon said, indicating the man on the bench.

"That's César, their boss. And those are the Muslims," he

said, leaning his head the other way toward the men on the opposite side of the yard, gathered around a middle-aged man with a white skullcap. It was easy to tell the two groups apart. Simon said the gangs were evenly matched and had established a fragile truce. The other prisoners, ones like Simon, were a minority of foreigners, mostly white. As long as they minded their own business they were mostly left alone. Some ran errands and did dirty work for one side or the other.

Simon and Nethery walked through the center of the yard and the chattering coming from both gangs slowly died out. A few small groups of men that were playing soccer and handball stopped playing as well, and there was total silence. Nethery could feel the eyes of everyone in the yard following them. Then it began, one or two voices at first.

"*C'est ce qu'on fait!*" from the Corsicans.

"*Vive Travis!*" from the Arabs. Eventually more voices joined in until both sides were chanting. Nethery understood that it was directed at him, but he didn't know how to respond, so he just kept walking, eyes straight ahead toward the far side of the yard, where there was a high chain link fence topped with razor wire. Beyond that he could see a grass field and a forest.

Lily walked into the hotel lobby. Now that she had come this far there was no going back. She was very calm. Her heart had slowed down and it was beating calmly and evenly. She made her way across the lobby, found the elevator, and pushed the button for the fourth floor. When the doors opened she got out and followed the signs until she found room 412. She removed the scarf from her head and stuffed it into her bag, making sure that the gun was on top of everything. She teased up her hair and knocked. Fabio answered and a grin spread across his face. She felt his eyes move up and down her body. She sensed a change in his demeanor. It became something darker. After a moment that seemed very long to her, he stepped aside to let her into the room. Marcello was reclining on the bed and when Lily stepped into the center of the room he sat up.

"Hello, my dear," he said, smiling.

Lily looked at him. He was wearing a shiny shirt made of silk or something similar, unbuttoned halfway. Lily looked at his hairless chest, and then imagined she could see under his skin and she wondered what his heart looked like, if it looked the same as everyone else's, a warm lump of throbbing flesh. But the image that came into her mind was that of red meat on a shelf at the market. Lily felt a surge of revulsion and her body heaved slightly, but her heart remained steady and calm.

"Would you like a drink?" Fabio asked, drawing her attention momentarily away from Marcello on the bed.

"You are so very beautiful, my dear," Marcello said, "so desirable."

Fabio had walked over to the mini-bar and was mixing a drink.

"We're very happy that you came to see us," he said, looking back at her for a second. He turned his attention back to mixing the drinks. Lily stepped over next to him and reached into her bag. It would be the last time she heard either of them say "my dear."

A cleaning woman was out in the hall, pushing her cart past room 412 when she heard a very loud noise and the door shook slightly. She stopped for a moment, and then got frightened and hurried down the hall toward the next room. As she reached the door of room 418 she heard three more loud bangs. She fumbled with her master key and eventually got the door open. She began to push her cart inside and caught a fleeting glimpse of a woman with a dark green scarf on her head coming out of 412, turning away and walking toward the elevator.

Nethery ambled across the prison yard. He saw a concrete bench out near the fence and headed for it. Simon walked alongside him, looking around nervously. The shouting of the gangs began to fade, but Nethery could sense that everyone was still looking at him. Three men were sitting on the bench and when they saw him approaching they stood up quickly, stepped off to the side and indicated that Simon and Nethery should take the bench. Simon veered off to talk to the men and Nethery sat down. He looked over and noticed that one of the men was talking to Simon very deferentially and with a lot of respect, bowing slightly and making praying gestures with his hands. A pair of men from the Corsican group came joined them, and they began having a serious conversation. Nethery turned away from them and looked out into the grass field. It was about the size of a soccer field. Beyond was a forest. He thought of Lily. What she was doing, how she was coping. Inexplicably and out of nowhere he was overcome with a sense, a kind of knowing, and he knew that at that moment she was safe. What had happened would fade enough that she could move on. But for him it was the end. There was no such optimism. He would never leave this place, or one like it. He accepted it with a cold and fatal resignation. The future had been snuffed out, and he was devoid of emotion, except when he thought about her. That aroused an ache that was pleasant in its pain. He stared at the grass field before him, perfectly groomed and a vivid green. The sun overhead was bright, and the temperature was perfect. Simon finished talking with the men and joined him on the bench.

"Something's going down," Simon said. Nethery did not hear him, and continued to gaze out upon the field.

"Hey, mate. Earth to Travis," Simon said, and he placed his hand on Nethery's arm. Nethery turned to face him.

"What?" he said.

"Did you hear me? Something's going down. The Corsicans are planning to bust out."

"Oh yeah?" Nethery said, disinterested.

"Yeah. The prison is short of guards. A lot of them have been called away to help with all the shit you started. The Corsicans know this, and they're giving it a go. They told me to tell you to get ready."

"Why would they do that?"

"Because you're coming with us."

"I am? Why?"

"Get it through your head, mate. You're a big deal. They think you're like Carlos the Jackal or something."

"Carlos the Jackal? He was a phony. In it for the fame. Money and chicks. I don't think he believed half of the shit he spouted," Nethery said flatly. "I'm no terrorist leader."

"Well mate, you might not have much say in it. Sometimes life has other plans."

Simon cocked his head to the side and looked at Nethery.

"I don't get you, mate," he said. "Shit's falling apart out there, man. We can be kings. This will be a fucking jubilee."

Nethery said nothing.

"Don't you want to get out of here?" Simon asked.

"I guess so," Nethery said, drowsily.

"Well, you better get ready anyway, because you're coming with us. You just don't say no to the Corsicans."

Simon stood and walked off in the direction of the Corsican group and Nethery turned his attention back to the field. After a few moments a small bird, probably a sparrow, flew out of the forest at the far edge. The forest looked excessively colorful and his vision flickered for a moment. He was so warm and comfortable he was lulled into a strange state. He felt almost half-asleep. Sounds faded and vanished. There was only the forest, and the sky, and the colors swirled and then came together. And then his eyes were drawn to something across the field. Lily. She appeared from behind a tree, vivid, clear, as if she wasn't so far away. She was wearing a black long-sleeved sequin dress. She moved closer and disappeared behind another tree. She seemed to be floating, as if she wasn't walking but gliding over the ground. She appeared again, and disappeared again, over and over as she made her way out from the depths of the forest. She cleared all the trees and was at the edge of the forest in shin-deep brush, at the very edge of the shade. She raised her arm, smiled, and waved. She moved out of the shade, there was a flash of light, Nethery squinted, and when his vision returned she was gone.

A group of seven or eight Corsicans had gathered behind the bench. They formed a screen between Nethery and the guard towers. One of the men, stocky, with greasy hair and severe facial features, put his hand on Nethery's shoulder and held out a cell phone, an old beat-up Nokia.

"What's this?" Nethery asked.

"You know a man named Klaus? He is your friend, yes?"

"Uhhh, yeah, yeah, sure I know Klaus," Nethery said, puzzled.

"He is our friend too. He has arranged for you to have a phone call. You must hurry. Only one or two minutes."

Nethery took the phone from the man and held it up to his ear. "Hello?"

"James?"

"Lily? But . . . are you okay?"

"Yes, yes, I am fine. We do not have much time. I must tell you something. I thought I would be fine here by myself but I am not. I need you."

"But Lily, I'm in prison. They'll never let me out."

"Listen to me. They cannot kill you. They cannot keep you. This I know. Come to me. Please. I will wait."

"Okay. Okay, yeah."

The Corsican snapped his fingers a couple times and indicated Nethery hand the phone back.

"Lily? I will get there. I'll find you," Nethery said, and then he had the phone pulled from his hand. The group of Corsicans that had shielded him dispersed back to their side of the prison yard.

Nethery heard a loud crack and at the same time it felt like he'd been kicked in his side. The bullet had passed between the backrest and the seat of the bench. He toppled off the bench. He heard people shouting, his cheek was pressed against the warm pavement of the yard, and he could smell the asphalt. He heard more loud cracks as if they were somewhere in the distance and he saw dust and dirt kick up off the yard a few feet away and bullets were hitting the concrete bench and spitting up little clouds of fine white dust. Simon appeared, kneeling next to him.

"Mate? Can you hear me?" Simon said.

"It's okay," Nethery said, "I had it coming . . ."

"What are you talking about, mate?"

The shooting stopped. Simon stood and yelled for help. Another man joined him, and they sat Nethery back onto the bench. Nethery fell over onto his side again and continued trying to look at the forest, at the spot where he had seen Lily. His vision grew smaller until it was a small circular area, and outside it everything became blurred. After a few moments he felt a kind of warmth sweep through his body that immediately began to fade and was replaced by a gradual coldness, not from without but from within as if a block of ice were inside his chest. Nethery felt his body filling up, a kind of pressure in his torso. He lay on his side and stared off through the fence at the forest, the dark green of the trees turning black. He felt his life ebbing away. He thought about letting go. It made complete sense in a way. In a way, it was right. It was just. A half hour ago, he probably would have. But now, he couldn't. He wouldn't.

He heard a sound in the sky, a helicopter approaching. There was gunfire again and men shouting all around. He could only see the forest, but the sound grew closer and louder. He felt hands on his body, and he was being lifted up. Simon's face appeared before him, smiling, and then one of the Muslims, wearing an embroidered white kufi. He saw César, the leader of the Corsicans. There was more gunfire, closer and farther away, and the bullets made whizzing sounds. He felt himself being carried by Simon and another man, his feet dragging on the ground.

"Hang on, mate, we're almost there!" Simon shouted.

"It's okay. I had it . . . coming. You do too," Nethery said, so unheard over the noise. The helicopter grew louder and louder and they were fighting an incredible wind. They lifted Nethery into the chopper. Everything was blurry and there were many voices. The engine of the chopper began to whine, and it took off straight up into the air. Bullets hit the side, and sounded like rocks striking the side of a car.

The chopper reached a certain altitude, tilted steeply, and began accelerating away from the prison. César and the leader of the Muslims were sitting across the cabin from him, and they began shouting at each other, both of them gesturing wildly. Nethery felt hands on his shoulders, and he was pushed up into a sitting position. Someone had removed his coat. Simon had broken open a First Aid kit and was wrapping a wide bandage around his torso. His hands were bloody. When he was finished,

Simon helped him get his coat back on. Nethery no longer felt his life dissipating. He no longer felt as if he were fading into oblivion, and the intense cold buried deep within his chest had vanished, replaced by a bonfire of determination and human will, fueled by adrenaline and hot blood. Lily was the match. He felt his strength returning. This wasn't the end of everything, as he had thought. It was only the end of one thing.

He hooked his arm in a strap hanging from the roof of the compartment and dangled at the edge of the door. He stuck his head out into the wind. He looked down. They had just crossed the coastline and were heading out to sea. He turned his face into the wind and closed his eyes. He grinned.

Author photograph by Robert Nethery

ABOUT THE AUTHOR

TOM HANSEN is the author of *American Junkie*, a memoir of his life as a heroin addict and drug dealer. He writes for *The Nervous Breakdown* and is an editor at *Knock Magazine*. He lives in Seattle.

Printed in the United States
by Baker & Taylor Publisher Services